THE CURIST

VINCENT CALFAPIETRA
&
JULIE DONOFRIO

From Vincent:

For my wife Maureen – Your undying love encouraged me to write this novel twenty-two years ago, enabling me to overcome my doubts of being a writer.

Your loving spirit inspired me to partner with Julie to finally finish the novel.

This novel and your loving memory will go hand in hand forever.

From Julie:

For my wife Gina – Who is my everything.

PROLOGUE
AN EMPIRE LOST, A CITY BORN

1536 – The Andes mountains of Peru

The Inca warrior raced up the mountain pursued by the ruthless Spaniards. He knew his life, and the lives of many others, depended on keeping the slim lead he had on his hunters. The warrior was sure on a different day he could easily stop running, become the pursuer, and kill the enemies chasing him, but not today. Today was different. He couldn't risk any delay in meeting his father, so he blocked his desire to engage and kill, and quickened his pace up the mountain. The once great Inca Empire had been reduced to ruins by the Spaniards with both their brutality and diseases. *Today,* was the day his noble father had chosen for the beginning of the new Inca Empire.

The air was bitter cold, the wind was ripping around the mountainside and the sun was fading in and out as large, bright cumulus clouds moved quickly through the sky. As the warrior looked up the mountain, he saw the peak glistening white, from the early fall snow. He imagined his father waiting in his adobe a few thousand feet above him. Just another hour or so he thought, trying to maintain his calm. Somehow the Spaniards had found out about his departure, he was not sure how, but it made no difference, now he just needed to maintain his distance from them. Although they had been chasing him for the last few hours, they had not been able to make up any time. Their plan was obvious; they would continue to chase him until he ran out of mountain—he, of course, had his own plan.

He paused for a second, looking up at the sky, estimating he had about two more hours of daylight. An hour to reach his father and then one last hour of light would be just enough for them to get to their final destination on the mountain. Although they were very familiar with the mountain, traveling along the dangerous cliffs and paths would be too difficult for his father at night. His heart was pounding as he climbed, getting ever so close to his father, and thinking about the wonderful and mysterious future that lay ahead for his people.

The Noble Melka sat at his wooden table, anxiously waiting for his son, trying to avoid the cold draft coming from the window of the small space. Melka had always been revered by his people, but the once proud leader and great warrior was now a shell of his old self. His body had been beaten down by age and arthritis, and he'd been reduced physically to what he never wanted to be, a tired, crippled old man, past his time. His mind, however, was as clear as the days of his youth, but ever wiser because of his life's experience. The breakdown of his body might have been easier if his mind was cloudy. Then he would not have to bear knowing the carnage the Spaniards had brought to his people, nor would he have to carry the burden of his singular knowledge and personal mission. Over the past year, Melka had carefully been recruiting people to join him in a new place, not yet discovered by the Spaniards. They had secretly been building homes, planting seeds and preparing to cut themselves off from the Spaniards, and painful as it might be, from the rest of their people. Melka felt this was the only way to keep their race from disappearing forever.

His hope for the future had helped him summon the strength and energy he had needed over the last year to direct the preparations and to complete a lifelong project—adapting their Quipu method of communication into a crude written language and recording their history. He believed this was another necessity to ensure the record of his people was never erased from the past. He placed his hands on the book that lay on the table in front of him. It contained guidance for the new community, as well as a record of their history. He was proud of what it contained and felt confident that his son could and would follow the path he outlined. The writings encompassed all that he had learned and all that his people needed to know to resurrect and rebuild the Inca race. He had worked tirelessly on the writings day and night for the last three months, so much so that sleep was rare, nights and days were now a blur. He smiled knowing he had finished, and that the long-awaited rest he so welcomed, was near. He closed his eyes and thought about what had brought him to this—the final day of his life.

WORLD WAR II

WORLD WAR II

CHAPTER 1

May 30, 1944 – London

Josephine was getting ready for her evening with the American colonel. She was standing in front of the mirror in her bedroom, admiring her beautiful body, and beautiful it was. She could easily have passed for a Hollywood pin-up girl, with her long raven hair shining as it fell down her back, deep and penetrating blue eyes and her silky white skin radiant in the reflection. At twenty-eight years old, her body was in pristine condition, which pleased her vanity, but was also a necessity for her employment. Josephine was very good at her job. So good in fact, that in just a few years, her talents had enabled her to become one of the top German spies during the war. That success had empowered her to rise from the slums of Paris to the wealthy and aristocratic lifestyle of London, something she had always desired. Her body was her tool, or more like her weapon, to extract the most classified secrets from men who had no power to resist her. She had them spouting out every worthwhile fact they knew that would help the Germans in their cause and had them begging for a chance to do it again once they had tasted her fruits. She understood men, their needs, their weaknesses, and that if she did things right, they would provide her with the life she wanted. She could care less about who wanted to rule the world.

It was two years into her spying career that her superiors started ordering her to murder her targets once she had extracted the desired information. They said it was necessary to keep her identity a secret. At first, she was uncomfortable with it, but after a while she began to enjoy the thrill of the kill, and she became known as 'Black Widow'. The Germans went to great pains to keep Josephine safe. They provided her with all the protection and resources she needed, and she never stayed in one place too long.

Tonight, Josephine would need to look especially ravishing, in order to give the performance of her life. Her last victim, a young British Captain, had revealed that the Allied invasion of France was scheduled for the first week of June, but not where the landing would take place. There were too many different theories and rumors about where the Allies were going to invade, many of which the Allies had started. Germany's high-ranking military officers surmised that Normandy was the most logical place for the invasion, while Hitler and his advisers were convinced it was Calais. This being the 30th of May, she knew time was precious and she would have to discover and confirm the exact date and landing place in order to give Germany a chance to defend their positions.

The German intelligence community had spent the last few months tracking several high-ranking officials they thought had specific knowledge of the plan. Their intel had them focusing on a certain American Army Lieutenant Colonel. Not only did they believe he had information about the invasion, they believed he was also one of the Allies top spies, known to be cruel and merciless, responsible for the deaths of dozens of German agents. To the best of their ability, they had tracked the colonel's habits and patterns, where he ate, where he drank and who he associated with. Their research revealed a man who used women, alcohol and drugs all at a frenzied pace, but seemed to somehow maintain control.

In a quiet little pub near Covent Garden, Josephine managed to meet the colonel a few days ago. When she walked in, he was standing at the bar. His piercing blue eyes followed her as she walked up next to him and ordered a drink. She turned to him and smiled radiantly, he struck up a conversation with her, she happily responded. After a bit they moved to a quiet booth, where they had a few drinks and continued their conversation which turned somewhat evocative. Josephine suggested they meet again, dinner at her place with her hinting it might be more. The colonel gladly accepted, and they had settled on tonight as the date.

Interestingly, Josephine was looking forward to tonight's job more than usual. The American was handsome, mysterious, and if he lived up to his reputation, it would require all of her skills to complete her mission, a challenge she was more than up to. She took one last look in the mirror, adjusted her red sheer and satin dress, applied a powerful matching red lipstick and a seductive French perfume, gave a nod of satisfaction to herself in the mirror and headed to the bathroom. She opened the medicine cabinet and removed a small, unlabeled bottle. She shook two small tablets from the bottle onto her hand, paused for a second, and then added a third. With a spoon, she crushed the three tablets and poured the fine powder into a special dispenser shaped in the form of a cigarette lighter. The device would easily allow her to put as much, or as little, as she wanted, into the drinks she would be preparing later in the evening. The pills were a powerful combination of several drugs, that within minutes of entering the blood stream would begin to send a person's senses into overdrive. Everything was enhanced for the user, sight, sound, smell, taste, and especially the sex drive. The drug did that for her, but she knew enough to use it sparingly for herself, she could not afford to lose her edge.

With transfer of the powder complete, she returned the bottle to the cabinet and re-entered the bedroom. She laid down on her large, oval-shaped bed, and moved to the exact position she would be in later this evening. Reaching out behind her, she pressed a hidden panel on the wall which slid away to reveal a small compartment that contained a shiny Beretta pistol, complete with silencer. She grabbed the weapon, checked to make sure it was loaded, made a mock firing gesture to where she expected her victim to be, then checked to make sure the safety was off. She put the gun back and closed the secret compartment. The spider's lair was ready.

Josephine got up from the bed and headed to the kitchen. The one domestic trait Josephine enjoyed was the preparing, cooking, and eating of gourmet food. She had four excellent bottles of wine, the best caviar, a savory beef Wellington cooking in the oven and other samples of fine culinary delights. She knew tonight would bring three things—the location of the Allied invasion, great sex, and the death of the Colonel.

CHAPTER 2

Lt. Col. Keith Strickland was in the back seat of the private car Josephine had sent for him. The driver, a closed mouth, rather ugly Brit—or a German trying to act like one—said nothing for the entire ride. When they pulled up in front of her building, he finally spoke, something vaguely resembling English, and told the colonel which number to go to. As soon as the colonel got out of the car, the driver sped away, giving the impression he was not coming back anytime soon. The colonel stood on the quiet street and surveyed his surroundings, the building he was meant to enter, the adjacent buildings and finally the alleyway, satisfied with what he saw, he entered Josephine's building. He passed through the dimly lit vestibule and climbed the stairs leading to the second floor. He glanced at the numbers and saw the one he was looking for on his left. Before knocking, he took a deep breath, focused his attention on the mission ahead and reminded himself to stay relaxed and to be careful. Always be careful.

He knocked on the door, and the sound echoed in the quiet building. In a moment, Josephine opened the door looking beautiful in her revealing red dress.

"Good evening, Colonel."

"Good evening, you look stunning, and please call me Keith."

"Okay then, Keith, please come in."

Josephine turned and led him into the large and luxurious flat. It was very well decorated with antiques, paintings and exquisite furniture dating back to some early period, none of which he could name. His eyes moved quickly around the main living room, taking in everything, the windows, the doors and the other rooms. Even if he had not known where he was going, he would have felt as if he walked into a spider's lair; her code name definitely suited her.

"You're on time. I like that." Her voice was very soft-spoken, well-versed in English, with no accent.

"It's part of my training, second nature."

"Please sit down and make yourself comfortable."

As always, Keith was carrying a black overnight bag. Tonight, it contained all of the tools he would need before the evening played itself out. He put down the bag and sat on one of the oversized sofas.

"I see you plan on staying a while," she said, glancing at the overnight bag.

"It's just my tooth brush and a change of clothes. This war has us all scattered. I never travel without them."

Josephine smiled ever so slightly, "Relax, while I pour us a drink. White wine, very dry, okay with you?"

"Yes, that's fine, thank you. You have a nice place, very nice. Very you."

"Thank you. I admire the finer things in life, and I like to surround myself with them."

"You certainly have done that," Keith said, eyeing her seductively.

Josephine went over to the bar, opened a bottle of wine and poured it into expensive crystal glasses. She brought over his glass and their eyes met for a moment before his eyes moved over her body. She sat down on a matching sofa across from him so they were directly facing each other, her dress barely containing her ample cleavage. Keeping her eyes fixed on him, she raised her glass and offered a toast, "To the start of a new friendship and a beautiful evening." She took a small sip of her wine.

Keith raised his glass and returned the toast, "To us." He took a sip of the wine. Buried ever so slightly under the fine taste, he detected a hint of a foreign substance. He was no stranger to drugs and he recognized what this was, mostly opium, and a quality product, but he suspected there were a few other substances also. It would be too much for most men, but with his hard-living lifestyle over the past ten years, he'd developed an extremely high tolerance for drugs and alcohol. This was definitely going to be an interesting evening.

"The wine is excellent, from the Burgundy region, if I'm not mistaken."

"I'm impressed. What other areas of expertise do you have?" Josephine wanted him to feel comfortable, for his words to flow without hesitation or thought. She had learned that the truth comes easy once her victims start to ramble. What better way to start than to let a man boast of his particular qualities and attributes, whether true or not. It was all part of the game.

"I'm an expert at many things. Wine," pointing at the glass, "women," nodding at her, "military strategy and invasions," this was what she wanted to hear, "weapons, explosives, murder … only German agents of course, have you seen any lately?"

"I don't know, what do they look like?" she said innocently.

"Nothing like you, that's for sure."

"Well, that makes me feel at ease. I see you have a full slate of expertise, Colonel, excuse me, Keith. I also detect some cynicism."

"You don't have to try hard to detect it. It's there. For most people the war has screwed up their lives. For me, it started well before that, and the war has only made it worse." For a moment Keith's face darkened and he seemed a million miles away.

Josephine motioned to his empty glass and asked, "Another drink, Keith?"

"Yes, thank you."

She moved gracefully, very confident and self-assured. Josephine took Keith's glass, went to the bar and poured him another glass of wine, exactly the same as the first. Through the large mirror behind the bar, she could watch him. This was a position she had been in many times, like a seasoned actress knowing her mark on the stage. She saw he was not watching her as she poured, rather, he was admiring one of the paintings. She returned and handed him the refilled glass, which he promptly emptied like he hadn't had a drink in a month. *God, he would never feel the bullet when it enters his head.*

"Let me check on dinner. It should be just about done."

"Good, because it smells wonderful and I'm starving."

She went into the kitchen to check on the food. He would only be out of her sight for a couple of minutes, so she didn't worry about leaving him alone, but that was an eternity for a spy! When she exited the kitchen with their dinner, he was in the exact spot she had left him. She put the food on the table and invited him to join her.

They savored each bit of food she had prepared, drank most of the wine, and left no topic uncovered. The body language and chemistry between them promised a brilliant conclusion to the evening. As Josephine had surmised, she was easily able to get Keith to reveal the information on the invasion. She sensed no lies, only a bitter man, weary of the war and of life, who didn't care any longer. He told her the invasion was scheduled for the sixth of June, which matched what the young British captain had told her, and confirmed Calais was to be the invasion point. He was so brazen, he probably thought he would kill her before she could tell anybody anything. *How foolish,* she thought.

Realizing there was no more to gain from continued conversation, Josephine said, "Shall we prepare for dessert?"

"Sounds great. What are we having? Something special I hope."

"Something very special, that I'm sure you've never had before." She was surprised that he seemed to show very little effect from the drugs and alcohol—very unusual. Josephine made the first move as she got up from her seat slowly, and seductively walked over to him.

"Let me take you to the room where dessert will be served."

His eyes said yes as she bent over and gave him a very light kiss on the lips, ever so soft. She paused, looked him in the eyes and followed it up with a more passionate kiss that sent a rush to his brain and loins at the same time. He reacted quick as a cat, lifting her up with his powerful arms, keeping their lips locked with their tongues dancing. He found her bedroom and bed just in time for them to come up for air.

As he laid her down on the bed, she whisked away her dress in one motion as if it didn't belong to her to begin with. He pulled off his shirt, and undid his pants. She attempted to remove his briefs, but he gave her a firm push back onto the bed. "Save your energy. You're going to need it," he said confidently.

"Hmmm, I like the sound of that." She smiled at him and said, "Please excuse me for a moment. I won't be long."

"Of course," Keith said as he nodded.

Josephine rose seductively out of the bed and entered her bathroom, leaving the door slightly ajar so she could see him from the mirror. She opened a drawer and took out a piece of paper which had two words already written on it—Place, Date. She took out her eyebrow pencil and wrote Calais, 6 June, and signed the paper BW. She put the paper into an empty lipstick case, and still watching him in the mirror, she lifted up a floor tile revealing a small tube that went down through the floor. Josephine dropped the lipstick case down the tube, it descended out of sight, on the way to the anxious recipients. She quickly put the tile back in place, sprayed some perfume over her body and redid her lipstick. *Now for the best part of the job*, Josephine thought as she prowled back to the bed and her waiting prey.

As she walked back into the bedroom, Keith was laying across the bed, completely nude. He smelled the intoxicating cologne and noticed the freshened lipstick, "You didn't have to freshen up on my account."

"I didn't do it for you."

Keith smiled broadly, "Well, okay then."

She leaned over and kissed him, setting off both of their desires.

A while later, Josephine sensed his climax was near. She rolled him over, placing herself on top. She opened her eyes to steal a glance, and saw that Keith was in pure pleasure, as he should be. She could feel the magic moment coming for both of them. This was the time for her to act. She bent over to kiss him and reached for the secret panel, with the movement of their bodies she missed on the first attempt, but was able to open the compartment with her second. The shock of what she saw froze the blood in her veins, removed all the heat that her body had generated and literally took the air from her lungs. The compartment was empty, the fucking gun was not there! How could that be? She put it there herself earlier, just before he arrived. Her mind started to breakdown, but her body was on autopilot. She continued to move her body, he was climaxing, she wasn't, she felt a deep cold inside that she had never felt before. She couldn't understand what had happened and fear, not passion, was now her strongest emotion. She saw that his face had completely changed. His look of pleasure was still there, but he also had an evil smile across his face. With one last movement deep into her, he tensed and then groaned with pleasure. He was done.

Keith opened his eyes, "Looking for something, my dear?"

"You are as good as they say." Josephine said as she realized she'd been taken at her own game by the American spy. She had been too confident in her own abilities to see any danger. She didn't know how or when he had removed the gun, but it didn't matter now. She knew there was no sense in begging for her life. She wouldn't stoop to that now anyway; she knew she was finished. For Josephine, it was better to taste the best that life had to offer for a short time than to toil forever in strife and poverty. *No one lives forever*, she thought. As he raised the barrel of the gun to her head, Josephine's mind flashed back to a memory of her mother braiding her hair. Keith fired the gun. Josephine's head slumped back as he lifted her off of his body.

With practiced efficiency, Keith got up and went to the bathroom, soaked a towel in cold water and washed the blood from his body. He returned to the bedroom and wiped down all the blood spatter he found. He got dressed, retrieved his bag from the living room and opened it. With rope and tape, he secured her hands and legs together and wrapped her still warm body in the bloody sheets. He loosened some straps on the overnight bag and it was transformed into a large carrying bag. After placing the body inside the bag, he wound rope through the straps to allow him to easily carry and maneuver the package.

After turning out all of the lights, he went to the window in the living room at the back of the flat, took out a flashlight, aimed it down towards the alley and flashed the light twice. A few seconds later a return light flashed twice from the bottom of the alley directly below the window. He opened the window and lowered the package into the darkness down the backside of the building. When it reached the bottom of the alley, he climbed out the window and attached a hook to the windowsill. Letting the weight of the window keep the hook in place, he used the remaining rope and hook to scale down the building. When he reached the ground, with a rehearsed motion he spun the hook out from the window, letting the window shut, and causing the rope and hook to fall harmlessly into his hands.

The driver opened the trunk of the large black sedan, and the colonel immediately loaded the body in there along with the hook and rope. The mission was clean, orderly and precise, just the way he liked it. The driver and the colonel exchanged no words until they were on the outskirts of London, far from the scene.

"Did everything go as planned, sir?" the driver asked.

"Yes, the intelligence boys were right on, everything down to the last detail." Strickland knew that ninety percent of his success depended on the information he was given ahead of time. He had been advised of the drugs, her preferred kill method, and the layout of the flat, all he had to do was stay cool and pull the trigger—which he did very well. The one thing the Americans had over the Germans was the quality of their intelligence research. Strickland didn't know for sure, and he didn't really care, but he was convinced that the German code must have been broken, the information was too good, too accurate.

Despite the flawless operation, the colonel had little sense of satisfaction. He actually despised that this was what his life had become; he was a dispassionate killer, seemingly incapable of remorse and feelings. If his family saw him now, they wouldn't recognize him. He didn't recognize himself, and he just didn't care about anything anymore. It was too late to change his path, but sometimes he wished for a mission that he would not return from, a mission that would end the misery that was his life. The car turned in to the drive of a farmhouse outside of London. This would be his safehouse until his next mission, which was just hours away.

CHAPTER 3

May 31, 1944 – Somewhere on the back roads of England

It was early morning. The fog was dense in some areas, patchy in others, and a steady rain was falling. The large sedan with its lone passenger drove steadily through the weather towards the destination. The driver, an Army corporal who had no idea who he was driving or why, knew that it was imperative that he get his passenger safely, and quickly, to the airfield. It had to be important, as the duty carried with it a two-day pass to London! With all the war activity going on in the last few months, along with the rumors of the pending invasion, a one-day pass was nearly impossible to get, but two days was unheard of. He had picked his passenger up in the pre-dawn hours, exchanging only the required code words. The heavy, frosted glass that separated the front of the car from the back was difficult to see through. At best the corporal saw the shadow of a tall man, wearing what looked like Army fatigues, but no features were recognizable. That was the way it was supposed to be, the corporal having no idea what his passenger looked like. *This guy must be the President or something,* thought the corporal, *who else would get this kind of big wig treatment?*

The road was slick, but that wasn't a problem for the corporal. He had been racing cars since he was a teenager back in the States and had handled worse roads than this, at twice the speed. His commander knew he was an excellent driver and had hand picked him for this task. At one point, with the rain and speed, the sedan began to fishtail, the corporal quickly and expertly regained control of the car and continued on.

"Everything okay up there?" said Lt. Col. Keith Strickland from the backseat.

"Yes, sir, my apologies. It won't happen again," replied the corporal.

Strickland leaned his head back and closed his eyes to relax and try to get some rest before this mission started. After last night with the Black Widow, he only had a few hours of sleep before the car had arrived to transport him to the airfield. He was able to doze off for a bit and when he awoke, he checked the time on his custom-made watch, the only one of its kind. A Swiss clockmaker had created the special design a few years ago, with some extra features not readily available on standard watches. It read 5:15 AM, giving them another forty-five minutes of travel. The rainy weather didn't seem to be delaying them much; the corporal seemed to be living up to his driving reputation. *The kid was earning his two-day pass*, thought Strickland. He looked out the side window, watching the rain bounce off the glass. It seemed that all it ever did in England was rain. The weather was atrocious. He hated the country for what it wasn't: it wasn't the USA. He hated a lot of things these days, but despite all he had been through, he loved America. He was a true patriot, and he would do whatever needed to be done for his country, regardless of the price he might have to pay.

The colonel started to think about how he got to this place in his life. He had been a West Point graduate, top ten percent of his class. He was a prime physical specimen, athletic and handsome, well-liked by his peers and superiors alike and best of all, he loved the Army. He wasn't in the military because of family pressure or a desire for a future political career, Keith Strickland wanted to be a soldier in order to serve his country. After West Point, he'd done well in the Army. He met and married a beautiful woman he was very much in love with, and they had a child, a boy. Strickland could not be happier. His family life was great as was his career. He made Major at the age of twenty-five and was on the fast track to becoming a General. It was 'a sure thing' he was constantly told by his superior officers. At this point in his career, he should have been up for his second star, maybe even his third considering all the chances that were available for promotion during the war. But his entire world changed in just a few minutes on that ill-fated day almost ten years ago.

The events were permanently scorched into his memory, every last gruesome detail still vivid. He relived them so often, he felt like he was physically transported back in time as his mind told him the story, always the same story, always horrific …

It was a bright and sunny day in their small midwestern town on the ninth day of July, 1934. A perfect day for a family picnic down by the lake. The young Army officer, his wife Kathy and their four-year-old son Tommy piled into their Ford and headed out. First, a stop at the bank and then on to the lake. There was no parking available anywhere near the bank because the street was being repaired, so Keith kept the car running and double parked as Kathy and Tommy went in to the bank together. Keith was fiddling with the model sailboat they brought along, hoping to finally get it to navigate more than a few feet before sinking.

Several minutes had passed, when all of a sudden, Keith heard sirens and the screeching of car tires stopping in front of the bank. He looked up from the sailboat and fear shot through his heart as he saw the black and white police cars. The policemen were jumping out and approaching the bank with revolvers drawn. He jumped out of the car and ran towards the bank yelling, "Kathy, Tommy!"

One of the officers grabbed his arm and pulled him back, "Stand back buddy, there is a bank robbery taking place, we don't need you gettin' in the way and gettin' hurt!"

"Let me go, my family is in there and—"

Just then all hell broke loose. Shots were coming from inside the bank, Keith could hear screams and shouting, and then the cops started firing into the bank; it was utter chaos. In just a few moments the shooting stopped as quickly as it had started. Several policemen cautiously approached and entered the bank. Keith broke away from the officer holding him and pushed his way into the bank yelling, "My wife and son are in there! My wife and son are in there!" He forced himself through the mob of people around the entrance, some trying to get in, most trying to get out, until he was in the middle of the bank lobby. He looked around and was desperately screaming, "Kathy, Tommy!" Then he saw three bodies on one side of the bank, he went closer and realized they must be the bank robbers; they all had masks on and all appeared to be dead.

He quickly turned his head in the other direction looking for his family. There was a gathering of people and policemen in front of one of the bank teller's window. The police were barking out instructions, "Get back, get back now." Keith walked uncertainly in that direction. As he did, the crowd opened up like the parting of the Red Sea.

As Keith got closer, his fears were growing, and his heart was sinking. He moved through the opening in the crowd of people and looked down. Keith stopped and then dropped to his knees, horrified by the sight of his wife and son covered in blood, both of them dead! Kathy was still holding Tommy. Apparently, she had tried to shield him when the shooting started. For a moment his limbs couldn't move, and his throat was paralyzed. Keith reached out and gathered them both in his arms, rocked them gently and started wailing a horrible, mournful sound.

The sergeant in charge barked at Keith, "Hey buddy, whadda ya' think—", Keith turned around and stared at the sergeant, his eyes penetrating deep into the officer's soul. The sergeant took a step back, he had never seen that look before and would remember it to the end of his days. He saw the Devil's face.

Keith turned back to his family and held them for a long time. Finally, he kissed them both, gently laid them down and covered them with a sheet someone had put next to him. Still on his knees, he stared for a while longer at their covered bodies. Every second brought with it more shock, contempt, rage and hatred. Every second also took away part of his heart and soul. He eventually got to his feet, and quietly walked out of the bank, covered in the blood of his family.

Strickland woke with a start; his emotions were raw from the nightmare memory. It was still raining outside the car, but the fog seemed to have lifted. It was reported in the paper that miraculously only two people besides the bank robbers died in the bank shootout. But that was not entirely true. There was a third casualty that day, only no one knew it yet, no one except Keith Strickland. He also died that day, even though his body went on, he was never the same person again. Their deaths were unforgiveable for him. When he closed his eyes, he could picture his wife trying to protect their son and he could hear her screaming, "Noooo!" From that day on he blamed everyone—the police, every thug, gangster, bad guy and criminal out there—for the deaths of his wife and son. Move over Adam and Eve, a new original sin had been committed in Keith Strickland's world. His memory of the months following the tragedy made him feel bitter and cold. His family had been brutally murdered and that was all he knew. The Army gave him some extended leave but it hadn't helped. Strickland changed. He no longer cared about the world, his life, the people around him, or even God. Especially God, who he blamed more than anyone else for what happened. His only salvation was the Army, but not the Army he had originally known. He started volunteering for every dangerous, suicidal mission he could, but the result wasn't what he'd hoped, to his constant disappointment, he returned from every mission. He learned, as did his superiors, he was very, very good at covert operations. He had found a new path, one of spying and killing. After a few years and some additional training, he was one of the best operatives in the Army, which proved invaluable as World War II began.

"Sir?" said the driver.

"Yes?"

"We'll be at the airfield in less than ten minutes."

"Okay, thank you."

The kid must have really been putting the pedal to the medal, as they were about twenty minutes ahead of schedule. *I'll have to ask for this corporal again*, he thought. When the corporal turned the wheel and drove the car past the high brush that helped to conceal the airfield from the road, they ended up in a large clearing, where a C-46 cargo plane was waiting on the runway. Strickland had been here before, but this was his first mission that required a plane with so much range and capacity.

This was also the first mission where he hadn't been briefed ahead of time; he would not know the details until the mission was underway. The only thing he'd been told was this mission was of the greatest importance and extremely dangerous. *That's what they say about ALL my missions*, thought Strickland wryly. Just a few years ago, he would have balked not knowing the job ahead of time, but even he realized the reality of war had everyone adjusting to constant flux.

The corporal pulled the sedan to within a hundred feet of the plane and brought it to a stop. He was under strict instructions not to get out of the car nor take notice of his passenger. The corporal did not want to mess up his two-day pass, so that is exactly what he did. Strickland got out of the car and stretched his legs a moment. The rain had finally stopped, but everything was wet and soggy. Strickland took a few steps in the mud to the driver's window and bent down to say something, at this point the corporal couldn't help but make eye contact with his passenger.

Politely, and in a very low, monotone voice Strickland offered the corporal a well-deserved compliment, "Good job, son. Excellent driving. Perhaps we can do this again."

"Thank you, sir," said the corporal, smiling ever so slightly.

Strickland turned around and started walking towards the plane.

CHAPTER 4

The colonel heard the sedan pull away but kept his attention directed toward the door of the C-46. There were no other vehicles or planes in sight, and as far as he could tell, he was the only human being in the vicinity. He opened the holster on his Army issued Colt .45, put his hand on the butt of the gun and started walking towards the plane. As he approached the door of the plane, an unexpected feeling of dread overtook him. He paused for a moment and checked his surroundings. Through training and experience, he had learned to always trust his gut instincts. As he started towards the plane again, the pilot came out the door of the plane and startled at the sight of the colonel.

"Oh! You're ahead of schedule sir," the captain said, trying to regain his composure.

"I think my driver had a date to catch," Strickland replied trying to be funny, casual humor was not one of his strengths.

The pilot smiled, trying to be polite, "Captain Scott Turner at your service, sir."

Strickland climbed the stairs, shook the captain's hand and followed him into the depths of the plane's cargo hold. As the colonel looked around, he could see the plane had been heavily modified in order to carry dozens of fifty-five-gallon fuel drums. *Where the hell am I headed with all of this fuel?* he wondered.

"Sir, all your gear, orders, and anything else you need is in those two crates, sir." Captain Turner pointed to his right, the crates were next to a makeshift bed, another modification of the plane.

"How 'bout we leave out the sir crap?"

"Yes, sir … I mean Colonel."

"Perfect, just call me Colonel, and what should I call you?"

"Everyone calls me Scotty."

Strickland took a good look at the captain. He was tall, blond with a standard issue crew cut, good build, but a baby face that made him look like he wasn't old enough to drive, let alone fly a military plane. "Ok, Scotty it is. Are you a good pilot, Scotty?" the colonel asked looking directly into his eyes.

"Number one in the air squadron, probably the best in this theater if I may say so myself, Colonel," he answered proudly.

"Good," said Strickland, doubting if that was at all true. "Tell me, what exactly are your orders?" Strickland was curious to find out exactly how much, if anything, the captain knew about the mission.

"My orders are to get you airborne by 0800, fly on a heading due west, altitude eighteen thousand feet, speed 175 knots for sixty minutes and then wait for additional orders from you. That's all I know."

"Okay, that sounds good. Let's get this gasoline tank into the air."

Without any further conversation, the captain started going through the checklist and procedures that were required for takeoff. After watching him for about twenty seconds, it was clear that the kid knew what he was doing, at least with the airplane. Within ten minutes, the C-46 had taken off and was nearing its prescribed altitude, speed and heading. Strickland then began the task of opening the two crates that held the gear and information regarding his next mission. Most of it was standard stuff, clothing, weapons, rations, ammunition, radio gear, and maps, which Strickland didn't bother to study yet. Once everything had been unpacked from the crates, he turned his attention to the leather briefcase that contained his orders.

Strickland opened the briefcase and pulled out a brown envelope, marked TOP SECRET in big red bold letters. He always wondered how many people had read these orders before they got to him. He opened the brown envelope which was simply sealed by a metal clasp and took out the file within that held the orders for the mission. He smirked to himself about the consistency of this procedure—the orders, in the file, in the brown envelope, in the leather briefcase. In ten years, they had never deviated or waivered on this protocol. Glancing at his watch, he noted he would have to give Scotty additional orders soon, so he started reading.

After a few minutes, he looked up from the papers in disbelief. From what he read, he doubted he would be coming back, barring an act of God, it would be his final mission. His emotions were mixed. On one hand, he felt some relief. Hadn't he wished for an assignment like this many times? On the other hand, he was disappointed that his superiors did not seem to really know him. They didn't tell him the details about the job until it was underway, because they thought he would try and get out of it. They were wrong, he would have taken the mission regardless. The Army and his country were the only things he had left in his life that he cared about, and he would never let them down. He got up and headed to the cockpit, it was time for him to give Scotty new orders.

"Scotty, put us on a heading of 220 degrees South-Southwest."

"Yes, Colonel," the captain said as he made the adjustment.

"Looks like this is gonna be a long ride. We're headed to South America."

"South America?!" Scotty sputtered.

"Yes, Peru to be specific."

"That's gonna take us over thirty hours."

"Yeah, I figured it would take us that long to get there. I gotta say, I was almost as surprised as you were with our destination. Do you have the instructions concerning the modified fuel system for the aircraft?"

"Yes sir, but I'm pretty sure I got it covered, I was fully briefed on the system last night by the engineers. Simple really. All I gotta do is flip the switches on this control box." Scotty pointed to a control box next to his seat that had a bank of labelled switches. A bunch of wires and cables, all taped together, came out the back of the box and snaked through the cockpit into the back of the plane. "Once the fuel gauges go below forty percent, I flip the switches in order. I had a trial run last night, everything worked just fine."

Strickland looked at the makeshift rig, "Okay Scotty, I'll leave the fuel system in your hands." He could tell it was a last-minute fix, but it seemed simple enough. Strickland now knew why the C-46 had been rigged to accommodate the additional fuel. The aircraft range was only 3,100 miles. To get from England to Peru and then to get Scotty and the aircraft back to a safe airbase was going to be almost 10,000 miles.

"Sir, can I ask you a question?"

"Sure Scotty, and drop the Sir."

"Sorry. Colonel, have you ever seen a fuel setup like this?" he asked apprehensively.

The colonel was beginning to understand why Scotty was on this mission and not preparing for the invasion. He talked a good game, but seemed like a Nervous Nelly. "Yes, I have. Nothing to worry about," he lied. *No need to give the kid anything more to worry about*, he thought.

"Alright, Scotty, I'll be in the back getting some shut eye, but feel free to wake me if you need me for anything."

"Roger that, Colonel."

Strickland went to the back of the plane, sat down on the bed and set the alarm on his custom watch to alert him in six hours. His orders had included a black and white photo of two men, he pulled the picture from his pocket and studied it again. His mission was to eliminate one of the men in the picture, Erik Wendt, a high-value German spy. He would have loved to eliminate the other man in the photo, he and several million other Allied supporters would have loved to eliminate that man—Adolph Hitler. He put the photo back in his pocket and laid down. His last thought before sleep overtook him, *never would I have thought it would all end in Peru.*

CHAPTER 5

It was 1500 London time and Scotty was all business flying his important cargo. The weather was good, but they had a pretty strong headwind, so he noted that the fuel usage was a little more than expected, but still within mission parameters. He was excited about this mission and that he was finally getting the opportunity to do an important task. His previous missions had been fairly boring, flying dignitaries and cargo up and down the British coast. His superiors told him he was performing a needed service for the Allies, but he never felt that way. It was hard to feel like you were really doing your part when everyone around you was flying combat missions and you weren't. He had wanted so badly to be a combat pilot, but early in his training, it was apparent to everyone that Scotty did not have the nerve and fortitude for the job. The only reason he was still flying for the Army was because his uncle, a two-star general in Washington, had pulled some strings.

Strickland was sleeping on his side, and with the smooth flight, he was actually getting a restful sleep. His watch sounded the alarm he had set, and he was awake in an instant. He opened his eyes, and from pure habit, quickly checked his immediate surroundings for any sign of danger. He noted the plane, the extra fuel tanks and the mission parameters filled his head. He rose from the bed and walked to the open cockpit entrance. There, he found the captain engrossed in flying the plane, checking his instrument panels, and keeping a strong grip on the control wheel.

"How are we doing, Scotty?"

The captain almost jumped out of his seat, he hadn't heard Strickland approaching. "Good, Colonel. Did you get some rest?"

"Yes, a bit."

"We're on schedule, weather is good so far, and everything as expected."

"Okay, good. I'll be in the back. Holler if you need me."

"Will do, Colonel."

Knowing he had a lot of time to kill, Strickland walked back and sat down on the bed, took the top-secret file out of the envelope and began to read through it for the second time. The mission orders read more like a fiction novel than intelligence data. Erik Wendt was his target, they were calling him 'The German'. The background on The German said he'd been a university professor who studied ancient civilizations. He had come to Hitler's attention after a state dinner where the two met and briefly discussed some of Wendt's research, the black and white photo Strickland had of the two men appeared to have been taken at that state dinner. Hitler was normally mistrustful of professors, believing their educated status would have them balking at the Nazi way and Nazi beliefs. Despite that, Hitler and Wendt had hit it off and started corresponding via letters. In a somewhat unusual move, Hitler setup a compound in the Andes mountains of Peru, and asked Wendt to head up the research team there. The compound was well hidden and well protected, and it was even rumored that Hitler had visited the site. The mission orders didn't give Strickland an exact location, but a range of coordinates over several square miles of terrain, he would have to find the compound on his own. The belief was that Wendt was in Peru studying the Inca civilization, and their ancient myths and legends. The concern was that his findings would lead to a new weapon, perhaps even an advanced biological weapon that would give Germany the advantage in the war. This was the reason the US government wanted Wendt taken out.

The mission was to eliminate The German and destroy the compound. When complete, Strickland would have to extricate himself from the area and make his way to the city of Cusco, a trek of several hundred miles, over very rough terrain, without the assistance of air or motor crafts. Although this extraction plan was possible, Strickland didn't see it having a high probability of success. On the surface it all seemed plausible, but what if the intelligence was wrong this time, very wrong?

He recalled what he knew about the Inca civilization. One day they were on top of the world, an empire twelve million strong in charge of their own destiny. Then a visit from Pizarro and a band of Spanish conquistadors started their rapid decline. After a few decades of systematic destruction, desecration, and the melting of gold and silver artifacts by the Spaniards, the Inca's were no more.

Strickland went up to the cockpit a few hours later, "Hey, Scotty."

"Hi, Colonel."

"Can you put this thing on autopilot?"

"Yes, of course."

"Okay, good. Go ahead and put on the autopilot. Show me what to look out for and you go grab some rest. We still have quite a ways to go."

Scotty seemed hesitant and replied, "I'm good, Colonel. I don't need to sleep."

The colonel got a hard look on his face and said, "It's not a suggestion Captain, it's an order. We still have twenty hours to go, and I need you to be at top form when we get to the jump spot, now go."

"Are you sure, Colonel?"

Annoyed now, Strickland said, "Yes, Scotty, I'm sure."

Scotty quickly checked his instruments, set the autopilot and showed the colonel what to watch for.

The colonel sat down in the co-pilot seat, and trying to soften the mood a bit said, "Nothing to worry about, Scotty. If anything goes wrong, I can just wake you up, right?"

"Yes, sir, no problem."

Nothing unusual happened while Scotty slept. When he woke several hours later, he returned to the cockpit to find the colonel right where he had left him. The colonel was just staring into the dark night sky.

"Hi, Colonel."

"Hi. All quiet up here."

Scotty reviewed the readings on the instrument panel. All was normal. They sat in silence for a long while and then Strickland told Scotty he was going to rest again.

After several hours, as dawn was breaking behind the plane, Strickland returned to the cockpit and sat next to Scotty. When they finally saw land in the distance, Strickland gave him a new heading. As they turned, the plane started to bounce around encountering some clear air turbulence. Scotty changed their altitude a few times trying to find a smoother ride, but had no luck. The constant bouncing was more annoying than it was a cause for alarm.

"Colonel, would you like me to change altitude again?"

Strickland thought about it for a second. "No, let's keep it at this altitude and see how it goes. As long as it doesn't get any worse, I think we'll be fine."

CHAPTER 6

June 1, 1944 – Somewhere over the Andes mountains of Peru

They bounced around for almost an hour until Scotty said, "Colonel, we're just a couple of hours from the drop point coordinates you gave me."

"Okay, I'm gonna do one final check on my gear."

Strickland went to the back and double checked all of his gear again, both the pack he would be jumping with and a secondary chute that had the rest of his supplies. This second pack was essential for him to have any hope of making the extraction trek to Cusco. He'd gone over the maps several times and felt he had a good understanding of the terrain and potential routes, as good an understanding as he could without having been there himself.

Scotty was now on the final approach to the jump spot over the Andes mountains and light turbulence had picked up again. His pulse quickened, as he knew he had almost made it. This mission was very important to him, it was his chance to show the Air Corps they were wrong about him and that he could successfully execute his mission. His excitement was quickly abated as he checked the fuel level and called out in a panicked voice, "Colonel, I think we have a problem!"

Strickland went to the cockpit and asked, "What's the problem, Scotty?"

"The fuel gauge is down below thirty percent."

"Well, did you flip the switches?"

"Of course, sir."

"Did you flip the right switches?"

"Yes, I did," Scotty replied, the panic evident in his voice. "The fuel was at thirty-eight percent, so I flipped the next set of switches and the fuel level started to rise as expected. That was about twenty minutes ago, but now we're down below thirty percent."

"How high did the fuel level go during the last refuel?"

"Um, well, I saw that it was rising, so I didn't really pay attention to how high it got, but there has to be some problem now that wasn't there before."

Strickland closed his eyes and took a deep breath so he could speak calmly. "Scotty, can you flip the next set of switches please?"

"Yes sir, flipping now."

They both watched the fuel gauge rise slowly, very slowly, it stopped at forty-five percent.

"Sir, it's, it's not working, the tanks aren't full."

"Calm down Scotty, I can see that."

"What do you think it is, sir?"

"I don't know, but now is not the time to panic. We still have plenty of fuel, and we'll figure this out."

Strickland started by checking out the box with the switches. He verified that all the cables and wires were secure. He was staring at the fuel gauge again, thinking, when it finally hit him.

"Shit! We must have a damn leak in this rigged up fuel system." He knew he would have to find the leak, and fast, in order to save the mission and both of their lives. They might make it to the drop point, but without the fuel system working, Scotty would never be able to safely land the plane away from the mountains, and there was no way he would survive parachuting out and making the trek to Cusco.

"Scotty, take her up to maximum altitude and level off, I'm gonna look for the leak."

"Roger, Colonel."

Strickland went to the back of the plane to examine the entire setup. He found the main fuel line coming from the extra drums in the cargo area and followed it into the under belly of the plane. Crawling carefully over the lines, wires and cables he found the point where that line entered the standard fuel system. The engineers had added an external fuel filler neck in order to pass the fuel from the drums into the plane's standard fuel system. That's where he found the problem, the filler neck was no longer attached to the main tank and fuel had been spilling out everywhere. He figured the idiots who put the system together had probably never tested the whole system, or even this connection. Once the pressure of the reserve fuel had run through the connection, the seal wasn't strong enough and it had loosened, probably more with every refill, and the turbulence hadn't helped the situation either.

He had to somehow reattach the filler neck, so the reserve fuel would make it to the standard tank. In all likelihood, it would still leak, but it might just be enough to save them and the mission. He needed help, so he stuck his head up and yelled out, "Scotty, I found the leak, I need your help down here. Put the plane on auto-pilot and bring the tool kit and some rope if you have it."

Scotty got out of the pilot's seat very panicky, their fuel level was dangerously low, and he couldn't remember where the tool kit was. He spun around frantically and then spotted it behind the cockpit door. *Thank God*, he thought. He picked it up and started for the back of the plane, he saw some rope near the colonel's gear and grabbed that as well.

"Here's the tool kit." There was no room for the tool kit in the belly of the plane, so he set it down on the floor.

"Give me the longest screwdriver in there and a bunch of screws. And cut me an eight-foot piece of rope." Strickland reached up, took the screwdriver in his hand, put the screws in his mouth and went back down to try and secure the fuel filler neck with the screws. He was going to use the rope as a secondary measure to help hold the fuel line in place by tying it to one of the plane's struts.

Then, the plane suddenly dropped, sending everything skyward. They were both slammed hard against the plane. Strickland banged his head, Scotty came down awkwardly on his back and the contents of the tool kit spilled out all over the floor. Heavy bouncing of the plane continued, the worst turbulence they had yet encountered. There was another huge drop and unexpectedly the plane banked hard to the left and started to descend.

"Oh my God," whispered Scotty, his face white as a ghost. He tried to get up and run to the cockpit, but the force of the plane's movement made it almost impossible to move.

Strickland knew it was over when he saw the expression on Scotty's face. The kid forgot the autopilot. Jesus, with all he had been through—he outwitted the best spies in the world, never failed at any mission, beat numerous attempts on his life—to go out like this because of an inept American pilot, how ironic. *The kid did have some guts*, thought Strickland. He didn't have to go back to the cockpit. He could have died a coward crying to the colonel and asking for forgiveness. In those last few seconds, Strickland found some respect for the kid. *God, forgive him.* Thinking of God, Strickland looked up and yelled, "Alright, you bastard, if you do exist, you owe me an explanation, face to face, of why my wife and son were allowed to die. I want to see you bullshit your way out of that."

Scotty continued his struggle and eventually crawled into the cockpit and pulled himself up into the pilot's seat, but it took him too long to get there. As he grabbed the yoke, a mountain peak was looming larger than life in front of the plane and they were approaching fast. Scotty pulled on the yoke as hard as he could, spurted out "Dear God!" and screamed.

Scotty's last-minute effort to get control of the plane only provided them with a few more seconds of life. He was just barely able to avoid the first peak when the next one, much larger, appeared in front of the plane, but he had nowhere to go. The plane hit the side of the mountain, the front of the C-46, and the pilot Captain Scott Turner, were pulverized on impact. The plane broke apart, the fuel tanks exploded and the wreckage tumbled down the mountainside.

CHAPTER 7

When Strickland came to, he did so screaming. It took him several minutes to be able to focus on anything other than the excruciating pain he felt. He was in a position where his head was laying a bit higher than the rest of his body, allowing him to see the incredible damage to his body. There was blood everywhere, his legs were broken in several places, he assumed his back was damaged, but there was no mercy there, he was still able to feel the pain throughout his body. He couldn't see his right arm, it was flung over his head, and the pain when he attempted to move was too much to continue. He could see the bone popping out of his left arm, and in what seemed like a surreal out of body experience, he saw his torso was ripped open and his organs and intestines were spilling out. He could not understand how he was still alive, but he didn't think he would be for much longer.

As a student at West Point, Strickland had written an essay considering the existence of God, any God. It was very well received by his professor and had been printed in the student paper. After his family died, he had abandoned any and all thoughts of God, but now, as he lay on the mountainside bleeding to death, he knew he would finally find out the true nature of God. Strickland felt drowsiness starting to overtake him, his eyes became blurry and finally closed. *This is it*, he thought. *Good, let's get on with it.* He then heard a voice, a deep and authoritative voice, but he couldn't understand what the voice was saying. Strickland struggled to open his eyes and to try and stay conscious, but he couldn't.

The final report on LTC Keith Strickland, was clean and concise. He was killed in the line of duty trying to stop a German spy, code name Black Widow. He was given the Medal of Honor, posthumously of course, for succeeding in his mission, while giving his life for his country.

He was a fine soldier. All of the correspondence, secret orders and evidence regarding the mission to Peru were destroyed. It never happened.

General Turner in Washington opened the letter, fully aware of its contents.

> We regret to inform you that your nephew, Captain Scott R. Turner was killed in the line of duty, flying a critical mission in support of the Allied Invasion of France. His plane was shot down by German ground fire. He received posthumously, the Medal of Honor for his bravery. He was a fine soldier.

CHAPTER 8

July 22, 1944 – Andes mountains

Erik was preparing the final report he was sending back to Germany and the Fuhrer, he expected they would be pleased that his years of research had finally yielded results and that his investigation into the Inca myth was true. He wasn't the first to make a discovery like this, in his previous life of academia, he had studied the work of all the explorers, both successful and unsuccessful. He had studied the findings and works of the father of modern Peruvian archaeology and Andean culture, the famous German, Max Uhle, whose diggings took place in the 1890s. He learned all he could about Hiram Bingham, the Yale University adventurer and explorer, who discovered the lost Inca city of Machu Picchu in 1911. The city was found at approximately eight thousand feet above sea level. Bingham's exploration, which was significant, went no higher than this point. Erik thought this was a fatal mistake, not looking any higher up in the mountains because it was believed impossible to build, farm and live above this altitude. Bingham later discovered the city of Vilcabamba, lower on the mountain, and that solidified his theory there was no reason to search at higher altitudes.

Erik was convinced he knew where to find the entrance to another lost city, and the report would convert the non-believers back in Germany who did not support his research. His analysis had consisted of piecing together known history, Peruvian folklore, and most importantly, hundreds of personal conversations he had with the locals he encountered during his travels through the mountains. The research led him to explore the upper ranges of the Andes mountains, some of which were as high as eighteen thousand feet. It was here, well-hidden in these peaks, he was certain he would find the entrance to the lost city. But it wasn't just a lost city he expected to find, but a fully functioning city with true descendants of the Incas alive and well, possessing all of the Inca knowledge and treasures. It was Erik alone who could provide Germany a path to the lost city and a path to the treasures that would be used to fortify the German military. An influx of unlimited wealth would turn the tide of the war and ensure a German victory.

He would send off the final report and then anxiously wait for official word from the Fuhrer to be allowed to enter the city. Erik truly felt he deserved this honor for the sacrifices he had made. While most of his peers had gotten accolades and promotions for their work for the Third Reich, he'd been asked to lead a life of seclusion and near destitution in Peru to carry out this special mission. He led the charade of the mountain compound being a spy camp for the Germans while almost everyone there knew it was just a cover for him to do the tireless research required to make this discovery. He felt like a prisoner, the sacrificial lamb, and that the best times of his life had passed him by. This could only be justified in his mind if he was allowed to go after the Inca treasures.

CHAPTER 9

August 3, 1944 – Berlin

Two months after Colonel Strickland's plane hit the side of the Andes mountains, a German cargo plane, heavily modified to accommodate extra fuel for a long trip, was taxiing for takeoff on a remote air strip fifty miles outside of Berlin. The cargo, besides the fuel, was one very important passenger whose destination was Peru. No sooner did the plane level off then the passenger opened his briefcase and pulled out a blue folder containing a rather lengthy report. The reader tossed aside the first page of the report, knowing what it said and immediately focused on the top of page two—*Final Evaluation of the INCA Legends.*

Two hours later after reading the report for a second time, the passenger put the folder back into the briefcase and cracked a menacing smile that would have frozen the face of Medusa herself! The report was convincing, the research thorough. *Could it be true?* he wondered. The war was no longer going in their favor, the invasion had all but finished Germany, but they were a proud people and still holding on. If the legends were true, if they were able to reach the Inca treasure, they would turn the tide of the war once more and be victorious. What a delicious thought!

CHAPTER 10

August 4, 1944 – Peru

Erik was resting in his quarters, awaiting the arrival of the German official, when there was a knock at his door.

"Come in."

The compound's senior officer opened the door and said, "Sir, we've just received word from the transport. Weather permitting, your guest should be arriving in three hours."

"Excellent, thank you. Let's make sure we are fully prepared to give our guest a grand welcome. Also, inform the cook to proceed with dinner preparations," Erik said as he sat up on his bed.

"Yes, sir."

The officer left Erik sitting on his bed, his eyes wide, his heart pumping fast, the adrenaline was flowing. He had not expected such a quick response from Germany, nor had he expected to be accompanied on the journey to the lost city, but those were his orders. Finally, the time was here. Tonight, they would discuss the plan and tomorrow they would leave to go to the lost city. It was so close. He was extremely well-prepared with his maps, supplies and, of course, his extensive knowledge of the Incas. Many long years of studying in this godforsaken mountain compound had finally come to fruition.

PRESENT DAY

CHAPTER 11

Summer – New York City

The temperature was in the nineties for the sixth straight day, and with the humidity over eighty percent, it was unbearable to be outside. Victor Panzetti, looking calm and cool, walks into the penthouse suite at the Plaza and sees his number two guy, Carmine 'The Whale' DeRosa, with his nose buried in the Daily News, reading about his beloved Yankees.

"Carmine!" Panzetti roared, "What the fuck happened with your Yanks? They almost got swept by the Red Sox? Pathetic, what a buncha bums!" Panzetti was a life-long Mets fan, and loved to give it to Carmine whenever he could.

"I don't wanna talk about it, Vic," Carmine responded. His was pissed about the series, but even more pissed about the five dimes he lost on it.

"Alright, alright. I'll give you a break today, but only today. Tonight is a big night Carmine, a big night. We are gonna have some fun." Tonight was Panzetti's 60th birthday party, and there was going to be one hell of a celebration.

"It's gonna be epic, Vic. I can't wait." The one love that Carmine had besides the Yankees, was the protection of Victor Panzetti. For years, he had worked his way up in the Panzetti family in the traditional way, from his start as an associate, to his position today. He was proud of the path he took, but often thought to himself, that traditions ain't what they used to be.

"Carmine, did you get the caterer to make the cake just the way I like it?"

"Yeah, I told 'em, all taken care of."

"Do you know where Toni is?" Victor asked.

"Right here, Boss," said Toni as she walked into the room. "Hey Carmine, your Yankees played great against Boston!"

Toni was Victor's tradition-bending number one 'guy'. *Same old Toni*, Carmine thought, *always busting my balls.* "I don't wanna talk about it, Toni. Geez," he said as he picked up his paper and stormed out of the room.

"You ever think of taking it easy on him?" asked Panzetti.

"Never," said Toni with a wily smile on her face. "Do you need anything before the party tonight?"

"No, I'm good, gonna just enjoy the view for a bit."

"Okay, Victor, see you later."

Panzetti went and stood at the huge picture window, looking down into Central Park. He gazed out over the city, thinking back at how he got to where he was now. The Boss of Bosses for all the East Coast families. He had power and he was ruthless. His resumé was typical of a man in his position, drugs, guns, gambling, murder, cyber-crime and even human trafficking. *Not bad*, he thought, *for a kid who grew up in the slums of Brooklyn.* His parents died when he was a teenager, and he and his younger brother Vinnie went to live with their grandma. He dropped out of high school to get a job and make some money, so they could all eat and keep a roof over their heads. It didn't take Panzetti long to figure out he could make more money in one day running numbers for the local wise guys than he would in a week stocking shelves at the local A&P. From that point on, he kept moving up the chain of command. Eventually he took over the numbers himself, then he became a lieutenant for the Brooklyn Capo. He was a good earner, and did whatever job was asked of him. He finally became a made guy giving him even more protection, which helped him survive the business. Ten years ago, he became Capo for Brooklyn and then after a necessary shakeup of the hierarchy, he became the Boss.

The only regret Panzetti had was not being able to have any children. It just hadn't happened for him and his beautiful wife, and he wasn't ever going to adopt a kid, just not his way. His wife passed ten years ago, and since then it was mostly the bimbo of the month club, never anything serious. He still had his brother, Vinnie, and of course his niece, Toni. The decision to put her on the payroll had turned out better than he could ever have expected. She was smart, had an Ivy league education, was a wizard with computers and brilliant in the world of international finance. She had helped to automate most of their operations, creating apps that enabled the movement of resources at digital speed. Now she was his number one, and she was making him money hand over fist. And then there was Carmine, the most loyal motherfucker out there. Carmine had been with him for over thirty years, not for his brains, but for his loyalty and trust. He was solid. Carmine was one of the last of his breed, faithful to the end, Panzetti knew Carmine would take a bullet for him. He smiled and looked down at his new Rolex, a birthday gift from Carmine. *I'll just check in with Carmine and then take a shower,* he thought.

Carmine looked down at his to do list. Victor had put him in charge of all the party details—the guest list, the menu from the caterer, the bartender, the entertainment (both kinds, during the party and after the party) and especially the security, which had to be air tight, a lot of VIPs were coming. They had rented out the top floor of the Plaza, taking all the penthouse suites, even those they didn't need. Carmine looked up as there was a knock on the door.

Panzetti stepped in, "How ya doing, Carmine? We all ready for tonight?"

"Absolutely, Boss, caterer will be here in fifteen minutes to setup and the band is already here."

"Excellent. You need anything from me?"

"No, Boss, all good, you just relax."

"Alright, I'm gonna get ready, catch ya later."

Carmine knew there was one last item on his to do list: the bartender. He had been vetted by Toni a couple of weeks ago. All that was needed was to give him a call and get him to the party about thirty minutes before it started. As far as Carmine was concerned, you saw one bartender, you saw them all.

Victor finished the knot in his bow tie, checked his cuffs and looked into the mirror. He smiled and thought, *Life is good,* and then he headed to his very last birthday party.

CHAPTER 12

Ken Stone was standing in his hotel room in front of the mirror fixing his tie. He was wearing a traditional black tuxedo, a typical bartender outfit, but this tuxedo was far from typical. It looked normal to the naked eye, but it had more secrets and tricks than an entire magic show. Ken knew that he would get frisked, but what his tuxedo was hiding would not be found by any of Panzetti's goons. He checked his hair again, the gray dye had finally dried, and the mustache was firmly intact. The large rimmed eyeglasses were a comfortable fit and looked as if they belonged on his face. He looked rather distinguished, he thought, not that it made any difference. This was not one of his best disguises, but it would do, and he would never see any of these people again, at least not alive.

Satisfied that he looked like a bartender, Stone went to double check his duffel bag on the bed. This was going to be a good night for him. Tonight was the last time he would take it upon himself to solve society's problems. From now on society would have to figure things out on their own, this was his last job. The truth was he was exhausted with all of it. He had solved hundreds of problems over many long years. He first started out by declaring his own personal war on drugs, taking out the dealers, and other scumbags, especially the ones who peddled to kids or used kids in their operations. His next battle was waged against human traffickers, bastards who were making a profit on modern-day slavery. Stone really couldn't decide what bothered him most: the child labor, the sexual exploitation, or the organ trafficking. He had finally come to the conclusion that his efforts were best spent going after the mob guys. They were organized, had the manpower and the money, and were the biggest cause of all the problems he was trying to fix. His mission the last few years was to totally and completely disrupt their organizations on a regular basis.

That was what led him to posing as a bartender for the night. Panzetti was truly evil, and he, more than any guy in quite a while, needed to be taken out. His removal from the human species would be a benefit for all of mankind. This man had taken the energy and life out of too many innocent people in his sixty years. Tonight, it would end, not only for Panzetti but for all of his friends and associates that were unfortunate enough to be attending his party. Stone knew there would be a few innocents there, like the call girls—most of them had no choice in the matter—he would spare them. Compassion for women like these was a soft spot in his armor. He knew that the female of the species had been, and likely always would be, taken advantage of by the men of society, especially powerful men like Panzetti.

Lost in his thoughts, Stone didn't hear his phone ring, but finally felt the buzzing in his pocket. He pulled it out and saw that it was Carmine, the number two guy. He had been interviewed by Toni and gave her the name John Knight, but since then, all of his communications had been with Carmine.

"Hello."

"Yeah, this Knight?" growled Carmine.

"Yes, it is," he said in a calm voice, part of his mild bartender demeanor.

"Get your fuckin' ass in gear. I want ya here now. The boss is thirsty."

"I'll be right there."

"Good," came Carmine's typical one syllable reply, and then he hung up.

Stone grabbed his duffel. Everything was in place. He knew Panzetti's boys would search the bag, but they wouldn't know what to look for. He went to the mirror one last time, took a quick look, and satisfied with his appearance he made his way to the door. As he walked to the elevator, a sense of relief washed over him. He was only a few hours away from completing his last job. Then he could pay his respects to the only people he'd ever loved, and do what he needed to do in order to complete his destiny. He didn't know what the end would hold for him, but he was ready for it. *But first, the party, and am I gonna be the life of it,* he thought as he chuckled quietly to himself.

CHAPTER 13

The last two detectives finally left her office and her partner, Kyle Jenkins, had left an hour earlier. Detective 1st Grade Abby Steel sat back in her chair, closed her eyes, and took a deep breath to relax. It had been a difficult couple of days for her. For the past few years, she has been chasing a vigilante killer responsible for at least fifteen murders, probably more, throughout the five boroughs. Her captain finally put a task force together for the case and put her in charge of it, telling her she was the best detective he had. The last few days she had been leading the task force, as they again poured over all the evidence from every killing, trying to find something to break the case. So far, no luck. "Fifteen murders and not one fucking clue," was how Abby vividly described the case. The perp was a ghost.

Abby wasn't a stranger to high profile cases or assignments. She did her job very well and commanded the respect of her peers and superiors. She had been to the prestigious FBI school in Virginia, was assigned to the anti-terrorist squad, had an excellent knowledge of weapons and explosives, and even did a stint on the bomb squad in a backup capacity. She was well rounded, fearless, and ballsy. But this guy, her gut told her the perp was male, was very good at his job also. He left no clues, each kill done with a precision unlike anything she had seen before. Strangely, the murders were done with a certain flair and style, like something right out of a fiction novel, throats slashed with no apparent fight or scuffle and then the bodies were posed in strange ways. The only upside of the case were the victims. They were the scum of the city, drug dealers, pimps, killers, most of them connected to the mob. This guy was unstoppable and had the criminals running scared. The public on the other hand, was cheering for him like he was a super hero cleaning up the city. Even she had to admit a tiny part of her was rooting for the guy, but it was still her duty to find him and put an end to it. Vigilantism was the beginning of a slippery slope, one she would not go down. She firmly believed in the rule of law, and that society needed it to exist.

Looking forward to a good night's sleep and a fresh perspective in the morning, Abby grabbed her bag, put some case files in it and headed to the garage.

"Hey Abby, wanna grab a drink or something?" asked Detective Peter Clarke as she walked by his desk.

"Maybe next time, Pete. I'm beat."

"Okay then. Have a good night."

"You too." Abby smiled as she walked away. She knew that Pete was a little sweet on her, and no matter how many times she turned him down, he hadn't given up, not yet anyway. Abby was thirty-nine and had been in the NYPD for almost twenty years. She had been married twice, first an insurance salesman and then a fireman. They were both great guys and she was still friends with them, but it was her long hours on the job that did both relationships in. She'd always wanted children, but was both glad and disappointed that neither marriage resulted in children; she sometimes wondered if she was able to have a baby. She was about five foot seven, long brown hair with red and gold highlights and had an athletic build. She had run cross country in school and still loved running; in fact, her regular morning runs had helped her solve more than a few cases. Something about the way her body relaxed and her mind worked when she was running helped her to make connections she had not made before.

Walking to her car she thought again of Pete's offer, she smiled and said to herself, "Nice to know the boys are still interested."

CHAPTER 14

Summer – Billings, Montana

Rabbi Saul Kuperman was just finishing a long day at the synagogue, where he met with various members, students and some local planning board personnel. He was exhausted, but it was a good feeling, knowing he'd gotten a lot accomplished. The recent growth of his congregation had prompted talk of expansion and new buildings and facilities. Some of the younger members had joined the board and everyone was excited about the future. This gave him hope and confidence in the continued success of his synagogue as a whole.

Despite his fatigue, Saul was looking forward to tonight because it was the night he had a regular chess match with one of his closest friends, who was also a leader in the community. It was always a fun and entertaining evening, but never much of a challenge for Saul, who played much better than his friend. Through the years, they had had many spirited conversations covering topics from religion to politics and from war to sports as they played chess and drank good wine. Upon returning home, Saul changed into casual clothes, ate dinner and put his regulation sized tournament chess set on the table he had custom made for it. The wine was chilling in the fridge and he had some time before his guest arrived to relax and get his mind ready for the games ahead. Saul was especially excited as he had been promised a surprise he would never forget. He had no idea how surprised he would be.

The doorbell rang and Saul went to the front door and opened it. "Hello, my friend. Here let me help you with that," as he reached for the bag his guest was carrying.

"No, no, it's no problem really," Crajack replied, but Saul took the bag anyway.

After the usual pleasantries, Saul opened the first bottle of wine, poured them each a glass and they sat down at the chess table.

Crajack said, "Remember I told you I have a surprise for you?"

"Yes, I remember."

"Well, here it is." Crajack took a beautiful mahogany chess box out of his bag and asked, "Why don't we play with these?"

Saul's jaw dropped as he immediately recognized the elegant 1950 Dubrovnik style chess set, the same style pieces that Bobby Fisher used in the World Championship against Boris Spassky in 1972.

"My gift to you, Saul, for our longtime friendship."

Saul was as giddy as a schoolgirl, "Look at these pieces. They are exquisite. I'll be afraid to touch them."

"Hogwash," said Crajack, "They're meant to be touched, especially for someone like you who loves the game and plays so well."

Saul was speechless as he carefully looked over each of the ebony and boxwood pieces as he put them on the board. They played a quick first game, where Saul won easily. The second game was underway and Saul was now struggling, not something he was used to in these games.

"You are making some interesting moves. Have you been studying?" asked Saul.

"Not really, I'm just feeling a bit lucky tonight," Crajack replied. What Saul didn't know was that his opponent was actually a chess master, and all these years, he'd been letting Saul win.

A few unexpected moves later Saul said, "Brilliant play, my friend, just brilliant. I must resign as I see no way out for me. Congratulations!"

"Thank you, Saul," Crajack said smugly. "Before I forget, I have another surprise for you."

"I think it will be pretty tough to top what you've already given me."

"Don't be so sure." Crajack said as he reached back into his bag and pulled out an envelope and then a plastic case about 12 by 14 inches.

Crajack gave Saul the envelope and said, "Here, open this first."

Saul opened the envelope and discovered a one-way, first-class ticket to Sydney, Australia. Also, inside the envelope was a cashier's check for one million dollars. Confused, as well as curious, Saul looked at him and asked, "What's all this about?"

Crajack's face suddenly twisted with a wicked smile as he said, "What's this about? It's about me being tired of you. It's about me having some fun and it's about where you'll be spending the rest of your sorry, pitiful life, Saul, on one condition that is."

Saul was now even more confused and worried about the mental state of his friend, "Are you okay? You're not acting like yourself."

"I'm fine, thank you, and I am actually acting exactly like myself."

"What are you talking about? Is this some sick joke?" asked Saul, "If it is, it's not funny, not funny at all."

"No, it's not a joke, Saul," said Crajack as he opened the plastic case to expose a Glock handgun, "I'm deadly serious."

Seeing the gun, Saul finally started to grasp the potential seriousness of his situation, but still could not believe it. He got up and said, "I think you should leave now, go home and get some rest. You are clearly not in your right mind."

"Sit down, you Fucking Jew!" screamed Crajack as he grabbed the Glock and pointed it directly at Saul.

Saul slowly sat back down again, real fear setting in.

"I have been putting up with your pathetic wallowing and your annoying ways for years now and it's time it comes to a stop. I just can't take it anymore. It's sickening me."

Saul could not understand why his friend was acting this way. He stared at him, trying to make sense of it all. *Did he have too much wine? Was he on drugs? Why was he saying these hateful things? And the gun?!*

Crajack stood up holding the gun. He reached back into his bag and pulled out a silencer, which he attached to the gun while he started pacing around the room.

"Okay, remember I told you there was one condition?" said Crajack. Saul stared at him.

"Do you remember?" Crajack screamed into his face.

"Yes, I remember," Saul whispered in response, eyes downcast.

"Good, here is my proposition—believe it or not, I will give you an honest chance to walk away from here tonight, alive and well. As pitiful as you are, I feel like giving you a chance. Doesn't happen often, in fact you would be the first, so try and be grateful, you disgusting Hebe."

"I'm sorry, my friend. I'm not following what you're saying," replied Saul very calmly, almost serenely, hoping it would help the situation. It doesn't help because Saul really doesn't know his friend at all and has no idea about the truly evil and disgusting things he has done in his life.

"Oh my God, you're a fucking idiot. I haven't even told you the condition yet for fuck's sake. Jesus Christ, why did I wait so long to take you out? Maybe I should just forget the whole thing and get it over with right now." Crajack put the gun up to Saul's temple, but doesn't get a reaction from him.

"Just kidding, buddy," Crajack laughs, "I still wanna have a little more fun tonight."

Saul is anything but calm, however, he is resigned to the fact he's dealing with a madman.

"Okay, so here is the condition—we play one more game of chess, you win, you go free, it's that simple. You take the check and plane ticket and go to Australia, never come back and never tell anyone about this evening. If you do win, which is very unlikely, and tell anyone about tonight, I promise you will suffer a horrible, tortuous death. If you lose, I plant one shot straight into your temple and boom, you're dead."

Saul sat in his chair in disbelief. "You want to play a game of chess ... for my life?" Saul squeezed his eyes shut. *Was this really happening? Would he wake up from this crazy nightmare?* He shook his head hard and then opened his eyes and looked around, everything was still the same.

Crajack took two pawns, one black, one white, mixed them up behind his back and then presented his closed hands and said, "Choose."

Saul just looked at him and did not move.

"No choice, Saul? Okay, then I will choose for you." Crajack opened his right hand to reveal the white pawn, "Ah, white, your favorite, you just might have a chance to beat me."

Crajack sat back down and put the gun on the table next to him. "Your move Saul, good luck!"

When Saul didn't move, Crajack stood up and smacked him hard across the face. "Wake up and play, you stupid Jew, or I'll kill you right now!" he was reaching for the Glock as he was talking.

The slap did the trick, Saul looked directly in his eyes and asked, "How do I know you will keep your word?"

"Well ... you don't. As you saw in our last game, I really am a master, so if you win, you deserve it. I will keep my word, but you have to win the game first."

Saul moved his first white pawn. He played slow and methodically.

54

Crajack moved his pieces within seconds.

Saul knew he wouldn't win the game, his opponent's aggressive moves were way beyond his ability to defend. And even if he did win, he was pretty sure he was not getting out of this alive. His only chance was to surprise his adversary and get his attention away from the gun.

"I know it's still early, my friend, but things aren't looking so good for you," Crajack confidently stated.

"Oh, I have one or two tricks still left in my arsenal," Saul replied, knowing what he had to do. He then placed his hand on his queen, kept it there for a few tantalizing seconds knowing that once he touched the piece, it must be moved. This surprise move caught his enemy's full attention—for a split-second Saul got his wish, the attention wasn't on the Glock—so Saul picked up his queen and made his move.

CHAPTER 15

Panzetti finally started to wake up. His body was numb all over and his mind was fuzzy. "What a fucking hangover," he mumbled to himself. It seemed that it was only a few minutes ago he was enjoying the party and sipping a drink. He hadn't put one on like this in a long time and he guessed his people were letting him sleep it off. As his mind started to clear, he realized with alarm that he was not in bed. He struggled to open his eyelids, which felt as heavy as lead weights. Panzetti quickly realized there was something very odd about the situation and that he didn't feel right. As his eyes opened and adjusted to the light, he tried to sit up. That was when he discovered he was completely paralyzed. Not a single muscle would respond. It was as if someone turned off that part of his brain that controlled all motor movements. Curiously, he could move his eyes, but he couldn't see much more than the walls and the ceiling and a few vague shapes in his peripheral vision. At least he knew where he was; he recognized the suite where the party had been. He tried to remember the party and when exactly he went blotto, but got nothing.

What the hell? Why was he, Victor Panzetti, laying on the floor in the party suite? Where the fuck were Toni and Carmine and his other bodyguards? This is what he paid them to prevent! All at once, his alarm quickly moved to fear as he realized someone had done this to him, some-one had gotten to him, and his people were nowhere to be found! Paying more attention now, Panzetti could hear noises, there was someone else in the suite, and it sounded like they were walking towards him. A man walked into Panzetti's line of sight, stood over him and stared down with deep, penetrating eyes, as if he could see Panzetti's dark, depraved soul. Panzetti thought he recognized his eyes, maybe he was at the party, but beyond that he couldn't place him.

"I saved you for the finale, Victor. Your elimination is my last prob-lem to solve, the rest of your lowlife associates were bonus points for good behavior … mine, not yours." A wicked smile appeared on the man's face. "Oh, pardon my manners, you can't see what I'm talking about. Let me fix that."

Stone maneuvered Panzetti into a sitting position against a wall. What Panzetti saw would have made him recoil in surprise and disgust, that is if he could move. He carefully focused to make sure what he saw was real. He saw Carmine, Toni, and his other six body guards lying in pools of their own blood, their throats had been slashed, their faces expressionless. They were neatly arranged in a circular fashion, with all of their heads together, and feet extended out. It looked like an overhead shot of the June Taylor dancers from the old Jackie Gleason show, only no one was dancing. He saw across the large suite, the bodies of some of his other associates, people who had been guests at his party. He couldn't see any blood over there, but he figured they were dead.

This is not good, Panzetti thought. In vain he tried to speak, but those muscles were also paralyzed. Fear was in Panzetti's mind, but not panic. He had been through some tough scrapes and had been close to death more than a few times, so he wasn't one to panic.

"Unlike your friends, who never knew what hit them, you now know what's coming. And although you won't feel the physical pain when I kill you, every second from now until then, you will feel the emotional anguish."

Panzetti stared at Stone, cursing him in his mind with every foul word he ever knew. If he could only move. This couldn't be the way he was gonna go down, Jesus, with no dignity. Now he started to panic.

"I know what you're probably thinking," Stone said. "Who is this arrogant bastard? If I could move, I'd kick his ass. Well, Victor, you can't move now and your ass-kicking days have officially ended."

Panzetti watched Stone go to a black duffel bag in the center of the room and take out a deadly looking knife with a razor-sharp edge. It had death written all over it. Stone walked back to Panzetti and bent down to do his deed. As the knife ripped through him, and the blood began pouring out of his body, Panzetti let out with a horrible scream, one that only he could hear.

CHAPTER 16

Saul dove across the table and shoved the sharp end of the queen towards Crajack's face, knocking the chess board and all its pieces off the table along with Glock. Saul knocked him over in his chair and landed on top of him. Crajack was caught off guard and was barely able to put his hands up in defense. He had definitely underestimated his prey. Saul quickly turned over, spotted the Glock and scrambled towards it. He grabbed the gun and jumped up, pointing it at the man he thought was one of his closest friends. He was surprised that there wasn't more of a struggle to get the gun once it had been knocked off the table. *I guess I really surprised him*, Saul thought.

"Pick up the chair and sit down!" Saul yelled.

Crajack slowly picked up the chair, righted it, and sat down facing Saul, who had the gun pointed directly at him.

"What now?" asked Crajack. "We both know you're not gonna kill me. It's not who you are, Saul." Crajack wondered, *how long do I let him revel in his moment of glory?* "Got to hand it to you, Saul. Didn't think you had it in you."

"Shut up, just shut up, you bastard."

"Saul, relax, it's me, your friend. The gun is just a joke. It has blanks in it anyway. The whole thing was a joke really, I was just trying to liven up our evening. I see now it was in very bad taste. I'm so sorry."

Saul is even more confused as he sees his friend's regular personality resurface. He wants to believe it was all just a bad joke, but something inside him knows it wasn't.

"Come on now, Saul, let me have the gun back and we can joke about this crazy night, and my awful sense of humor," Crajack said as he stood up.

"Stop, stop it right now or I *will* shoot you!" Saul yelled, his hands beginning to tremble.

"I know you aren't going to shoot me, and I really don't want you to hurt yourself. Please give me the gun, Saul." He took a step closer.

Saul backed up two steps, "Sit back down! Don't come any closer!"

"Okay, enough already," said Crajack clearly annoyed at this point, "This little charade is over." He walked straight towards Saul.

Saul fired two rounds right into his chest, his body jerked a bit, but it doesn't stop him. Crajack wrenched the gun out of Saul's hand and pushed him down onto the couch.

Saul looked up at Crajack, voice shaky, "You sick bastard, you did put blanks in the gun, you never had any intention of killing me. Why would you do this?" he asked.

"Well, Saul, I'm sorry to say you lost the game." Crajack then pointed the Glock at Saul's stomach and fired two rounds. Saul cried out in pain as the bullets ripped through him and blood started pouring out. "Oops," Crajack said with a laugh, "I guess they weren't blanks after all."

Saul looked down at the blood on his shirt, the stain getting bigger, he knew he was dying. The pain was intense and his body was starting to feel cold. As he lay slumped over on the couch, the last thing he noticed as darkness started to take over was the white queen, his queen, standing straight up on the floor. It was his last move in the game and also his last move in life.

CHAPTER 17

The Dodge Charger was speeding through early morning traffic, which was sparse at 2:00 AM, trying to get from lower Brooklyn to Central Manhattan as quickly as possible. Abby had gotten the call from Captain Kelley about a half hour ago, very early and very unexpected, Victor Panzetti was dead, and she was needed at the crime scene. She had gotten dressed and was out the door in less than five minutes. Her thoughts were racing around what little information she had. All the captain told her was that there was a major hit at the Plaza, where Panzetti was having a party. There were lots of bodies and it looked like the work of the vigilante they had been tracking. Again, the vigilante had taken out a true bad guy and for that she was grateful. She hated Panzetti and all the vile things he did. But she also knew she had to stop the vigilante once and for all, he was out of control. She screeched to a stop in front of the Plaza and was out of the car in a flash.

She was met by a patrolman, who was there to escort her directly to the crime scene. Not a word was said in the elevator, but Abby's mind was working furiously. Her captain promised nothing at the scene would be touched until she arrived, which was exactly the way she liked it. She wondered, *how did the guy get close to Panzetti?* Besides the slew of body guards, the perp would have had to get by Carmine and Toni, and she found that hard to believe. Her partner Kyle met her as the elevator doors opened on the penthouse floor and walked her to the scene.

"Good morning, Abby."

"Good morning, Kyle. What the hell do we have?"

"Panzetti is dead."

"Yeah, that much I got from the captain. What about his bodyguards, how did they get past 'em?"

"They're dead too."

"Carmine and Toni?" Abby asked surprised.

"Yep, Carmine and Toni are dead, altogether we have eighteen bodies."

"What?" shouted Abby as she grabbed Kyle's arm and stopped him in his tracks. "Eighteen bodies?"

"Yeah, it's a fucking nightmare," responded Kyle.

"Who are they?"

"All of 'em are bad guys, affiliated with Panzetti in one way or another, so at least there are no innocents. Reports are telling us there were sixty or so people at the party. Looks like these guys stayed for an after party and got way more than they expected. I gotta tell you, I've never seen anything like this."

"Eighteen, huh? Okay, show me the bodies," she said solemnly. Abby knew she was heading to something unusual if Kyle was shocked at what he saw. As far as Abby was concerned, Kyle had seen everything. Early in her career, she had heard the story of how Kyle had spotted a car that matched the description in an Amber alert. He had the day off, was working around the house and had run out to Home Depot to get some supplies. As soon as he saw the car, he grabbed for his phone to call it in, and too late, realized he left it at home, as well as his gun. Not wanting to lose the car and potentially the child, and having no alternative, he just started following the car. Ten hours and two states later he'd followed the car to a suburban neighborhood in Ohio. They had only stopped once, for gas at one of those huge truck stops with hundreds of trucks, cars and people. He had been too distracted by the thought of losing them to try and get help. Now there he was, a few houses down sitting in his car, no phone, no gun, clothes covered in paint, trying to figure out what to do. If Kyle left to get help, the guy might leave with the kid and he hadn't followed him for ten hours to lose them now. In the end, he did the only thing he could, he burst into the house unarmed, surprised the kidnapper, got shot three times and in the end managed to save the terrified six-year-old boy he found in a closet.

As they entered the room with the bodies, Abby looked around for a long time, just taking it all in. Kyle knew Abby went into a different mode at a crime scene and he never interrupted her. She would get a distracted look on her face, but in fact, she was laser focused on examining every detail of the scene. In this state she was hyper-tuned to everything going on, but she also heard and registered everything that was being said.

All of a sudden, an officer burst into the room and said, "I've got more bodies." Abby and Kyle exchanged a knowing look and followed her out the door. She took them to another room down the hall where six women, all dressed provocatively, were laying around the room. After closer examination, they realized the women were not dead, just seriously drugged and unconscious.

"Kyle, can you find out who these women are?"

"I'm on it," he responded.

Abby looked at the women and wondered to herself, *why are these women still alive? Are they supposed to be? Did he make a mistake, and finally we'll get a break in the case?*

Paramedics arrived in the room and started to treat the women. Abby decided to go back to the main crime scene; the women wouldn't be able to help her until they were awake anyway.

The sun had already been up for several hours and Abby was beat. There was so much blood, and so many bodies, it would take the crime scene techs days to get everything photographed, labeled and back to the lab. Until then, the entire penthouse floor was a crime scene and would be closed off as long as it needed to be, much to the dismay of the hotel's manager.

Kyle walked over to where Abby was standing, she asked, "They awake yet?" referring to the women.

"Nope, they're still out cold. But I did find out who they are."

"Okay, so tell me," Abby said.

"High-priced hookers, no major run-ins with the law, a couple of them don't even have rap sheets."

"Hmmm, interesting. Any other info?"

"Not yet, they're all at the hospital, I'll follow up and let you know as soon as they're awake."

"Okay, thanks, Kyle."

The women had been transported to the hospital so they could be closely monitored. Abby knew one of them might hold a key to bringing the vigilante down once and for all, and she wanted them as safe as possible. Abby was guessing they had been drugged with some sort of powerful sleeping barbiturate, a dosage just short of being deadly, but enough to keep the women out a long, long time.

The medical examiner walked over to Abby and Kyle to report on his preliminary findings regarding the bodies, "Whoever did this knew their shit about drugs. Also, it's hard to tell without a full autopsy, but my best guess is that the murder victims were drugged and put into a cataleptic state before they had their throats slashed."

"Thanks," Kyle replied, he then turned to Abby, "What're you thinkin', partner?"

"I don't know, I'm thinking a lot of things, but nothing that makes sense. It seems like our guy, but he hasn't used drugs before. I'm hoping when the women wake up, they can give us something we don't have now. Otherwise, we'll work the case like we always do and hope to catch a break, not that we've had any luck on this one yet."

"Sounds good to me. Why don't I hang around here, you go home, get some rest, and I'll call you when someone wakes up so you can interview them."

"No, I'm good, I'll stay here with you."

"Abby," Kyle stepped closer and lowered his voice, "Starting up this task force has been exhausting for you. I know that better than anyone. Just go home for a couple of hours and recharge your batteries. We're partners and I got this."

Abby looked at Kyle, he looked engaged and alert, way better than she felt. "Okay, I'll take just a couple of hours, but call me if anything happens, got it?"

"Yeah, I got it," Kyle said grinning.

On the drive home, Abby's brain was going a mile a minute with all the questions she had about the crime scene. It was clearly a pro hit, no witnesses (so far), no noises, no warning, no clues, just eighteen fewer scumbags in the world. This guy was good, the timing alone was nearly impossible to figure. How could everyone just fade off into some drugged state at the same time without some suspicion being raised? He would have to be a freakin' Houdini. This guy had nerves of steel to even think he could pull it off. Panzetti no less! Why did he save the hookers? Did the vigilante have a heart? And how did he know they were hookers and not associated with Panzetti? Four of the victims had been women, but they were known associates of Panzetti. How do you commit eighteen cold-blooded, cold-hearted murders, but find it in your heart to spare six high-priced call girls? It didn't make sense to her. One of the oddest things at the crime scene was the look on Panzetti's face, pure terror, maybe it was a revenge hit? Another odd fact was the strange arrangement of the bodies. What was that all about? Did the vigilante have a sense of humor, or was he sending a message? Was it even the vigilante who did this? She had no fucking idea.

Abby was back at her apartment and after a shower and some comfort food, she was getting ready to nap for an hour before she went back to the crime scene, but then her cell phone rang, her dad.

"Hi, Dad."

"Abigail, my dear, how are you?" asked her father, Dominic Steel.

"I'm good, Dad, just a little tired. I've had a long couple of days."

"Oh, I'm sorry, I really needed to talk to you, but if this is a bad time …"

"No, it's fine, Dad, you know I love talking to you, anytime."

Dominic could hear the smile in her voice, so he continued, "Well, if you're sure, I really don't want to wait."

"I'm sure, and now you have me intrigued. What's going on?"

For the next ten minutes, her father talked and she listened intently. He told her he was investigating several deaths in his hometown of Billings, Montana. He was a long-time newspaper reporter and editor, first in New York City, and now he ran a small paper in Billings. He was calling them 'suspicious deaths', even though they had been fully investigated by the police and ruled as accidents or natural causes. His concern was that there had been so many of them in such a short time, his gut told him there was something more there, something the police had missed. He didn't really have proof of foul play and no known motives, but had uncovered some coincidences and circumstantial evidence. He wondered if it was too much for a small-town newspaper guy to ask his big city detective daughter to come to Billings and look over his evidence.

Abby was conflicted, she knew her dad wouldn't call her like this unless he had some very serious concerns, and she wanted to help him, but the only thing she could think about these days was the vigilante case. There was no way she could leave now after the multiple murders last night.

"Wow, Dad, that's some story. You really believe they weren't accidents, and you have evidence?"

"Yes, Abigail. Not sure if it would stand up in a court of law, but it's damn convincing to a newspaper man."

"Well, I hope you know I'm happy to help. Let me talk to the captain and see if I can come out in a few weeks."

"A few weeks?" he said, clearly disappointed.

"Dad, are you okay?"

"Yes, yes, I'm fine."

"Is there something you aren't telling me?"

"Well, it's probably nothing, but it does have me pretty uneasy."

Anxiety and nervousness were not emotions her father usually dealt in; with him it was all about the facts. "Tell me what it is Dad, please." She was beginning to worry about her father now.

"Okay so, a local rabbi was brutally murdered in his home last night."

"Oh my god, that's terrible, but what has that got to do with the accidents you were talking about?"

"You're right, it's probably nothing."

"Come on, Dad, tell me."

"I think they're related," he blurted out. "My intuition has been screaming at me since I found out about the rabbi's murder and I just can't shake the feeling that the suspicious deaths and last night's murder are related somehow. I know the police chief isn't even gonna entertain the idea, since his department investigated and ruled every one of the other deaths an accident, so I really need your help, Abigail."

"Dad," she asked carefully, "Does anyone know about your investigation for the paper?"

"A few people do, why?" he asked, then it dawned on him, "Oh."

"Okay, Dad, I'm sure there is nothing to worry about. Listen, I'm gonna talk to the Captain and get some leave and I'll be out there as soon as I can. Please just keep a low profile until I get there."

"A low profile? That's crazy, I think you're overreacting."

"You're the one who called me with your crazy theory, right? So, let me do what I do best. Keep a low profile until I get there and then we'll figure it out together, alright?"

"Alright, let me know once you've made the travel arrangements."

"Okay, I will see you soon. Love you, Dad."

"Love you too, Abigail."

CHAPTER 18

Ken Stone was a perfectionist. In his line of work, he had to be. Over the years, he'd learned from experience what precautions absolutely had to be taken in order to ensure success and survival. He knew most people in his business made their mistakes after the hit, rather than during it. His preparation for his final hit had been meticulous, and he did not deviate from the plan. He had a date with destiny and didn't want to spend the next two weeks looking over his shoulder. As soon as he had killed Panzetti, Stone started to disengage himself from the scene. He immediately returned to his room, took a quick shower and changed clothes. He packed everything he'd brought with him into a duffel bag, he knew to never leave anything behind or trust it to the garbage, the police would track it down within hours. He threw a small container of bleach down the sink and the shower drain, wiped down every surface and walked out carrying his bag. The lobby was quiet as Stone walked through, acting casual, blending in. He exited the hotel, turned right and walked to the end of the block. He pulled out a burner phone, called 911 and reported that he heard some noises from the penthouse of the Plaza, maybe gunshots, the police should send someone right away.

Using a couple of different cars he had staged earlier, and some backtracking to avoid being traced through video surveillance, Stone made his way back to the boutique hotel he had been staying at. Just fifty-seven minutes after killing Panzetti, he was in his room sipping Johnnie Walker. He rarely drank, but usually had one after every hit. Since this was his last hit ever, he had two. He was asleep moments after his head hit the pillow, and he slept like a baby.

In the morning, Stone showered, dressed and called a car. He made it to the airport in record time thanks to the Benjamin he gave the driver at the start of the trip. The power of the almighty dollar never ceased to amaze him. He had two different tickets, with two different names, and two different destinations, just in case something unusual happened. He often followed his intuition, ready to change his plans in a moment, but today it was all quiet and his preferred flight was on time, so he grabbed a paper and boarded.

Abby had been running around the last couple of hours trying to get everything settled before her trip. She was finally at the airport, had checked her gun at the desk and now had a few minutes to call her Dad and give him her flight information. Her call to the captain had not gone well initially. He couldn't believe she wanted to leave after what had happened to Panzetti and his associates. She told him her Dad was not doing well and she needed to go out and help him, which was true, but wasn't completely honest. In the end, he relented and granted the personal leave she wanted. She dialed her dad.

"Abigail, hello."

"Hi, Dad. I just wanted to give you my flight information. Do you have a pen?"

"Yes, just hold on a second," Abby could hear him rustling through a drawer, "Got it, go ahead."

"I'm on Prestige, flight 320. I get in just after five o'clock."

"Okay got it, I'll send a car for you. Listen, honey, did you bring a nice dress with you?"

"Why?" Abby asked suspiciously, her dad was always pulling stuff like this.

"Well, it's just that there is a little thing tonight—"

"*Dad*, I thought we agreed you would keep a low profile!"

"Now don't get mad at me, it's the annual Chamber of Commerce dinner and you know I have to go. That's why I'm asking if you brought something to wear, so you could go with me, keep me safe so to speak."

Abby could hear the smile in his voice as he talked, and she knew there was no getting out of it, she sighed and said, "I have something that will work."

"Great! I'll meet you at the house when you arrive. Love you, honey."

"Love you too, Dad."

68

A brisk walk to her gate after going through security, and Abby was boarding the plane. She sat down in her aisle seat just in time to get a drink before takeoff. First class had been the only option available, and now it looked like all the seats were full, so she knew she was lucky to get on the flight. Her drink was delivered, she took a big sip and settled further into her seat, finally relaxing. She turned to see who was sitting next to her in the window seat, but could only judge that it was a tallish man, since his face was buried in the *New York Times*. Just as well, she was in no mood to talk to a stranger. She wanted a couple of drinks and a chance to catch up on the sleep she missed out on last night.

Ken was just finishing the *New York Times* article on the murders of Panzetti and his inner circle. He was impressed with the accurate details and thought the police must have revealed every gory detail to the lucky reporter. He couldn't have written it any better himself. From the intercom he heard, "Please fasten your seat belts, we're ready to taxi and take our place for eventual take off." He folded up the paper and turned to see who was sitting next to him. Unexpectedly, the woman turned to look out the window at the same moment and their eyes made contact. His reaction was immediate and rather obvious, but not at all what he had expected it to be. He was staring at an incredibly beautiful woman who brought back a face he hadn't seen in many years, too many years. When he looked more carefully, the resemblance faded but not the good feelings. Ken stayed unsettled only for a few seconds, but knew he had to say something to break the awkwardness.

"I'm so sorry. I didn't mean to stare, but you remind me of someone I haven't seen in a very long time."

"No need to apologize. I was kind of staring myself," the woman said blushing, "In fact, I was wondering, are you that movie actor ..."

"No, I'm not, but thank you for the compliment," Ken said smiling.

"Oh, thank God, because ... I mean ... well, I really don't know what I mean," her face was turning a bright shade of crimson and she knew it. "Please, let me start over, my name is Abby, Abby Steel, at least it was when I got on the plane, and I don't usually act silly like this, I apologize."

"On the contrary, Ms. Steel, it's I who should apologize for staring at you. I was startled, and I'm sure you noticed. I'm Ken." He reached out and they shook hands. Ken laughed, and continued, "And sometimes I do act silly like this, especially when I see someone as beautiful as you."

Flattery will get you everywhere, you big hunk, Abby thought, graciously accepting the compliment and smiling. So, he wasn't a movie actor, but he was a good looking man, tall, dark and incredibly handsome. His brown hair was graying slightly, his neat goatee was mostly gray and he was smartly dressed in a nice pair of jeans, a dress shirt and sport jacket. His blue-eyed stare had started a warmth in her body she hadn't felt in a long time and she unconsciously backed up a little in her seat. From the cockpit, "Folks, we are number one for take-off, please ensure your seat belts are securely fastened." They sat back as the plane accelerated down the runway.

A mess of conflicting feelings were going through Stone's mind as they took-off. He was instantly drawn to this woman, and it had been a very long time since he felt this. He was on a mission to complete his destiny. This life and all it had to offer had become too much for him to bear; he could not let emotions sway his thinking, but there was just something about this woman, Abby Steel, that had moved him deeply in just a few minutes.

In the air, Ken asked, "What's taking you to Billings?"

"My father lives there, and he asked me to come out and help him with some things, and honestly, I could definitely use a few days of vacation." She was silent for a moment, deciding whether she should continue the conversation or just politely end it. *What the hell,* she thought, *I have nothing to lose.* "And how about you, Ken?"

A slight pause, and then, "I have some family there I want to say good-bye to, and then I'm starting on my retirement."

His statement was somewhat odd, but she didn't want to push it. "How long will you stay?" she asked with her fingers crossed, wondering if he might be a pleasant addition to her time in Billings.

"Probably about ten days." Ken had no set timetable, but was anxious to get everything in order as quickly as he could; he had been planning this for a while. He was not usually one for casual conversation on a plane, but he was so attracted to Abby, he decided to allow the conversation to take its course. He thought, *what harm could come from a few hours of friendly conversation with a beautiful woman he would probably never see again?*

The next few hours went by very quickly as Ken and Abby told each other stories about their lives. Surprising to both of them, they touched on more than the typical safe topics strangers were usually willing to share. As the flight and the conversation continued, their connection and feelings towards each other deepened. Ken told Abby that he had been an art dealer and talked about the many places in the world he'd visited, focusing mostly on the last few years, but he stayed away from his personal life. Everything he said seemed sincere and Abby didn't feel the need to probe in that area. She in turn, told him about her life, some of her childhood, her college days, a little about her father and his newspaper background, and that she worked for the police department. Abby did not elaborate on what her job was there; she had learned from experience not to tell potential suitors that she was a homicide detective. It either turned them off, or they were too interested in her work in a creepy kind of way. She thought that Ken might be different, but she wasn't ready to lay the detective scene on him just yet. She laughed her way through the stories of her two marriages and admitted that she would have liked to have had a child.

From the flight attendant, "Ladies and Gentlemen, we've been cleared for landing, please fasten your seat belts, and ensure your tray table and seats are in the full-upright and locked position."

As Ken put up his tray table, he was thinking about the plans he had made. On one hand, he didn't want to start anything he couldn't finish, but on the other hand, this would probably be one of his last chances to be in the company of a woman, especially a woman like Abby. As he thought further, he realized that it was more than that. Abby was nothing like any woman he had been with, or even met, in many years. Under the soft layer of her external beauty, and there was plenty of that, was a radiating inner beauty. Ken could see it and feel it, she had warmth, humor, and a sincerity that was real, as real as anything he'd known in a long time, something maybe she didn't even realize. He knew that she hadn't been totally truthful about her job, but it didn't matter, he had done the same and he felt that she had done it for his benefit. Ken's problem was simplicity. He knew that he should keep his life uncomplicated, no new connections, no new involvements. Why did he have to meet her now? Was this fate? Or God playing with him again? He finally realized that he was not going to keep his life simple, and though he found it hard to believe, he felt like he was falling in love.

For Abby, in just a few hours, she had developed an incredibly strong attraction for Ken, one that was more than just physical, and she was pretty sure he felt the same way. A thought formed in her head, one she would normally have rejected, but in this case it felt right, so she decided to go for it. She paused for a second to compose herself for the potentially awkward moment that might follow.

"Ken, I may be making an ass of myself, but what the hell, I've done it before and managed to live through it. I need a date for a Chamber of Commerce dinner that my dad asked me to go tonight. It'll probably be boring and a little old-fashioned, but with you there I'm sure I'll have a good time. Would you like to go? Are you married? Going to see a girlfriend? Or just not interested?" Abby couldn't believe the words came out of her mouth!

"Yes, no, no, no, and I like old fashioned."

"Awesome!" Abby said with a huge smile on her face.

CHAPTER 19

Crajack was relaxing on the deck of his mountain retreat, which was about an hour outside of Billings, drinking a glass of Riesling. He bought the property when he first came to Billings ten years ago. Considering the modest occupation that was his cover story, he told the local towns-folk that his favorite uncle had left him a nice sum of money, which allowed him to afford such a purchase. He had about ten acres of land which included a two-story house with a basement, an updated barn, lots of trees and a little pond in the backyard. He never had anyone visit him at the retreat, preferring to keep it very private. If he needed to do any entertaining, he would use the residence he had in town. He'd put quite a bit of money into his retreat for surveillance. He had a state-of-the-art system with a 360-degree view around the main house, the latest computer and communication equipment as well as motion and heat detectors throughout the property. It would be difficult for anyone to notice these updates, even if they knew where to look, which was just the way he liked it. In his true profession it was just smart business to be prepared, and though the threat of a full-on attack didn't worry him; he didn't like to be surprised.

Despite the grey competing with the dark brown in his hair and beard, and a little middle-age spread, he didn't feel a day over twenty-five. Time had been very, very good to him. He was medium in stature, about five foot nine, but had the strength of a much larger man. Throughout his life, he had sought education and knowledge all over the world and his quest had brought him wealth, and with that, power. The things he'd done and seen in his lifetime would probably have filled the lifetimes of ten normal men. Crajack spoke six languages fluently, was an expert in small arms, chemical weapons, explosives and all kinds of new specialized weapons that were coming out rapidly these days. He had lived for a time on every major continent and was able to afford the best that money could buy everywhere he went. After a while, he realized his life would be easier if he had a normal everyday cover story and job. With that decision, he established an underground logistics network that provided him with anything he needed: documentation, weapons, IT skills, dark web communications, and ways to move money that were untraceable. He did all this, without ever meeting with his network face to face, he considered that a top priority and a key to his continued success.

Since his youth, Crajack knew there was evil in his heart and he rejoiced in it. He was vicious and malevolent with an extreme desire to eliminate those he despised or deemed unworthy and to inflict maximum pain and misery whenever and wherever he could. He had not started out as a paid hit man, but when the opportunity presented itself—to kill for money—he knew he'd found his perfect calling. This opportunity occurred in Las Vegas, where he spent quite a bit of time acquiring and mastering another of his skills, gambling. His favorite game was craps. He always had an innate feel for how the dice would land. Another game he loved was blackjack, he was one of the first to understand and use card counting techniques to win, years before Ken Houston wrote a book on the subject. His gambling success enabled him to make important friends and contacts in Sin City and also gave him his nickname—Craps and Blackjack—Crajack.

Through his connections, he often played in private, high-stakes poker games. One night, he was eight hours deep and over twenty thousand dollars in the hole at a game hosted by one of the top mob guys. All night the cards he was getting were crap. Even with his exemplary skills, he couldn't do anything with his four card flushes, kangaroo straights and second-best hands. During the course of play, the conversation between two of the other players, Tommy and Junior, centered around the problems they were having with a rival casino owner who was causing problems with the Las Vegas police, problems that were spilling over to the other casinos.

"We need to have the son of a bitch whacked, but not by anybody who is known," said Junior.

"Yeah, but I don't think anyone will be able to touch the fucker. He's too well protected. It'd be suicide for the whacker," Tommy replied.

Crajack saw an opportunity and butted into the conversation, "What's it worth to have this guy whacked?"

"Why the hell do you care? You ain't gonna do it, now mind ya own business," said Junior brusquely.

Crajack quickly assessed his losses which he put at $23,000 dollars and then said, "I'll whack the guy for thirty-five grand, and I'll do it in the next two days."

"Hey asshole, are you crazy or something? You ain't never whacked nobody before, why you gonna start now?" said Junior.

"Why I'm gonna start now is 'cause I'm down a shit-ton of money and this seems like an easy way for me to get flush. Cash me in as even tonight, consider it my advance. Then pay me twelve grand after I make the hit."

Junior stood up and said, "I think it's time you leave."

"Junior," says Tommy quietly, "He's got some balls on him, dontcha think?"

"Yeah, but—"

"We're gonna let him do it, or at least let him try to do it," said Tommy with finality. Clearly, he was the one in charge. "We got nothing to lose, and maybe the crazy fucker will pull it off."

"Yeah, okay, Tommy," said Junior.

"Thank you, gentlemen. I promise you will not be disappointed," Crajack said smiling as he got up from the table.

That hit was more than just an ordinary hit as far as the mob was concerned. They were convinced that it could not be pulled off, not without the hit man himself being whacked. So, when Crajack not only killed the target, but did it with ease and without a trace of who put out the contract, his career began and he became the mob's go-to hit man. It was the last job he did for less than $50,000 dollars, and the last time that he ever met his target face to face.

Through his association with the mob, word got around about his particular skill set, and he became one of the highest paid hit men in the world. As the hits accumulated, so did his wealth. He had used almost every possible method to take out his targets, from explosions, to poison and lethal gas, and more, he was an expert at staging *tragic accidents*. His last paid hit was in Vegas where he got his start and his name. For that one, he had very much enjoyed taking out the target from over one thousand yards with his prized, custom sniper rifle. He had what he'd always wanted, power, wealth, influence and the ability to inflict pain and death on the weak and innocent. From his early life in Europe to where he was today, the journey was more than he ever expected or could have imagined, and it was spectacular.

CHAPTER 20

For Abby and Ken, the flight could've lasted another four hours, but they landed in Billings right on time. As they taxied to the gate, Abby turned to Ken with a smile and handed him a card, "My dad has a car waiting for me. Here's his address, and my phone number. I'm not sure where the Chamber of Commerce dinner is, but I'll find out. I think it would be easiest for you to meet me at my father's house and we can leave from there. Is that good with you?"

Ken looked at the address and then his watch and gauged that it could take him up to two hours to get a car, get to the hotel, shower, get another car, and get to Abby's dad's house. He had planned to do a few things tonight, but they could wait. He wanted to see Abby again and soon.

"I'll be there as soon as I can, but it could be as late as 7:00 PM."

"That's fine, but take your time, Ken," Abby felt that she could call him by his first name now. "We don't have to be the first ones there."

"What about your dad? Will he be upset that I stole his date?"

"Are you kidding? He'll be ecstatic that I have a date. Now he can leave for the dinner early, and make sure that all the festivities are in order. That's the way he is."

A few minutes later the plane was safely parked at the terminal and Abby and Ken deplaned with the rest of the passengers and walked towards the front of the terminal.

"I have to get my luggage. Did you check any bags?" asked Abby.

"No, I'm all set with this here," Ken indicated the duffel he was carrying.

"Well then, I expect to see you around seven. Please call me if for any reason you might be late. I don't take well to being stood up, and especially not for my first Chamber of Commerce dinner." Abby smiled, gave him a friendly kiss on the cheek and then headed off towards baggage claim.

Ken watched her walk away and then turned and headed for the exit. He requested an Uber on his phone, and as he waited, he could not get Abby out of his mind. His car arrived and he was quickly headed down Highway Three towards the hotel. He stared out at the sky, so blue it did not seem real, and thought about what happened on the plane. He had everything planned, his last job was over, he was tying up loose ends and then he had planned to just fade away into the sunset. No one would miss him. No friends, no family, no acquaintances, no one who knew or cared where he was. His journey had been long and painful, and he needed to finally call it quits, but then he met Abby, and a little bit of doubt started to creep into his mind.

How could a plane ride with one woman cause him to reconsider everything he had planned? He'd known and been with many beautiful women and many smart women. Abby possessed both qualities, but she had something more than that: an inner light that had made a huge impact on him. She had it all. This trip was supposed to be simple, and being with Abby would not be simple. He reasoned he should probably let her go. It would be easy to do right now, but if he met her tonight as planned, he knew they would get involved and then easy was out of the question. It wouldn't be fair to either one of them, especially her. He could call and tell her he was sick and couldn't make the dinner. Or he could not call at all, she didn't have his number. The other side of his brain offered him a different argument. He didn't think even a woman like Abby would cause him to reconsider his plans, so why not spend his limited time in Billings enjoying himself and in the company of an amazing woman?

"We're here, boss," the gruff Uber driver barked as he screeched to a halt in front of the Northern Hotel.

Built in the early 1900s, the hotel had undergone extensive renovations in the last few years. Ken had been lost in thought when the cab driver's voice, it was right out of *Guys and Dolls,* pulled him out of his daze. He hadn't really paid any attention to the driver when he got into the car, since he had been preoccupied thinking of Abby and his future. When he finally looked at the driver, he was slightly taken aback. *How did this guy end up in Billings, Montana?* The driver looked about fifty, average height, stocky build, dark blond hair worn long and dark sunglasses. He was wearing a sports coat, but underneath was a black Rolling Stones t-shirt that had seen better days.

78

"Thanks for the ride," said Ken as he pulled a twenty from his money clip and handed it to the driver.

"Yo!" The driver turned his head and looked at Ken, taking a quick glance at the remaining bills on the clip. "Let me know if ya need any more rides, boss. Here's my card, just call and ask for Sal, and I'll be there on the double."

Ken looked at the card, *Sal Chieffo At Your Service.* Just a phone number and at the bottom of the card a slogan, *We please with speed, no questions asked!* Ken didn't have a car, and he hadn't planned on renting one; he really hated driving. He realized it would be very convenient to have a personal driver for his time in Billings, and he had a good feeling about this guy, even if he might be a little strange.

"Where you from, Sal?"

"Brooklyn, New York. And please don't ask how I wound up in this cowboy town, that's another story ... from another time."

Ken had no intentions of asking.

"Can't you tell from my accent?" asked Sal.

"Well, I knew you weren't from around here."

"Nobody's from around here."

That was a strange reply Ken thought.

"Are you?" asked Sal.

"No, not really."

"See what I mean?"

Ken smiled, he really, really liked this guy.

"Sal, I have a proposition for you."

Sal raised his sunglasses and stared at him, concern on his face, and asked, "Exactly what kind of proposition?"

Ken laughed, "No, no, nothing like that. Just wondering if you were interested in being my personal driver for a week or so?"

Sal's face lit up with a big smile of relief, "Yeah, yeah, sure, no problem, but it'll cost ya."

"Okay, how much?"

"Fifteen hundred, plus expenses."

"How about five thousand, you take care of expenses."

Sal looked shocked but responded in a way that Ken had not seen in a long time, with sincerity. "No way, boss, that's too much, unless you want me to drive ya to the moon. Three grand, I cover expenses, and ya got a deal."

Ken put out his hand to Sal, and as they shook, he said, "Deal, you start right now. Here's five hundred in advance."

"So where we goin' first?"

"Give me thirty minutes. Enough time to take a quick shower and get into some fresh clothes. We're going to a dinner, but first to this address." Ken gave Sal the card with the address that Abby had given him on the plane.

"I know this place. The newspaper guy lives there, Dominic. I take him around town sometimes."

Ken was pleasantly surprised. Sal would definitely come in handy, very handy.

CHAPTER 21

Abby was on the way to her dad's ranch outside of town, riding in a late-model Lincoln Town Car that her dad had arranged. He never spared any expense or luxury when it came to her. She was the sparkle of his life, especially since her mother had died. He still did not communicate with his other daughter Gina, which really bothered Abby, but none of her efforts to heal that rift had succeeded. It was the death of Abby's mother that had caused the split. Her death was tragic and sudden and sent the two sisters spiraling in very different ways. Gina was in her third year of college, on her way to becoming a doctor when their mother died. Within a few weeks she had dropped out of school and started self-medicating with drugs and alcohol. For years she had been on that heartbreaking path, in and out of several rehabs, jobless, homeless and begging for money. Abby was only eighteen when her mother died and she had planned on going to college, but her mother's death, really it was her mother's murder, prompted her to join the police academy after graduation; however, she found out she was too young. Not deterred in the least, she became a paramedic and started taking college classes until she had the required number of credits to join the academy. Since then the police force had been a huge part of her life. Gina eventually straightened her life out; she had even gone back to school and finally became a doctor. She was doing very well, but their father was still not willing to talk to her. Abby and Gina had a relationship, but not a strong one. They spoke a few times a year, but had not seen each other in person in a very long time.

During the ride, Abby thought about Ken Stone. She liked him, a lot, and she knew he liked her also. She also liked the air of mystery that surrounded him. It added a little spice to the potential relationship, and who didn't like a little spice? If her father liked him that would make it even better. He hadn't liked most of her previous boyfriends and had only tolerated her two husbands.

When the car pulled up in front of his house Dominic Steel was already outside, ready and waiting to greet his daughter. He was sixty-four years old and in good shape; the ranch and all the outdoor activities in Montana kept him that way. He was just under six foot, with a slim build, his full head of hair was a medium grey, cut in a military fashion and he sported a full mustache. His smile went from ear to ear, and he was always cracking a joke. He came to Montana from New York City, where he had been a hot-shot editor at the *Times.* He was still in the newspaper business. He owned and ran the *Billings Journal.* It was his passion, and he loved the relaxed lifestyle out here compared to what he'd known in New York. As part of his relaxed life in Billings, he had taken up painting and loved to paint nature scenes. His eyes lit up when he saw Abby. His love for her overflowed and it showed.

"Abigail!" he exclaimed as she got out of the car.

"Dad, oh Dad, I missed you."

"I missed you too, honey." They hugged each other for about ten seconds with tears coming from both of their eyes. Abby's filled up first. God, she loved her father.

The driver had retrieved her bags from the car and put them on the front porch.

"Thanks, Ralph." Abby's dad squeezed a fifty-dollar bill in the driver's hand for getting her there safely.

"Anytime, Dom."

"Let's get inside, Abigail. I want to show you some new stuff around the place."

"Okay, Dad, sounds good. I know we have some pretty heavy things to talk about, but I'm not up for it right now."

"No problem, honey, I kind of figured it would be best to wait until tomorrow. Whenever you're ready."

"Oh, I almost forgot, I have a date for tonight's dinner. I met him on the plane."

Her dad turned to look at her, real concern on his face, "You met a guy on the plane and you're bringing him to the dinner tonight? Now, honey, do you really think that's a good idea?"

"I know what it sounds like, Dad, I really do," Abby laughed, "But he isn't a jerk or a snob or an asshole, I promise! This guy has his head on straight and we just really connected, it was a huge surprise to me too, but I really do think you'll like him."

"Well, if he's as good as you say, then I'm happy for you. But I'm reserving my final judgment until I meet him in person. Got it?" he said, now smiling.

"Got it."

Abby's father spent the next twenty minutes giving her the ten-cent tour of the house and the barn, showing off the renovations since her last visit. After, they sat down at the kitchen table with a couple of glasses of iced tea and chatted about simple things in both their lives, nothing too serious. He talked about some of the stories he'd worked on and things happening around town that were of interest. Abby realized she was preoccupied with thoughts about Ken, so she asked to cut their talk short so she could get ready.

"Okay, Abigail, no worries, you go get ready. And since you have a date now, I'm gonna leave a little early to check on any last-minute details that need checking on."

It was just as Abby had told Ken. Dad was Dad, very predictable. She smiled and said, "Sounds good. I'm gonna go hop in the shower."

"Alright, honey, I'll see you at the dinner."

CHAPTER 22

Crajack was getting ready for the annual Chamber of Commerce dinner, somewhat looking forward to it, only because it was the last one he would ever have to attend. He felt at ease in his current cover and had never had any problems carrying out the charade, he just felt it was the right time to move on. He marveled at how easy it was to fool people. There really was no reason for anyone to suspect that he wasn't who he presented himself to be, but that didn't stop Dominic Steel. He had recently overheard a conversation between Dominic and the library-woman Donna and learned that Dominic seemed to have gotten in his head that something was not quite right about the high number of accidents befalling the younger citizens of Billings, and that Dominic was investigating the deaths on his own. Crajack had made sure all of the investigations concluded that they were truly accidents or natural causes, so he was not very concerned with it. He wouldn't be around Billings much longer anyway, so he would just keep an eye on Dominic and if it was a problem that needed solving, he would just make it look like an accident, right?

Dominic got to the dinner venue quickly, as there was little traffic. He checked that everything was ready, and it was. Since there were no last-minute problems for him to take care of, he went in search of Donna Stapleton, the Director of the Billings Library. She was a very good friend and often helped him with research for stories his paper was working on, though none of the other stories were as potentially dangerous as the one he was currently investigating. He was very happy Abigail had agreed to visit; he wanted to show her what his investigation had uncovered, knowing she would be able to tell him if he was on to something or if he was just being a mistrustful reporter. Either way, her reassurance was needed.

Donna had told him yesterday that she had some additional information to share, but he told her to wait until they saw each other in person. Maybe he was being paranoid, or maybe he was just being extra safe.

He found Donna checking the seating arrangements. She finished up and they sat down together at one of the empty tables near the back. The dinner guests wouldn't start arriving for another hour, so they had the place to themselves. Donna Stapleton had been the Library Director for almost fifteen years and she had worked at the library for over twenty years. She was extremely intelligent and at fifty-eight, she was surprisingly good with all the latest technology, which was one of the reasons Dominic relied on her for research; he never quite adapted to the new digital age. Looking at her, one would never guess she was a librarian with her slim athletic build and shoulder length light brown hair cut in a modern style. She was also a very sharp dresser who looked like she would be more at home in a New York advertising agency than in a Billings library.

"So, what do you have to tell me from your latest research?" asked Dominic.

"I would say you're not going to believe it, but you were the one who brought it to me, so I'm pretty sure you will believe it" Donna chuckled.

The latest research she had done for Dominic was way beyond the typical scope he asked for, which was usually related to current events, medical issues and politics. This was serious, maybe even deadly serious. There had been at least fifteen deaths of young, healthy adults in Billings in the past two years. All of them had been investigated by the police and they had determined the deaths to be accidents or natural causes. Dominic came to her saying he thought the number of deaths was suspicious and he had a strong feeling they were connected. He didn't have anything concrete, just some circumstantial stuff and a reporter's gut feeling and he wanted help looking into it. Just recently, Dominic had gone to speak to Chief Wagner, the head of the Billings police department about what Dominic was now calling, the suspicious deaths, but the chief had just confirmed what the original investigations had determined. When Dominic challenged him that there might be more to the deaths than the investigations showed, and that all of these deaths might be related, the Chief laughed. He told Dominic that lots of people die young and die tragically, but that doesn't make them related or a crime.

After meeting with the chief, Dominic's gut was even more convinced that there was an evil presence in Billings that was responsible for some, if not all of these deaths, and maybe more. Dominic had asked Donna to try and find links between the people who had died, anything they could use to make a connection. Their work was quickly rewarded—they discovered that all the victims were Jewish, and with the exception of the car accident, all of the victims had died while they were alone. There were three people who perished in the car accident; they had not been alone when they died, but there were no survivors, which was almost the same thing. Dominic had asked Donna to go deeper and try to find other connections, but also to look at each death individually to see if anyone had a motive.

"As you know," Donna started, "I didn't find anything related to their finances that linked more than a few of the victims, and looking at each victim and their circumstances, there wasn't anyone who would gain anything significant upon the death of one of the victims. No links related to educations, place of birth, children, careers, the variety in all the categories I looked into was almost too random to be normal."

"Like someone was specifically picking victims with different backgrounds to avoid suspicion?" asked Dominic.

"Yes, almost. But since the victims were all Jewish, that link seems to be in stark contrast to everything else related to their backgrounds. An enigma."

"Agreed. So, what did you find out? Because I know you found something."

"I did find something," she responded, her eyes twinkling with excitement. "I started thinking of random activities that we all do in our daily lives, grocery shopping, license renewals, getting a bank account, stuff like that, just trying to think outside of the box. So, I have this thought process running around in the back of my mind for a few days and one day I go out to get the mail. For some reason the Billings Adult Education brochure catches my eye, so I glance through it. Did you know they offer a Dog Training class?"

"No, I don't think I knew that, why is it important?"

"Did you know that Chief Wagner raises golden retrievers?" asked Donna.

"Yeah, I think everyone who has ever met the Chief knows that." Dom said with a smile.

"Did you know that Chief Wagner sometimes teaches the Dog Training class?"

"Donna, please, what're you getting at? Just tell me before I go crazy."

"Over the past three years, thirteen of our victims attended a Dog Training class that was led by Chief Wagner, and I found three more potential victims using that information!"

Dominic sat back, stunned into silence for a few moments. He stared at Donna as she nodded her head in affirmation. He had thought there was something to the investigation, but this was more than he could have imagined. "A lot of things start to make sense to me now," he finally responded.

"What do you mean?" asked Donna.

"All the investigations coming back as accidents or natural causes and the way the chief laughed me off when I suggested there was more to the deaths, that they might be murders. If he is involved, of course that's the way things would be. I never thought it would be the chief himself."

"Wait a minute, Dom, aren't you jumping to a really big conclusion? This is just one link. It doesn't mean the chief is responsible. They were all Jewish and you never said that Rabbi Kuperman was responsible. Why are you making assumptions now?"

"It's not an assumption, it's logical thinking. Rabbi Kuperman travelled a lot and he wasn't around when several of the deaths happened, so he was never on my radar. For that matter, neither was the chief, but this is too much of a coincidence to be a coincidence, don't you see that?"

"Not really. I think you're still making a huge assumption," Donna responded.

"My gut tells me I'm not," he paused for a second, "But the reporter in me sees your point. I wouldn't publish a story with evidence like this. I'd need another link or some more concrete information before I would even think about publishing something like this. So, we'll just keep digging. If the Chief is responsible, there has to be something else we can find and we will."

"Promise me you won't do anything rash before we have a chance to better verify what I found? Please, Dominic?"

"Of course not, I promise. You were right, I did jump the gun a little. I'm gonna talk to Abigail about the investigation, maybe there's something her cop eyes will see that we missed, something that will remove all doubt."

"I thought you didn't want to talk about this except in person. That's why you made me come early tonight, remember?"

"Oh, Abigail is in town. I called her after Rabbi Kuperman's murder and asked her to come out. I needed an expert opinion. She's gonna be here tonight at the dinner," he said smiling proudly.

"Oh, how lovely, I can't wait to meet her. Does she know anything about what we've been looking into?"

"I gave her a little bit of information, but she just arrived this afternoon and I haven't had a chance to go through it with her in detail. We're gonna do it in the morning. So I promise, I will take no action until she gives me her opinion, okay?"

"Okay, thank you, Dom. This is serious and I'm starting to get a little worried."

"It is serious, Donna, but no one knows you're helping me with this, right?"

"Right."

At that moment, Reverend Lephit and Chief Wagner walked into the dining area. Both of them had drinks in their hands and were having a spirited conversation.

"Oh no, I can't even look at him," said Donna in a timid voice.

"Donna, look at me. Chief Wagner is just Chief Wagner, no more or no less. Just think of him as the same guy. Like you said we don't have any concrete proof yet, just a link. You can do this."

"Okay." Donna took a deep breath and said, "I can do this."

They both got up and went over to say hello to the early arrivals.

Ken was back down to Sal's car in thirty-two minutes. Abby had not said what the dress code was, so he was wearing a jacket, but no tie, smart casual is what they called it these days. Sal was deep in thought, reading the scratch sheets, getting his picks for the next day. He got his bets in through the local bookie. Even Billings had a bookie. The ponies were his weakness. It cost him his marriage, at least that's what his ex-wife said at the divorce hearing. Sal's version was somewhat different. He claimed that since he was married to a horse's ass. He might as well bet on them. Either way, that was his life until football season came around, of course. Actually, Sal would bet on a cockroach race if the odds were right. He was a gambler like all real Brooklynites.

Ken knocked on the driver's window surprising Sal, who rolled down the window looking at Ken with a smile.

"Right on time, boss. I like that."

"Close enough," Ken said getting in the back seat.

"We'll be at Dom's house in twenty-five minutes, give or take. How you know him, boss, if you don't mind me pryin'?"

"I don't know him. I know his daughter."

"Oh, the daughter, okay, I don't know her. For a second, I thought yous was going to the dance with Dom. Hey, I got no problem with that if you was, but the daughter, that's good. Is she a looker?"

Ken gave Sal a look as if to say, *what do you think?*

"Okay, boss, I get the picture. No more questions."

"Right." Ken knew the guy meant no harm, but he was not in the mood to talk, at least not about Abby. He was still not sure that he was doing the right thing.

Sal got to Dominic's house in just under twenty minutes. Downtown traffic was nothing to speak of and once outside the city it was easy cruising, Sal was not a man who was afraid of the gas pedal.

"Stay right here, Sal. I'll be out in a few minutes."

"Okay, boss."

It was clear to Ken that his name with Sal was gonna be 'Boss'. That was okay with him. This guy was a real character and he would enjoy his company over the next week. He was smiling as he went up to the door and knocked.

Abby opened the door, also smiling, and greeted Ken with a polite kiss on the cheek as if they had known each other for years. She wished they had.

"I guess you found the place without any problems," said Abby.

"Not exactly. It's more like I found a wacky Uber driver who knows every place in this town. He's our designated driver for the night and mine for the rest of the week."

"My, my, Mr. Stone, our own personal driver. You flatter a girl."

"Well, I do what I can. You look divine, Ms. Steel."

"Just something I threw on for a first date. Take me out a second time and I'll really dazzle you."

Abby did look good. She was wearing a slightly revealing emerald satin dress that highlighted her figure. It wasn't what she had planned to wear when she was going with her dad, but now it was different. It was a date. She wanted to look good, and she did. Besides, she hadn't been out in so long, she thought, *What the hell, let's do it up.* She had her hair up in a French twist and wore a pair of dangling diamond and gold earrings that complimented the dress very nicely.

Ken was hooked solid. What Abby didn't know, is that he was hooked even if she wore rags and smelled like she lived at the zoo.

"Where's your father?" Ken asked.

"Just as I said, as soon as he found out I had a date, he took off early to make sure everything was in order."

"Then shall we go?"

"Yes, we shall." Abby felt like a kid going to her first dance. She was enjoying the evening already.

Ken offered his arm and Abby took it as they walked to the car. Sal, seeing that Ken was coming, quickly got out, ran around to the passenger side and held the door to the back seat open for them as they approached. He wasn't sure that this was the right thing to do, but he figured that his new boss would appreciate it. Abby wasn't sure what she had expected, but Sal's unusual dress and manner surprised her from the start.

"Where did you find this guy?" she whispered.

"He found me, and don't let looks fool you. He's cool. Trust me on this one."

"Okay," she replied.

Ken paused at the door, "Abby meet Sal, the most knowledgeable driver in Billings."

"Nice to meet you ma'am," Sal replied with a big smile.

Abby immediately liked his warm smile and familiar New York accent, "Pleasure to meet you, Sal." She returned the smile.

After Ken got in the car, Sal hustled back into the driver's seat. He fixed his rear-view mirror while sneaking a glance at Abby's cleavage, which in Sal's estimation was definitely major league.

"Where to, Boss?"

"Boss?" she said laughingly as she looked at Ken.

Ken looked at Abby, opening his hands at the same time, a gesture asking her to respond to Sal.

"Oh, right, you don't know where we're going." To Sal, "Moss Mansion downtown please. It's on—"

"I know the joint. I've taken your old man there a few times."

"You know my dad?"

"Sure, everyone knows Dom."

Sal headed back to town and proceeded to tell Abby and Ken some of his crazy driving stories. They were quick, funny, and obviously exaggerated, at least Abby thought they had to be embellished. It was as if he was on stage at a comedy club and had twenty minutes to tell a hundred cab driver stories to win a contest. Sal saw that he was getting through to Abby; she was laughing like a kid, so he added some color and language to the stories which made them even funnier. Abby saw why Ken liked the guy. He was indeed an original.

Before they knew it, they were at Moss Mansion. There was a large sign in the front of the building advertising the Annual Chamber of Commerce Dinner. They pulled up into the valet parking area where Sal abruptly slammed on the brakes and brought the car to a sudden stop.

"We're here, Boss."

"And almost in one piece. Jesus, Sal, a little easier on the brakes, please."

"Sorry, Boss, old habit. I'll do better."

An attendant opened Abby's door. Before she got out, she gave Ken a look that told him she was slightly annoyed with Sal's driving, or rather, his stopping. Sal saw the look in the rear-view mirror.

When Abby got out Sal said, "She looked a little pissed, Boss. Did I screw up?"

"No, Sal. I think you just startled her."

"I don't want to mess up with her, Boss. I like her."

"I'm sure it's fine. You made her laugh all the way here. Don't worry about it."

"Okay, Boss, whatever you say."

"So, Sal we're gonna be a few hours at least. You should find yourself a good place to relax and catch up on your sports." Ken could tell that sports were Sal's life.

"Don't worry about me, Boss, I got the whole night mapped out. Gonna catch the Yankees on ESPN and if your still cuttin' some rug, I'll work on the ponies."

"Dinner and speeches will probably end around 10:00 or 10:30," Abby said.

"Alright, Sal, if we want you earlier I'll call, otherwise we'll see you at 10:30 right out in front."

"You got it, Boss. Have a blast."

As they walked into the grounds of Moss Mansion, Abby said, "He's quite the find. I like him, but I'm not sure how many more of those stops I can handle."

CHAPTER 23

Moss Mansion was a very elegant and well-maintained estate built in the early 1900s by the prosperous Billings citizen, Preston Boyd Moss. Members of his family lived in the mansion until the 1980s, and since then it has become a popular tourist attraction and great location for weddings and other events. As Ken and Abby walked into the entrance hall which was adorned with lush dark wood and antique lighting, they saw an elderly gentleman in a tuxedo, sitting at a small table with a seating plan and name cards. He had a look on his face that was begging for someone to give out their name, so he had something to do. Abby walked up to him.

"Steel and guest."

"Oh yes, Dom's daughter, table thirteen. You're at the head table with tonight's honorees. I hope you have a good evening."

"I'm sure we will," she said.

Ken chuckled to himself when he saw the number. Abby noticed and asked, "Let me in on the joke?"

"No joke, not really, just seems if there is a number to be assigned, I'm always getting lucky thirteen, or unlucky thirteen, depending on your point of view."

Abby grinned and took Ken's hand. They walked into a stunning pink room where the walls were adorned with intricate woodwork, and at the center of the room was a beautiful fireplace. There was a bar setup where cocktails were being served and guests were mingling. Next to the bar, there was a sign sitting on an easel with the names and positions of the people who were being honored tonight. The names were printed in large black lettering, very distinct, something the town was obviously proud of.

Mr. Cort Wagner – Chief of Police
Mr. Rupert Stockwell – Mayor
Mr. Dominic Steel – Editor, Billings Journal
Rev. Harold Lephit – Billings Fellowship Church
Ms. Donna Stapleton – Library Director

The surprise hit Abby just as Ken asked, "Did you know that your dad was being honored?"

"I had no idea. He never told me. Wait until I get my hands on him."

They ordered drinks at the bar, a wine for Abby and club soda for Ken. They headed outside where dinner would be served under the event tent. It was a gorgeous evening and they both appreciated the beautifully maintained grounds, and the white lights that had been strung through the tent and grounds, giving everything a wonderfully soft glow.

Ken noticed a small dance floor was setup with a four-piece band playing some pleasant background music. He asked Abby, nodding towards the dance floor, "Would you honor me with a dance later, Ms. Steel?"

"Absolutely, I love dancing, I just hope you can keep up," she said playfully. She was so enjoying his company and their fun, easy banter. Her feelings for him were growing with each passing moment. As Abby was glancing at the tables, taking notice of the numbers so she could work her way towards thirteen, Ken noticed that a number of people, mostly men, were staring at her.

"Looks like cleavage is news here in Billings," whispered Ken good-humoredly. "I hope the EMTs aren't too far away."

Abby looked around and saw several men look away quickly, "Seriously? Hasn't anyone seen a woman in a dress before?"

"Perhaps they are seeing more of you in that dress then they're used to."

"You better watch out, you are skating on thin ice right now," Abby responded smiling.

Ken said nothing more, but his face showed that he was amused. Abby was slightly embarrassed at the attention. She thought, *Where the hell was table thirteen when you needed it?* Abby finally saw her dad at a table and headed over. Dominic saw them as they approached the table and stood up with enthusiasm to greet Abby.

"Abigail!" He exclaimed as he gave her a hug and then a kiss on the cheek.

"Hi, Dad. This is Ken."

"Glad to meet you, son."

"Likewise, Mr. Steel."

"Call me Dom, Ken. All my friends do."

Ken was immediately impressed with Dominic as he shook his hand. He started to understand a little more about Abby and how she got to be who she was. She clearly came from a good family.

"Dad, why didn't you tell me that you were being honored tonight?"

"Oh, it's no big thing, honey. They had some awards left over from last year, so they decided to give me one. Here, let me introduce you to everyone at the table."

Dom started to introduce Abby and Ken, "Donna, this is my daughter Abigail and her friend Ken …"

"Stone." Ken chipped in.

"Donna is our Library Director and has been for almost fifteen years."

"I am so pleased to meet you, Abigail. Your father talks so proudly about you. I'm Donna Stapleton."

"Pleased to meet you also and please call me Abby. My father is the only one who insists on calling me Abigail."

"Pleasure to meet you," said Ken as he shook Donna's hand.

Abby and Ken followed Dominic around the large table being introduced to each of the remaining guests.

"Well, that's everyone here now," Dominic said as they sat down. "The mayor, police chief and the reverend are at the bar; I'll introduce you when they return. They're probably having a serious debate about nothing serious. They just like to argue with each other."

Over the next thirty minutes Abby and Ken engaged in typical dinner conversation with the other guests. One of the chamber members was telling Abby of all the social, cultural and athletic events that Billings had to offer. It was the standard Chamber of Commerce pitch as to why it was a great idea to visit and stay in Billings. Abby was agreeing with him, but he didn't realize it and just kept going with his spiel. While that was going on, Ken was discussing favorite books and authors with Donna and Dominic.

As the mayor, the police chief, and reverend came back to the table, Dominic got up to do introductions. Ken went to stand up also but was struck by a piercing evil presence right in front of him. He faltered for just a second but recovered and was able to shake hands with each of the newcomers as he and Abby were introduced. He didn't think anyone noticed his reaction. This ability to sense evil was something Ken had been able to do for a very long time. When it first came to him, he didn't know what it was, so he did extensive research into all kinds of supernatural abilities like ESP and telekinesis to try and figure out what was going on. He knew that ancient civilizations in South America had referred to this as *Suka*; it was rare, but it was not unheard of. He learned to just accept it, and once he figured out it was never wrong, he was able to use it in his work. But this presence was stronger than any he'd come across ever before, even stronger than Panzetti's. He found it hard to believe he would come across such a presence in Billings. This type of evil in Billings just didn't fit.

"Ken, are you okay?" asked Abby. "You look like you've just seen a ghost."

"Yes, I'm fine." Ken said, realizing that Abby had noticed something. "Just a little acid reflux, sudden and strong, but it's all gone now. I'll be fine as soon as I get some food in me."

"Why don't you have one of the dinner rolls for now to help settle your stomach?" Abby suggested, with concern showing in her face.

"Sounds like a great idea. I'll do just that," he said as he reached for the bread basket. He smiled and said, "I'm fine really."

"Okay, but let me know if you want to get out of here early."

"No way! You promised me a dance, and I intend to collect," Ken replied, his eyes twinkling mischievously.

Abby turned to say something to her dad, which gave Ken the opportunity to reflect on what he felt. He didn't feel anything at all until the three men had come to the table. So, one of them—the chief, the reverend or the mayor—was the cause of the evil presence. He would have to be on his guard for the rest of the night to try and figure out which one it was without alarming Abby, of course. As he sat at the table trying to figure out which of the three men had the evil soul, he realized something about this presence seemed almost familiar, like he had felt this Suka before, but he could not place it. Soon after, they served the first course and everyone's attention turned to dinner. The conversations were light-hearted, Ken mostly smiled while listening attentively, looking for anything that might give him a clue. Nothing.

Crajack sat down after meeting Dominic's daughter and her date, and began to feel a strange, prickly sensation in the back of his mind. Something about one of those people was starting to put him on edge, and based on his experience, he knew he had to figure it out quickly. His instincts told him to be wary and alert, observe everything. If anything unusual happened, he would deal with it when the time came. His more immediate problem was Dominic and Donna. When he arrived at Moss Mansion, they were both seated at a back table, intently focused on the discussion they were having. Without being obvious, he watched them closely, trying to read their lips, and he was able to catch a few of their words. It was rumored by most of the old bitties in Billings that Dominic had the sweets for Donna, but this conversation was not about their next date. Quite the contrary, they were discussing Dominic's investigation into the high number of deaths of younger citizens in Billings. Crajack had heard Dominic whisper 'over the past two years'. The police didn't find anything suspicious in the deaths, so the fact they thought there was something to investigate was very troublesome. They might not be close, but the fact they were discussing it, made them too close, and he would have to act soon to fix it. The prickly feeling was growing stronger as Crajack turned his focus to the dinner table and conversation. As they were finishing up the main course and dessert was being served, the band started playing again and Donna asked Dominic if he would like to dance. He agreed and they proceeded to the dance floor, not realizing they were being carefully watched or by whom.

After they left the table, Chief Wagner turned to Abby and said, "Dom tells me you're the head of an elite detective squad in New York City."

Abby threw a glance towards Ken and he raised his eyebrows in question. She had told him she worked for the police department, just not what she did, but he certainly knew now. "I'm not sure about being elite, but we manage to get quite a few bad guys."

"Dom said you have an uncanny ability to see through all the noise surrounding your cases and zero in on the facts that will solve it," replied the chief.

"Well, I've been at this for a long time, and no two cases are the same. Sometimes the evidence is very clear, but sometimes I surprise myself when I figure out a key piece of evidence we were stuck on. I would like to think it's because of my experience, but sometimes I think it's just blind luck … maybe it's actually a little bit of both," Abby said thoughtfully and then continued, "Dad said you recently had a high-profile murder here in Billings. Rabbi Kuperman?"

"Yes, we did, just a few nights ago. Tragic situation. The initial investigation clearly points to murder, but my guys have had a very hard time finding any evidence to help us solve the case. It's one of the cleanest crime scenes I've ever seen. So tragic and sudden. It's obviously very difficult for his family to deal with."

"It sounds heartbreaking. I feel for the family and his synagogue. Billings sure isn't New York City, but I'm sure you get your share of crime and unfortunately, murder happens everywhere."

"Isn't that the truth," said the chief. "Speaking of murders, I've been following the stories about the New York City vigilante. That last hit, there were about a dozen killed, right?"

"Actually, there were eighteen victims," Abby replied.

"Wow," said the chief.

"He's getting quite the exposure in the media, isn't he?" Rev. Lephit chipped in. "Lots of headlines and some are even calling him a hero."

"Yes, Reverend, he does get a lot of media attention," Abby responded. "I've been on the case for the last three years, the toughest of my career." She thought her dad might have already shared that information, so why hide from it?

Ken's full attention returned to Abby and the discussion as soon as he heard the last statement. His mind started racing and his heart started sinking. *Oh no*, he thought, *she is on the vigilante case? This beautiful woman I just met and am falling for is trying to capture me and put me in prison. Fate certainly is a fickle bitch. I came out here to put every-thing behind me. Instead, I meet the one woman in the world who probably hates me more than anyone, and I'm on a date with her. Hello, irony, welcome to the party.*

"He's a cunning devil, but like all the rest, he will make a mistake and when he does, I'll be there to catch him." Abby went on, "As for being a hero, to me he isn't, he's a murderer. But in New York, the press has a powerful sway over public opinion, and that seems to be one of the upsides of being a vigilante: positive press."

"It does seem like he's cleaning up the city's scum, maybe you should wait a while and let him do his thing," the reverend continued.

"That's a very slippery slope, Reverend. Law and order must prevail. That's what this country is all about, don't you agree, Chief?"

"Yes, I do agree with you, Ms. Steel, but I also agree with Harold. I can see both sides, the benefits and the conflicts. As a police officer, I must enforce law and order, but it really gets me riled up when so many of these guys get a pricey defense attorney and walk away scot-free. As a man, I think sometimes you have to walk along that slippery slope and I believe there are occasions when the end justifies the means."

"Well, that's not gonna happen on my watch," Abby replied. "The SOB won't walk; I can guarantee you that."

"I wouldn't want to be him, that's for sure," replied Chief Wagner.

"So, Chief, going back to Rabbi Kuperman, how would you feel about letting me look at the investigation file on his murder?"

"That's awful kind of you, Abby, but it's not necessary; I think we have everything we need."

"You'd actually be doing me a favor. Some of the best lessons I've learned in police work have come from looking at cases I know nothing about. You see everything a little differently when it's a crime that's not in your city. Really, you could be teaching me something."

"My dear," interjected Rev. Lephit again, "You are out here to visit your father and have some vacation time, why in the world would you want to get back to the business of death before you absolutely had to?"

"Exactly what I was thinking, Harold," said Chief Wagner.

"Police work is my life, and I really do love it. I won't take much of your time at all, how about fifteen minutes Monday morning?" Abby asked hopefully. Because of her father's call the previous day, she had an ulterior motive for trying to get a look at the file and she was pushing it a little farther than she normally would. The chief didn't know that though, and she wondered why he was being so hesitant, small town politics maybe, or something else?

"Okay then, why don't you give my office a call Monday morning and we'll see if we can work it out," the chief finally gave in.

"Great, thanks, Chief Wagner!" Abby said excitedly.

The mayor finally interjected with, "Okay, people, enough about death and murder and vigilantes. Let's enjoy the rest of the evening." He asked his wife to dance and they were off to the dance floor.

Ken looked at Abby, held out his hand, "I agree with Mayor Stockwell. Shall we?"

Abby stood up, grabbed his hand and pulled him behind her to the dance floor in answer. The band was playing an American Songbook classic, and when they started, it seemed as if they had been dancing together for years. About a minute into the dance, Ken asked, "Uh, so when were you going to tell me about you being Wyatt Earp?"

"Does it matter that I didn't?" she asked.

"No, it doesn't."

"Good. I wasn't trying to mislead you. I've found telling people I'm a New York City police detective is often more trouble than it's worth."

"I think I can understand that." As they danced effortlessly around the floor, Ken's mind was still reeling from the discovery of Abby's true role at the NYPD. Part of him wondered again if he should just end this—say goodbye tonight and get on with his original plans. The other part of him knew that wasn't going to happen. He told himself it would be fine; there was no reason for the vigilante to come up again in conversation in Billings.

As if on cue, Abby said, "I'm really glad we met. I have a good feeling about us." Then she pulled him closer and put her head on his chest.

"Me too," he replied. As he held her, his mind suddenly flashed back to the evil presence and started racing with questions. Would he have to tell Abby the truth about himself and the presence he felt? Was it a danger to her or possibly others? How would he explain this feeling without telling her everything else? He just didn't see a way to do it. He could guess what her reaction would be to learning he was the vigilante and what he was capable of, and there was nothing good about it. This is not what he had planned for his swan song. Not even close!

They danced to a few songs and then Jack Carson, Chairman of the Chamber of Commerce, went to the podium and asked the band to take a break in order to get to the awards presentation. Over the next half hour or so, the five honorees received their awards for community service in support of Billings, and each made a brief speech. After the final presentation, Mr. Carson announced the bar would be open for one more round and the band would play for another thirty minutes. He walked off the podium to a round of cheers from the evening's guests, while a line at the bar had already started to form.

After the last announcement, Dominic turned to Ken and asked, "Do you have any plans for the week?"

"Well, I'm here to take care of some business stuff, and I wanted to take a few days off, but I don't have any specific plans," replied Ken.

"Are you the adventurous type?"

"More so than most, I think. I'll try almost anything at least once." Ken looked over at Abby, who shrugged her shoulders indicating she had no idea where this was going. "Do you have anything particular in mind, Dominic?"

"As a matter of fact, I do!"

"Dad, please," pleaded Abby.

"Now Abigail, just hold on, let me at least tell him what I'm thinkin' of. We've had an excellent white-water rafting season. The Yellowstone River is flowing really good. Have you been rafting before, son?"

"No, sir, I have not."

"Then you're in for a real treat. Can't beat it for entertainment and fun. Listen, I know an outfit outside of town that can take the two of you on the river and show you a damn good time, interested?"

Abby pleaded again, "Daaaaad!"

"Hold on now, I think your dad hit on something, Abby," said Ken. "It sounds like it could be a lot of fun. What do you say?"

It had been a while since Abby did something even remotely spontaneous or a little on the edge. And it was another chance to be alone with this guy, and maybe find out what makes him tick. After a moment's thought she replied, "Okay, I'll go rafting with you, as long as you agree to do something with me, deal?"

"Well, what do you have in mind?" asked Ken.

"Nope, no questions. Deal or no deal?"

"Hmmm, I'm not sure I can agree to a deal like that without more specifics. I have my honor and reputation to think about," Ken said while keeping a straight face.

"What? Are you serious?" Abby asked confused. Then she saw the smile he could no longer hide and said, "Oh, okay, you're kidding. Bet you think your funny, right?"

"Maybe a little?"

"No, not funny, not in the least."

"My apologies, Ms. Steel. It would be my extreme pleasure to accept your invitation to do whatever your heart desires."

"Much better answer, thank you," said Abby playfully.

"Okay, then it's a deal. I'll check the weather and have Sal set up the rafting trip for Monday or Tuesday, whichever looks best."

"Do you mean Sal Chieffo, the driver?" Dominic interrupted. "He's quite a character."

"Yes, the one and same. I hired him to get me around town for the week. He definitely is a character, a little wacky, but I really like him."

The next few minutes were spent saying goodbyes while Abby pulled Ken away from the table. "So, I'll see you tomorrow?" she asked Ken hopefully.

"Well, why wait until tomorrow? You could come with me right now," he responded with a mischievous twinkle in his eyes.

Abby closed her eyes, thinking about how much she would like to do just that. She opened them and said, "I really, really would love to, but I have plans with my Dad in the morning. It's actually the reason I came out here."

"I could have you home super early in the morning …"

"I'm not sure I would want you to."

Ken sighed and said, "Then tomorrow it is. Can I pick you up?"

"That would be great. Let's say 1:00 PM."

Ken gave Abby a hug and a kiss on the cheek, whispering in her ear, "Can't wait for tomorrow." He gave Dominic one last hand shake and headed to his car where Sal was waiting as planned. Ken got into the back seat, and on the short drive to his hotel, he kept thinking about all the events that had transpired in the last forty-eight hours. From the Panzetti killings to meeting Abby on the plane and the evil presence he felt tonight. It was nothing like he had imagined or planned, but despite everything, he was very happy to have met Abby. He also knew he would have to be on his guard. The evil Suka was a lurking danger.

CHAPTER 24

Crajack was in deep thought after the dinner as he drove back to his retreat. He still had the prickly sensation and it had only grown stronger throughout the evening. It was turning into a feeling of extreme dread and he knew it meant something bad was about to happen. Something *bad* didn't really apply to him as it did to others, but there were still ways where his life could be altered forever, and he didn't want that to happen. The only thing different tonight was Dominic's daughter and her boyfriend. Crajack had never met either of them before, so his intuition told him the feelings he was experiencing were connected to the two new players at the table tonight. Despite the inherent dangers of being a hit man, he had only experienced this sensation one other time, and then something *bad* definitely happened

Crajack was in Chicago, waiting for his flight, when he received an unexpected message on his phone. It was a notification from an innocuous dating site that was also used as a communication vehicle for the dark web. The only thing that showed up on his phone was that someone was interested in him, nothing illegal about that, but the purpose of the message was to tell him to access the dark web site he used for getting jobs. He was just returning from his latest job and had no desire to do another one anytime soon. He was, however, very disciplined and professional in his business dealings, and his reputation was everything. So rather than ignore the message completely, he would just decline it. So he logged in to read the message.

Twenty million dollars! The request was for a hit to be done in the next twenty-four hours and they would double his fee. *No way*, he thought. He knew his success to date was his meticulous planning and timing, and he could not do that in twenty-four hours. Too much of a risk. Even with the extra money, it wouldn't be worth it, he still had to decline. Crajack started to respond to the request, and then he paused ... he was a greedy bastard and extremely confident with a huge ego. He thought, *if anyone can pull this off, I know it has to be me.* He thought about all his past successes, never a close call, and he didn't fear a close call in the future. He knew his abilities were unmatched anywhere in the world, but could he really take this job? Should he? It went against all his instincts, but in the end, his ego won out. He accepted the job and booked a new flight to the west coast of Florida.

Crajack was sitting with a hood over his head and his hands and feet secured to the chair he was in. *Damn*, he thought, *I should have paid attention to the bad feeling that started as soon as I booked the flight, but I had no idea what it meant. I guess I do now. Shit. Okay, I'm here now, just need to figure out how to get out of this. No problem.* Suddenly the cuffs holding his hands and feet were electronically released and he was told to take off his hood, which he did. Crajack quickly assessed his surroundings. He was in a glass cube that was ten feet on every side. The cube was in a large concrete room that looked to be fifty feet long and thirty feet wide with very high ceilings. There was a woman standing outside the cube right in front of him, two guys with AR-15s aimed at him, and another five operatives in the background.

The woman standing in front of him was tall and slender. Her dark brown hair was pulled back into a ponytail and in her black jeans and black V-neck top, she was an imposing figure. Her piercing brown eyes and square jawline added to her already striking features.

She asked him, "What's your name?"

"What's your name?" Crajack replied in return.

"That's not how this is gonna work. I ask the questions, you answer. You can clearly see you are in no position to negotiate."

"Well, the way I see it," said Crajack, "I'm still alive, so I must have some value to you, which I think actually does give me a little wiggle room when it comes to negotiations." He saw a look of irritation quickly pass over her face and leave. "How about this, you tell me yours, and I'll tell you mine?"

"Okay, you first."

"Call me Ralph, I like that name," he responded with a sarcastic grin.

"Ralph? That's really what you're gonna go with?"

"Sure. And you are?"

"Nina."

When they grabbed him, Crajack had heard their accents and assumed he was probably dealing with Mossad. They could also be well-paid mercenaries, working for the highest bidder, so he couldn't rule out the CIA or other intelligence organizations that might be looking for him. But when he heard Nina's thick accent, he knew it was Mossad, maybe even the Kidon, the most highly trained and experienced in Mossad. He realized he would be dealing with this skinny bitch. No one else was moving or appeared likely to say anything; she was clearly in charge. *Okay, let the games begin*, he thought, *let's see how good she is*.

"We know what you've been responsible for in the last few years," said Nina. "So please don't insult anyone's intelligence and waste my time by denying it."

"More like the last fifty years," he whispered to himself.

"Quite an impressive resume," she continued, not hearing Crajack's comment, "Politicians, CEO's, scientists, and the Deputy Minister of Defense for Israel. Those were all you, right?"

"Maybe, but why would I tell you?"

Nina took a deep breath and realized nothing would be easy with this guy. No problem for her. She had all the time in the world, and his future was short. She knew he was not getting out alive.

"Because I'm asking nicely?" Nina responded.

"Oh, that's sweet, you're asking nicely. Bullshit, I'm not giving you anything for free." Crajack fully expected to get out of this situation even if his captors thought differently. But before he did, he needed to know how they had found him, so when he got out, he could permanently eliminate that problem.

"Okay, what will it cost me?" asked Nina.

"Not much, just a little information for a little information. You give, I give."

"Exactly what information are you looking for?"

"Not to be condescending, but you and I both know, your *sophisticated* Kidon operatives could never have tracked me to this bogus hit without help." He was purposely being sarcastic to see Nina's reaction. "Who blew my cover?" Crajack asked.

Her face showed no emotion, just a constant stare with those cold dark eyes. "No one blew your cover," she said, looking slightly offended, "We finally figured out how to get you out in the open and vulnerable, and it worked didn't it? A guy like you has a huge ego and greedy pockets. That's all there was to it."

"Okay," she continued, "Now give me a little. Was Israel's Deputy Minister of Defense one of your hits?"

"Well, Nina, I would love to give you that information, but I feel you have been less than honest with me." There was truth in what she said about his ego and greed, but she had lied about how they found him, and he knew it. "I'll ask again my dear, and please don't lie this time, it's unbecoming of you. Who blew my cover?"

He showed no sign of fear, his voice was relaxed and matter of fact. Nina had seen people in his situation before, and they didn't act like this. He was different. She thought for a moment as she kept her stare up, *Damn, I need to know if it was him.* Torture could be an option, but she thought he would probably be able to handle it, so it might produce nothing. She turned and walked over to her second in command to discuss their options.

When Nina walked away, Crajack took the opportunity to further examine his surroundings. At the top of the glass cell he was in, there was a one-inch opening where a gas line was secured. He assumed it was fentanyl gas, or something similar, with options to release enough gas to render him unconscious or enough to kill him. He did not see any apparent hinges or doors anywhere in the glass cube, only a small passthrough window in the front, no way for a body to get in or out. But he did notice the thin steel cables connected to the top of the cube, *Ah,* he thought, *it must be raised and lowered from above.* Eventually he would need to convince them to let him out of the glass cube.

"Ok, here is the deal," Nina said as she walked back to stand in front of the glass cube. "I will write down the name of the informer, and in exchange, you write down every fucking detail of the hit on the Deputy

Minister, how you did it, weapon, time of day, escape route, everything." She knew it wasn't protocol but saw no harm in giving him the name of the informant. He wasn't going to be able to do anything with it.

"Okay, I'll give you the details, so you know I was the one who performed the hit, *but* I want to see the snitch's name first. Place the paper with his name flush against the glass."

"Sorry, Ralph, that's not gonna work for me. First, you give me all the details of the hit. If they match, then, and only then, will I give you the informant's name. Take it or leave it. I'm eighty percent sure it was you. That's enough for me. One hundred percent would be nice, but it's not necessary."

"Nina, Nina, Nina, I thought we had a deal. Now you're acting like my information means nothing to you. How do I know you'll give me the name of the snitch once I have given you what you want? This is very disappointing, Nina, very disappointing."

Nina stared at him and wondered, *was he really being sarcastic with her in his position? He must realize the situation for what it was. He was the one in the cube, weapons pointed at him, deadly gas only a press of a button away.* She was tired of being patient with him. She motioned to one of the operatives and he pushed a piece of paper and a marker though the passthrough on the front of the cube.

"Actually, you don't know I'll give you the name, but you don't have any other options. Now write!" she barked, her emotions starting to break through.

Crajack stood up and retrieved the items, then returned to his seat and began writing. As he did so, Nina wrote something on a piece of paper, put it in her pocket, and then waited for him to finish.

"I'm done," Crajack said.

"Put it in the slot."

Crajack walked over and put the paper and marker back in the passthrough, and then stood there waiting. Nina walked over and grabbed the items, quickly scanning what had been written. In just a few seconds she realized the words on the paper had nothing to do with the hit on the Deputy Minister, he had written the first part of the fairy tale, Hansel and Gretel.

Nina whipped around and yelled, "You've made a huge mistake, you asshole. You know you're not getting out of here alive, right?"

"I know nothing of the sort, my dear. In fact, I think I'll be out of here in time to see the sunset. I just love sunsets, don't you?"

Nina was infuriated, "Clearly you think this is all a joke, and you're not willing to cooperate, so I'm done wasting my time with you." She pulled her Glock from her holster and said, "Raise the cube!"

The two guys with AR-15's moved quickly into an active shooting stance and a third guy pressed a button on the control panel behind him. The glass cage began to lift towards the ceiling. As the glass ascended, Crajack slowly stood up from his chair and stared at Nina.

"Goodbye, Ralph." She fired two quick shots into his chest.

The gun fired, but nothing happened to Crajack. He flinched a bit and then stood there smiling.

"What the hell?" said Nina in disbelief.

Crajack started walking towards her and then bullets started flying. Nina emptied her magazine into him while the AR-15s fired dozens of rounds at him with seemingly no effect. Crajack covered the last few feet by leaping at Nina, knocking her down and taking her weapon. Nina was in disbelief and could not figure out what was going on. Why wasn't he bleeding and dying on the floor? Maybe somehow blanks had been switched into her team's weapons? No way that was the case with hers. She personally loaded her two Glocks and magazines with real ammo and they had not left her side. Crajack reached down and grabbed her ankle gun and started shooting at her team. They dropped one by one while he stood there, taking everything they shot at him.

Crajack turned and faced Nina. They were the only ones still alive in the room. "Stand up," he said to her as he pointed her own gun at her head.

Nina stood and stared at Crajack in disbelief. There was no blood on him. His clothes showed some signs of the bullets that had been fired at him, but not a scratch. Did he have some new bullet-proof technology she hadn't seen before? That seemed impossible, but what other explanation could there be?

"Start walking and get me out of this place," Crajack said, never moving the gun away. She turned and led him through a maze of rooms and corridors until they stepped out into the bright Florida sunshine. Crajack took a deep breath and could smell the warm salt air.

"I'm guessing you thought this would all end very differently, my dear."

"What the fuck are you?" she asked.

"Step back into the building please, just beyond the door."

"Fuck you," she yelled but did as he asked. Nina knew this business was dangerous and that she was always just one bullet away from her life being over, but she never thought it would end like this.

Crajack fired a round into each of Nina's legs. She immediately dropped to the floor, screaming in pain and agony. He reached into her pocket and retrieved the paper she had written on. Not sure what he would find, he was pleasantly surprised that the note actually gave the name of someone in his network, someone who had been very trusted.

"Thanks for the information, Nina." He moved closer to her, placed the muzzle of the Glock against her temple and pulled the trigger. He closed the door behind him and never looked back.

Crajack would not make the same mistake again. This time he was taking it seriously. The fact that the feeling had intensified since dinner told him he had to act on the offensive, be the first one to make a move. The lovely new couple in town was a danger to him, and he would have to take them out. He recalled the discussion of the rafting trip and decided it would be the perfect opportunity to do so. He still had the problem of Dominic and Donna with their investigation and potentially getting close to the truth. He would just have to take care of them also. He enjoyed the rush he was getting just thinking about the evil he was about to unleash.

CHAPTER 25

$\mathbf{A}$ loud knock on her bedroom door startled Abby out of her peaceful slumber. "Wake up, sleepy head. Breakfast in ten minutes," Dominic called to her.

She rolled over to peek at the alarm clock on the night stand, 7:30 AM, on Sunday morning no less. *You have got to be kidding me*, she thought. After the dinner, she came home with her dad, they sat up talking for a bit, and she didn't get to bed until a little after midnight. She needed more sleep! But she knew her father and knew that wasn't going to happen.

"Can we please make it fifteen, Dad?" she called back to him.

"Okay, but not a minute more. I know your new friend is coming to pick you up and I want to make sure we get through my files before that."

A half hour later Abby was on her second cup of coffee as she finished the last bite of her cheese and tomato omelet, one of her dad's specialties.

"My omelet was delicious, Dad. Thank you."

"My pleasure, Abigail. Once you finish up, I'll show you the files I've put together on the suspicious deaths I told you about."

Typical Dad, she thought, *anxious to get going*. She knew it had to be something important for him to call her with the urgency he demonstrated on the phone, so she understood. "Another half of cup, Dad, and I'll be ready to dive into your findings."

Dominic poured her a full cup. "Just in case," he chuckled.

They moved into Dom's office and on his desk lay a thick folder with multiple files in it, simply titled Current Investigation.

Abby picked up the heavy folder, "Dad, you really have done a lot of work here."

"I hope it all actually comes to something. I would hate to think someone is getting away with all these murders by making them look like accidents and natural causes."

"Okay, give me your summary again, the one you gave me on the phone and then I'll review each of the files in detail."

"That folder includes files on fifteen deaths over the past two years." Dominic continued, "All of them under the age of forty-five, so pretty young. All of them are Jewish, seven females, eight males. The deaths were either accidents, or labeled natural causes, although I don't think it's very natural for a thirty-seven-year-old soccer mom to have a heart attack. And another thing, all of the people were alone when they died, no witnesses, no one to call for help. Looking at each of the cases individually, there is nothing at all suspicious. What caught my attention was there have been so many of them. Looking at them all together like that, I think it's very suspicious. Most of the victims, twelve to be exact, belonged to the same synagogue. The rabbi I told you about who was murdered the other night? He was the head of that synagogue, and when I heard about his death, it made my suspicions go through the roof. I really think there's a killer here in Billings, preying on young Jewish people, and something sent him over the edge which is why he murdered Rabbi Kuperman."

"Let me put on my detective hat for a minute and ask a few questions."

"That's why I asked you here, honey, if anyone can figure this out, my daughter the finest detective in New York City can."

"First, fifteen deaths over a two-year period does not seem extremely unusual. I'm not an actuary, but I bet that number falls in the realm of acceptability."

Dominic went to say something, Abby put up her hand, indicating she was not yet finished. "How did the deaths occur?"

"It's all there in the files, but I know them by heart—two drownings, four deaths in two different car accidents, three apparent heart attacks, two apparent strokes, a married couple got lost and died on a camping trip, one fell off his roof fixing a gutter and one kidney failure."

"Were these deaths all investigated by the police or any insurance companies? I'm guessing since they all died alone, there had to be some investigation."

"Not sure about any insurance investigators, but Chief Wagner, who you met at dinner last night, had each death investigated by his people."

"What did he find?" Abby asked, "Anything helpful?"

"Nothing. He said that as far as they could determine, all of the accidents were accidents, and he found nothing suspicious in any of the natural deaths to think they were not what they seemed to be."

"Do you know the extent of his investigations? Did they get any outside help from other law enforcement agencies?"

"Not to my knowledge," Dominic replied. "Not sure anything like that is in the budget and the Chief doesn't really like to ask for help."

"Have you talked to the Chief about your suspicions?"

"Yes."

"And what did he have to say?" Abby asked.

"He listened to me for a bit and then kind of laughed the whole thing off. Said my reporter brain was working overtime, looking for something that didn't exist."

"I see." She paused and then asked, "Tell me about Rabbi Kuperman."

"One of the most gruesome crimes we've ever had in Billings, but from what I've heard from Chief Wagner, they're not having a lot of luck. There's little to no evidence at the scene and no significant clues or tips to follow. You would think with a murder like that, there would be something the police could go on."

"Right. Okay, Dad, last question. What makes you think these deaths are the result of foul play and not just what they appear to be, accidents and natural causes, except the Rabbi, of course?"

"You know me, honey, I was never one to jump to any conclusions … but my reporter's instinct is at work here. There are just too many coincidences. None of these people had any apparent enemies, and none had a large fortune where someone would benefit from their death. When I first thought something nefarious might be going on, I started to look into it. That's what reporters do. I didn't really expect to find much, but the more I dig, the more suspicious I get, even if I haven't found concrete proof yet."

"Alright, Dad, I think I have a good basis. Let me look through the files and then we can regroup."

"Skip the first page, Abigail, that's my summary and my conclusions," Dominic requested, "I want you to come to your own conclusions before you see mine."

There was a file for each of the alleged victims, ten minutes in, Abby remarked, "This information is well-structured and very concisely written. Who helped you?"

"It's that obvious?" Dominic asked.

"Well, from what I remember of your notes, they were never put together this well."

"You're right, Donna Stapleton the Director of the Library is my ghost writer, you met her at the dinner last night."

"Yes, I remember her." Abby had to ask, "Is there anything else going on between you and Donna? She seems like a very nice person."

"She's very nice. We do dinner a couple times a month, but that's it. She has made it clear on more than one occasion that just dinner is just fine with her. So no, to answer your question, there is nothing going on. So please, stop worrying about my love life and get back to the files."

Abby raised her eyebrows at her dad, smiled and went back to the files. As Abby read through the files, she made notes on the pages and on a separate pad of paper. Close to two hours later she said, "Okay, Dad, I'm finished."

"So, what do you think?" Dom asked with an inquisitive voice.

"Well, on the surface and in accordance with the findings of the Billings police and specifically Chief Wagner, you have a case of fifteen unfortunate deaths that appear to be accidents or natural causes."

"And below the surface, what does your detective instinct tell you?"

"There are an awful lot of coincidences," she responded.

"Yes, go ahead," Dominic said, encouraging her to share her thoughts.

"Okay, here goes," as she looked at her notes. "All the victims were Jewish, all were young, twelve of them belonged to Rabbi Kuperman's synagogue, no witnesses, all the investigations were done in house, and only two of the victims had an actual autopsy. That's what I see that falls in the coincidence category. Each item alone is acceptable and maybe when all put-together they are still acceptable, but, still too many coincidences for me."

Abby continued, "The strangest thing I found is having no witnesses at any of the deaths. The probability of that happening is extremely low. But all in all, I don't see a smoking gun here, and maybe more importantly, your chief of police doesn't see any either. I know that probably isn't the answer you're looking for, Dad. Sorry."

"It's okay, honey. No need to apologize. There is something I learned last night that isn't in the file yet, maybe that will change your mind."

"What is it?"

Dominic leaned forward in his chair and spoke softly, "Thirteen of the victims took a Dog Training class in the last three years."

"So that's another coincidence, but I don't see it adding much to the investigation."

"They had taken a Dog Training class that was given by Chief Wagner, what do you think now?!"

Abby looked at her dad, wondering what he was getting at. She happened to glance down and caught sight of her dad's handwritten summary of the case, the last line caught her attention. *Is the Chief somehow involved?*

"Holy shit, Dad! You think Chief Wagner is involved? Isn't that a huge assumption? You need to be careful who you share that information with. Nothing goes wrong faster than a cop who is unjustly accused of something. Wow, is that really what you're thinking?" she asked, looking directly at him.

"Honey, it's what my gut is telling me. I know I don't have the proof, no hard evidence, just call it my reporter's intuition. Maybe I am trying to force this information to fit my feelings, but I'm not forcing the feelings. Haven't you had the same kind of experience in your career? Where your gut takes you to a place that the facts didn't lead to?"

"Sure, I've had gut instincts, but about little things, not some huge conspiracy involving the Chief of Police."

"Well how about we go see our chief? I'll tell him you want to follow up on his offer to look at the investigation file on the rabbi's murder. Maybe from there you can segue into talking about some of the accidents. See how he reacts when you question him. What do you say?"

"I don't know, Dad. I'm happy to look at the Rabbi's file, but not sure I'm up to questioning the Chief of Police about deaths he has ruled as accidents and natural causes and that you think he's involved in. And it's not like we can go see him now. He told me to call on Monday."

"Abigail, please. Can we both see him tomorrow and try to get some more information? If nothing comes of it, I will think of dropping the investigation."

"You would really drop it after all the time you've put into it?"

"If you say there is nothing there, then I have to believe it."

"Okay, let's regroup in the morning. I'll have had some time to think about everything we covered today. Maybe something new will pop into my head. Tomorrow, we'll decide if we are both going to see the chief or just me."

"That works for me, honey."

"Alright then, I have a date to get ready for. Ken is gonna pick me up in less than an hour."

"Okay then, I love you, Abigail."

"I love you too, Dad." Abby headed off to the shower blowing Dominic a kiss. She was thinking she didn't like all the coincidences either.

CHAPTER 26

Right before 1:00 PM, Abby heard the loud screech of tires as a car pulled into her Dad's driveway. *That's gotta be Sal*, she thought as she grinned and went to the door. She was right. When she opened the door, Sal's car had just stopped and Ken was getting out of the backseat, a huge smile spread across his face when he saw her. She was wearing white capri pants and a flowing yellow and blue top, perfect summer wear.

"Hello, beautiful," Ken said.

"Hello yourself, handsome." Abby responded as they came together with a kiss and an embrace.

"I missed you last night."

"Good."

"Good?" Ken said surprised.

"Yes. Makes you more excited to see me today. I can already tell."

"Well, I am excited to see you today."

"Good. And if you wanna know a little secret, I missed you too!" Abby gave him another kiss, a little longer this time, and then said, "Okay, let's get this show on the road," as she headed to the car and got in the backseat.

"Good morning, Sal."

"Good morning," Sal replied.

As they settled in, Abby asked Sal, "Everything good to go?"

"Yeah, it's all as you requested Boss Lady, right down to the last detail."

"Great, and thank you, Sal."

"No problem."

Ken turned to Abby with a questioning look, "You enlisted Sal's help? Interesting."

"Of course, I did. He's a very resourceful guy."

"So I keep learning. So, exactly what am I in for today?" asked Ken.

Sal was the one who replied and said, "It's all good, Boss, just sit back, relax and enjoy the ride."

Not wanting to sound like a little boy pestering his parents on what the surprise is going to be, Ken sat back, gently took Abby's hand, raised it to his lips and kissed it. He said, "Okay, guys, I'm all in. Let's go." He honestly had no idea what Abby had in store for them, and again he found himself in a situation he'd never expected. When was the last time he was not in charge of his own time? He never would have been okay with that before he met Abby. She was changing him, giving him a reason to have hope when thinking about the future. Sal got the car headed east on I-94.

For thirty minutes or so, Sal drove through the rolling hills and farms outside of Billings. He then pulled in to Pompey's Pillar National Monument, a spot made famous by the Lewis and Clark expedition when William Clark stopped there in 1806. It was a beautiful park, with the towering pillar and an amazing view of the Yellowstone River. Ken wasn't sure if Sal had made a mistake or if this was the surprise, a day in the park! Although he had been to Billings many times, he'd never taken the time to visit this place. He'd heard it was a great way to spend a day, but spare time was never a luxury he had when he was in Billings. Unfortunately, his visits were in and out in a day or so as was the nature of his profession.

"We're here," Abby said to Ken smiling.

"Gonna pull around near where you wanted to be, Boss Lady." Sal went to the very end of the parking lot, hit the brakes hard, then remembered to soften it up a bit. Their stop was awkward, but better than some of the earlier ones. Abby was prepared this time and braced herself for the stop.

"Better, eh, Boss Lady?"

"Best stop so far, Sal. Keep up the good work." Abby said with a broad smile on her face. She glanced at Ken and saw he had a little grin on his face also.

"Okay, I'll get everything set up," Sal said as he exited the car.

Abby and Ken got out of the car and looked around at the park, enjoying the peaceful scenery, bright blue sky and the many shades of green in the leaves and waving prairie grass. It was a beautiful day with a light breeze blowing as Sal made a few trips from the car to an out of the way spot by the river. Abby went over to help Sal setup.

Ken asked, "Do you need any help?"

They responded in unison, "No!"

Up went a ten by ten portable screened room, blankets on the soft grass to create a floor, a couple of chairs and a few pillows for added comfort, and then a small table. Sal worked on setting up a portable speaker, and in just a minute or two, Frank Sinatra was coming out of the speaker.

Abby placed a cooler on the table and started to arrange the other items Sal had brought from the car. From a large picnic basket, she pulled out a tray of sandwiches, a bag of chips, a fruit plate, potato salad, coleslaw and dessert, some chocolate chip brownies.

Ken looked at the spread and said jokingly to Abby, "What, no ice cream?"

She turned around and gave him a hard stare he could not quite read, and then she opened the cooler and pulled out a tub of vanilla ice cream.

Ken started laughing, "You have literally thought of everything." He went over to Abby, gave her a hug and a kiss, while she playfully batted him away.

In less than ten minutes, everything was set up, Sal said, "Okay, guys, have a great time. Be back in a few hours."

"Thanks, Sal, you're a doll," said Abby as she blew him a kiss. He sheepishly smiled and disappeared into the parking lot.

"So, this is it?" Ken said. "What you had planned?"

"Yes," said Abby looking around at their little piece of heaven. "I haven't been on a picnic since I was a little girl, and I figured it was time. I've always loved coming out to Pompey's and it seemed like the perfect place to spend the afternoon. This is the first of many things I've been missing in my life that I plan on doing more of. Maybe we can do them together?" she said as she gave him a soft kiss.

"I would like that," he responded as he kissed her back.

Ken had to admit he was surprised. He thought she might have planned something a little more exotic or adventurous, but it was just the opposite, a simple picnic. The whole thing told him more about her—she was a woman looking to get back to enjoying the simple things in life. He liked that. But in the back of his mind, again he wondered if he should just cut ties with Abby sooner rather than later, he was supposed to be here to wrap things up and move on, not to fall in love. He kissed her again and thought, *I'll worry about it later.*

They filled their plates from the spread on the table and sat down to eat when all of a sudden Abby said, "Crap, I almost forgot the wine!" She pulled a bottle of Chardonnay out of the cooler and handed it to Ken. "Would you please open this for us?"

"It would be my pleasure," said Ken.

Abby got some glasses for them to use, Ken opened the bottle and poured, and they again sat down to enjoy their meal. And enjoy they did, the food, the wine, the beautiful scenery around them and most importantly, each other.

"I am stuffed," Abby said as she leaned back in her chair, "I might not have room for dessert, and that'd be awful!"

"Lunch was great. Thank you," Ken said. "Would you like to go for a walk, maybe go up to the top of the Pillar? We could work off some calories and then be ready for brownies and ice cream."

"Sounds like a fabulous idea!"

They walked hand in hand through the park, down to the river which was moving swiftly but quietly, birds in the trees were talking, rabbits and squirrels were running around, and they even saw a family of deer out in the grass. Finally, they climbed to the top of Pompey's Pillar and took in the beautiful view.

"It's so peaceful up here," Abby said.

"Yes, it really is. Thank you for bringing me here."

"It has absolutely been my pleasure, Mr. Stone."

When they got back to their setup, they heard a low rumble in the sky and they both looked up. It was the sound of thunder, and they could see storm clouds gathering in the West. "Damn, looks like it's gonna rain and we're gonna have to wrap up early. I'll give Sal a call," said Abby.

"What about dessert?" Ken asked feigning disappointment.

"Oh, don't worry, there is always time for dessert," Abby replied. She quickly called Sal, who was already on his way, and then went over to the table. She pulled out some bowls, put a couple of brownies in each one and then scooped the ice cream on top. The ice cream was pretty soft, but the combination was delicious.

Sal arrived about ten minutes later, barely screeching the brakes. They all packed up the car and then headed back to town. They were in the car just a few minutes when the sky opened up and the rain started pouring down.

"Cut that one kind close, didn't ya, Boss?" asked Sal.

"Yes, we did, but we're safe and dry, and the day is still young, right?" he said as he turned to Abby.

"Yes, the day is still young, and because I'm always prepared, I had a contingency plan in case it rained," responded Abby.

"There's more?" Ken asked.

"Sal, do you know where Holiday Circle is?"

"Yeah, sure, Boss Lady. You wanna go there?"

"Yes, please. Thank you."

Ken looked at Abby, "Another surprise?"

"Yes."

"Well, I'm in, of course. The first surprise was pretty awesome."

Sal made his way back into Billings and to Holiday Circle. He guessed where Abby wanted to go and softly stopped in front of Yellowstone Cellars and Winery. "This da place you wanted?"

"It's like you read my mind, Sal. Perfect."

Ken looked out at the sign, "A winery. I like it."

It was still raining out, so they quickly got out of the car and sprinted inside to find they had the place all to themselves, except for the bartender of course. They spent the next several hours sampling the different wines, talking to each other, listening to the rain and enjoying the afternoon, despite the weather. At one point the owner came in and they talked with him for a bit. He even gave them a tour of the cellars and equipment. The rain eventually stopped and the sun peaked out for a bit, but was on its way to setting. As the shadows grew longer, Ken sent a text to Sal and asked him to pick them up. He was there quickly and deposited them both back at Ken's hotel a little before 9:00 PM with a minimum of screeching tires.

CHAPTER 27

Abby and Ken walked through the lobby of the Northern Hotel to the elevator. Ken pressed the button to take them to the top floor.

"The penthouse. Nice," said Abby.

Ken just looked at her grinning and shrugged his shoulders a bit. Abby wasn't expecting any more than the standard hotel room, maybe a suite, and she didn't care as long as the bed was comfortable. So, when they went through the front door of the room and Ken turned on the lights, she was quite surprised. This was not an ordinary hotel room by any definition. One side of the main room looked like a library, shelves of books, and tables with books spread out all over, the other side of the room looked like a modern-day office. All the eye could see were books, computers, monitors, a few filing cabinets and more books. It was spacious and well lit, with very little furniture, a small kitchenette and some ancient looking paintings on the walls. From just inside the front door you could see that there were at least two other rooms.

"Jesus, where did this palace come from? I don't think the rest of the good citizens of Billings know about this cozy apartment. I'm not gonna ask how much. Shit, how much?"

"Not as much as you would think. The hotel did a renovation a few years ago so this suite was created at the same time."

"I guess there's more money in the art business than one realizes."

"I have been fortunate and done well in business, so thankfully, money is not an issue for me."

"I guess not," Abby said while still looking around in disbelief.

"Is it an issue for you?"

"No, I don't think so. You just surprised me. And you are certainly full of surprises, Mr. Stone."

"Perhaps you should look around the entire suite so there are no more surprises and then I can have your full attention."

"Okay, but first I have to call my Dad and let him know I won't be home tonight."

"How is he going to feel about that?"

"Well, I'm a grown-ass woman, and he knows that. I think he'll be fine with it. But just in case, I'll tell him we're in separate rooms."

Ken raised his eyebrows in a look of shocked surprise.

"Relax, Mr. Boy Scout. I was just kidding. I'm not gonna lie to my father. He's gonna be fine with it. I just want him to know I'm safe and not to expect me."

"I guess I need some time to learn your sense of humor."

"Okay, I'll make sure you have plenty of time with me to work on it," Abby said grinning.

A few minutes later, Abby was off the phone with her father; they made plans to go to the police station to see the chief late the following morning. Abby then went to explore the rest of the suite. She opened the door off the right of the main room and turned on the light.

"What the—," Abby was momentarily speechless as she looked around and took the bedroom in. "Seriously, this is your bedroom?" The room was huge. There was a king size bed with a glossy black headboard, a sitting area to the left with a large recliner and a table that was also filled with books. The décor was masculine, but it appealed to her; it was all done in very good taste and it gave her an instant sense of comfort.

"Wow, I don't think I've seen a bedroom this large before, not in person anyway," Abby said in amazement.

"I really don't spend much time in there," Ken said, "When I'm in town, I spend most of my time in my library doing research. Between the books and the internet, I have access to almost all the information I need to conduct my business. Usually I fall asleep on the sofa going through my research. I don't have any time for relationships."

"Not even once?"

"No, not even once," Ken said emphatically.

That was the truth. Ken never had any involvement with women in Billings. The hotel built the suite for him at his request during the re-model, he only gave them plans for the library and office. There were no requests for the bedroom, so the owner of the hotel hired a decorator to do the bedroom. Ken was fine with it. He hadn't asked for anything specific; he just wanted privacy, access to information, and convenience. The suite provided all of that.

Abby believed Ken was sincere when he talked about his lack of relationships. She turned from the bedroom, gave him a quick kiss on the cheek and went to open the door to the one remaining room she hadn't seen. After the gorgeous master bedroom, she was sorely disappointed. It was just a plain room, no furniture, just some artwork leaning against the walls and boxes stacked in one corner.

"Okay, so this is kind of a letdown," Abby said turning from the room and looking at Ken.

"So sorry the spare room does not meet with your approval, Ms. Steel. I will get someone on it right away."

"Don't bother, Mr. Stone. I don't plan on using the spare room."

"That sounds like a much better plan to me," Ken replied, grinning.

Abby walked over to the kitchen area and asked, "Do we have any bubbly?" She opened the refrigerator and found it was well stocked with several very nice bottles of champagne and wine, along with water, beer and, of course, Ken's favorite, club soda. Ken let Abby ramble on as she opened the champagne and poured a glass, enjoying her one woman play and her delight in exploring the suite and making herself right at home.

"I'm glad everything meets with your approval," he said during a pause in her monologue.

"Everything so far does, but let's not be too quick to judge," she looked at Ken mischievously and said, "I haven't sampled everything yet, so I will let you know in a couple of hours."

"Don't I get one too?" Ken asked as he gestured to the glass of champagne.

Abby poured champagne into another glass, picked it up and walked over to Ken. Their eyes locked as she handed him the glass. A fire was starting to kindle.

He raised his glass and said, "To this moment right now."

They gently clinked glasses and both took a long, slow sip as they stared at each other. As if on cue, they both put down their glasses, moved to each other and embraced with a passionate kiss. They moved to the bedroom and took their time undressing each other. Abby pulled off Ken's shirt and stopped.

"What happened to you?" she said as her fingers were tracing a long scar over his abdomen.

"Training accident in the Army. It wasn't serious."

She looked at him, "Are you sure? It looks pretty serious to me."

"It's completely fine. Now stop worrying about me and let's continue."

"I'm completely fine with that," she said smiling as she reached to kiss him again.

Abby had described her previous love affairs and sexual encounters to her closest friends and her therapist in many ways, and rarely did she describe it as making love. Sex was always the operative word. It took thirty-nine years, nine months and twenty-nine days, but after three hours of being with Ken, she knew what making love really was. The word sex never came to mind, instead it was replaced by feelings of love, sensitivity, sincerity, passion, kindness, fun, happiness, adoration, tenderness, yearning, and veneration. It was beautiful. The sacrifice of not experiencing it all these years was worth it. Her body, her mind, and her soul never felt this way before. It wasn't what they did, but how they did it. At times they were so tender with each other their bodies barely felt the other's presence. Their minds were engulfed to the fullest. They both found something wonderful and new in each other.

Abby felt herself change in these moments with Ken. It was as if a long-lost side of her personality, one that had been buried by cynicism, was finally released. A part of her that wanted more out of life than she was getting, a part that wanted to give more to life than she was giving. The energy and strength she once had were reborn.

For Abby, it was the beginning of a new life. For Ken, it was the beginning of a torturous few days. Abby was special in a way he never expected to find again. He hadn't loved anyone in a very long time, and he knew he was falling in love with Abby. It wasn't simple, and not what he had planned, but he believed she was feeling the same way, and for that he would gladly change his life plans and his destiny to live a new life with her. Somewhere between three and four in the morning, Abby and Ken fell asleep, entwined in each other's arms. They had not said it yet, but they both knew they were feeling it: Love.

Ken woke in the early morning, looked at Abby and smiled. She was deep into some beautiful dream that he would not wake her from. He tucked the covers around her as if to protect her and then he paused for a second to gather his thoughts. He remembered his plans, and realized he would do none of it, not if it meant losing Abby. She was worth altering his plans and his life. He gently pulled Abby into his arms and went back to sleep. He would figure out a way to make it happen.

CHAPTER 28

The alarm on Abby's phone went off at 9:00 AM. It had been a very late, but incredible night with Ken, the first in what she hoped would be many more, but she would have to make do with the sleep she had gotten.

Ken mumbled from under the covers, "Why are they bothering us?"

"No one is bothering us. It's just the alarm. I'm meeting my dad at the Chief's this morning, remember?"

"Unfortunately, I do remember that we must part this morning. I have a couple of things to do, but how about the three of us meet for lunch?"

"That sounds great. I'm sure my dad will be up for it. It will give him a chance to grill you about why I didn't come home last night!" Abby said playfully.

"Not a problem, I will tell him it was all you. I tried to take you home and you wouldn't get in the car."

"Nice try," said Abby as she threw a pillow at him and then quickly got out of bed. "He won't believe a word of it. I'm his little girl," she said over her shoulder as she headed to the bathroom.

"Oh well, I guess I'll just have to win him over with my charm and humor. Hey Abby, do you need Sal to drive you this morning?"

"No, I'm gonna to walk. It's just a couple of blocks and it's a beautiful morning."

An hour later, Abby had showered, dressed, had a coffee and muffin and was headed to the Billings Police Department. She waited outside for a few minutes and when her dad arrived, they walked in together. The desk sergeant said the chief was expecting them and to head on up. Dominic had been there many times, so he led Abby upstairs to the chief's office. Dominic knocked on the open door and the chief looked up and smiled.

"Good morning, Dom. Come on in," the chief said as he stood and shook Dom's hand. "Welcome, Ms. Steel. Nice to see you again."

"Thanks, Chief. Good to see you again too," Abby said with a soft smile as she also shook the chief's hand.

"So, Ms. Steel, you wanted to see the file on the Rabbi's murder, right?"

"Yes, Chief. Thank you for making the offer at the dinner." Abby made it sound like he had offered, but they both knew she really pushed her way in. And after going through her dad's files yesterday, she was now much more interested in looking at the file, but that was no longer her only reason for being there. She would eventually work up to discussing her dad's investigation, but first things first.

"Here you go," the chief said as he handed Abby a manila folder, titled Rabbi Kuperman with a number next to it. "I don't think you're gonna find anything new, but it never hurts to have another set of eyes look it over … I guess."

"Thank you, Chief Wagner," Abby replied, trying to show him respect by using his formal title.

"While she's looking at the file, Dom, can I get you a cup of coffee or maybe some water?"

"I know where it is Cort, thanks. I'll get it myself and make a few phone calls while you guys do your police thing." This was part of the strategy Dominic and Abby had worked out—for Dominic to be out of the room and give Abby an opportunity to bring up her dad's investigation.

"Ms. Steel, would you like anything?"

"No thanks, I'm fine," Abby quickly replied. She looked through the file carefully and ten minutes later handed it back to the Chief. "Looks like you've covered all the bases so far. I don't see anything I would have done differently." Abby knew at this early stage in the investigation, with no witnesses or obvious motive, the file would be thin, and it was. She also knew that not finding the perpetrator in the first seventy-two hours made the case much more difficult to solve.

"Yeah, not much to go on yet, but we'll find our killer. I'm sure of it," the chief responded.

"I have no doubt you'll find him," she answered, trying to give the chief some praise before she switched gears on him, and now was the moment of truth.

"Chief Wagner, I wonder if you could do me a huge favor, and frankly, make life a lot easier for me," she said softly.

"I'd be glad to help if I can. What can I do for you?"

"Well, I would like to talk to you about the investigation my dad has been undertaking for quite some time." She pulled her dad's file out of her bag.

"Stop right there, Ms. Steel," the chief said harshly. "If this is about the unfortunate and accidental deaths over the last few years, go no further. I've told your dad on numerous occasions that all of those cases have been fully investigated. We've gone over the files more times than I can count and I have found no evidence of foul play. None!" At this point the Chief stood up, but continued his rant, "For some confounded reason your dad just won't quit on trying to find something behind these deaths. It's become an obsession with him, and quite frankly, it's becoming an extreme annoyance to me and my department."

At this point, the chief came around and sat on the front of his desk. He forced himself to take a breath and said, "Don't get me wrong. I have a lot of respect for your father, and I admire everything he's done for Billings, but his reporter nose, as he calls it, is way off the mark this time. So, you can put that file away. I won't be looking at any of those cases again. As far as me and my department are concerned, they are a closed issue. Your father is just gonna have stop interfering and move on."

Abby was taken aback at the hard stance the chief took and the tone he used. He tried to soften it at the end, but she thought it was forced. She could tell the chief would not discuss it further, so she quickly decided to drop it even though she had gotten nothing from him. Actually, maybe she had gotten something. If she were in the same situation, would she respond so strongly? Was it another clue that he had reacted the way he did?

"Sorry, Chief. I meant no disrespect. My dad took me through his files yesterday and he tried to convince me there is something there. He asked if I'd talk to you about it, but I understand and respect your position. I'll talk to him about letting it go."

"I'm sorry if I seemed to overreact, Ms. Steel. I really am. It's just that your dad can be so damn persistent, it got to me."

"No problem, I know exactly how he can be. Thank you very much for your time, Chief. We'll be on our way."

As Abby and Dominic walked to meet Ken for lunch, Abby retold her dad the exact conversation she had with the chief.

"He stonewalled it, Dad. I think his reaction was over the top, but I don't know him as well as you do. For now, let's leave it alone. Give me a couple of days to give the whole situation more thought, maybe come at it from a different angle, okay?"

"Okay, honey. I'll wait a couple of days and then we can come back to it. But I want to ask you a question, and I want you to answer honestly, alright?"

"Sure, Dad, what is it?"

"Do you think I'm chasing my tail?"

Abby thought for a long time before she answered. "On the surface, it really doesn't look like there is anything there, especially not with the Chief being involved. But," she said and paused again, "something about your investigation has my detective sense tingling, I've been wrong before though. So, like I said, let's give it a couple of days and circle back, okay?"

"That works for me. I'm just glad you didn't tell me I was crazy," Dominic answered, smiling at his daughter. "Now let's go have a nice lunch with your new friend Ken, and we won't worry about suspicious deaths, or possible murder, or anything bad for at least the rest of the day!"

"Sounds wonderful, Dad. Let's go." Abby smiled and put her arm through her father's as they walked on.

Not too far away, Crajack was planning his moves for the next day, it was going to be a long one, but at the end of the it, he will have eliminated any and all threats to him. The only thing that annoyed him was that he was doing this for free. "Not good for my stock holders," he chuckled heartily to himself.

CHAPTER 29

Ken woke up and looked over at Abby. They had spent another wonderful night together, and this morning she was sleeping peacefully. Yesterday, after lunch and spending the afternoon with Dominic, they returned to the Northern Hotel for an evening in. After a room service dinner, they continued getting to know each other better in every possible way. The thought entered his mind that he wanted to tell her the truth about himself, and that had very much surprised him. He had never contemplated sharing his past with anyone, but in his heart, he somehow knew that to be with Abby, he would have to do exactly that. With her though, revealing the truth would be even more difficult. He could not imagine what her reaction would be when she found out *he* was the vigilante she has been chasing. He pushed the thought away. Today was not the day.

He kissed Abby gently on the cheek and brushed the hair off her face. She stirred, her eyes opened and when she saw him, her face lit up with a wonderful smile. She pulled him in for a nice, slow, good morning kiss.

"Good morning," she said.

"Good morning to you. Are you ready to get up? We have a big day ahead of us."

"I guess so."

"You guess so? That's not very enthusiastic of you. Come on, Boss Lady, it's time to hit the shower," Ken said grinning at Abby's expression.

"Boss Lady? Boss Lady? For that crack, you can get your ass up first and shower. Make it a long one, so I can get another few winks."

"I suppose I deserve that, so off I go." Ken got out of bed and glanced back at Abby. She blew him a kiss, then turned over while pulling the sheets up, implying she was indeed going to grab another few winks. *A deal is a deal,* he thought as he closed the bathroom door.

Ken got in the shower and let the hot water flow over his body, enjoying the steam and pounding from the water. Thoroughly engrossed in the shower, he didn't notice that his privacy was being invaded.

"Room for one more?"

Ken did not turn around to the voice, although he was pleasantly surprised to hear it. He responded, "Only if you know the password."

Abby stepped into the shower and slid her hands around Ken's waist, pushing her naked body against his, and said, "Mad, passionate, wild love."

"That's close enough for me," Ken said as he turned around.

He put his hand on each side of Abby's face and gave her a long, sensuous kiss. For the next thirty minutes, they picked up where they left off last night. The hot water aroused and energized them, heightening their sexual appetites. As they held each other leaning against the shower wall, Ken finally said, "We better get moving. Sal will be here soon."

"Sal who?" Abby responded with a slight laugh as she held him tightly.

"Funny girl," said Ken as he kissed her and turned off the shower. He stepped out and grabbed them both towels.

Abby was ready first and as she was waiting for Ken, she wandered around the suite checking out the books that were stacked all over the place. She noticed that a lot of the books had the same theme, they were about ancient civilizations, with multiple volumes specifically on the Inca Empire. *That's interesting*, she thought, *I wonder if it's connected to his art dealing.* She didn't remember anything about the Incas, she would have to ask him about it later.

They had a quick breakfast downstairs and then were in the lobby waiting for Sal. They planned to take a half-day rafting trip which would start at noon. The beginning of the trip was in a little town known as Gardiner, about 150 miles from their hotel. It would have been a long drive, but Sal had managed to borrow one of the town's rescue helicopters and a pilot, so they could get there in just forty minutes. Abby wondered how Sal managed to pull that off, but Ken just said that Sal knows quite a few people that owe him favors. That was good with her, but it was another reason for her to wonder about this guy and how he ended up in Billings, Montana. There was definitely more to him than meets the eye!

While they were waiting, Abby picked up a brochure on white water rafting. The flashy brochure mostly contained photos of people in rafts on the water, smiling and happy. There was also a list of common rafting terms with definitions.

"Might as well learn something about what we'll be doing," she said to Ken as she sat next to him and opened the brochure.

He had his face buried in the local paper, but looked up at Abby and the brochure, and chuckled, "Excellent choice, Rafting for Dummies."

"Excuse me," she quipped, "but are you calling me a dummy?"

He looked at her with a smirk on his face, "I would never."

"Okay, smart guy," she said as she looked at the first definition, "What is an eddy?"

"A guy I know from Brooklyn," he joked.

"Nice try."

She was about to fire out another definition when the distinct sound of screeching tires could be heard throughout the entire lobby. Apparently, he only softened his stops when they were in the car.

They looked at each other knowingly as Abby said, "Hmmm, I wonder who that could be?"

Ken just smiled as they headed out the door and got into the car with Sal.

There was no doubt in Abby's mind that Sal got his driving skills on the streets of New York City. He drove aggressively, a little wild at times, but was always in control. During the ride, curiosity got the best of her.

"Sal, did you drive a cab in New York City?" Abby asked.

"Yeah," he answered.

"What brought you to Billings, Montana?"

"Clean air," he responded, without hesitating.

She wasn't used to such short answers from him, and she was not going to let it go just yet. "There are lots of places with clean air, why this place?"

"Mountains, lots of mountains. I like mountains."

"There are also lots of places with mountains, why here?"

"The great weather."

"Okay." Abby realized this conversation was going nowhere. Either he was being completely honest, or he was evading the real answer, maybe it was somewhere in between. She thought he was probably evading the real answer, which made her wonder again about his past. He had helped her pull off the perfect picnic day, planned the rafting trip, managed to secure a helicopter. She wondered what other talents he might show them over the next few days.

Out of nowhere Sal added, "Lots of good people too ... very nice."

The drive to the helipad went without incident, they parked and got out of the car. Sal went to the trunk and pulled out a small cooler and a duffel bag to bring with them, which contained lunch and drinks for the trip.

Ken asked, "Got everything we need, Sal?"

"Yessir, Boss, no problem," he responded.

They all climbed into the chopper and put on their seatbelts and headsets. Sal introduced Ken and Abby to the pilot, Joshua. He politely said hello, gave a short safety briefing and then they took off. Trips in a helicopter were not new for Abby as she had done this many times while on the job in New York. She and Ken sat in the back two seats while Sal sat up front next to Joshua. Conversation was at a minimum while they enjoyed the beautiful Montana scenery. They were flying at about twelve hundred feet and they had an amazing view. The weather was perfect, creating a very smooth ride and before they knew it, they were landing.

Someone from the rafting company was waiting for them in an old Jeep and gave them a ride to the rafting launch site. Once there, they checked in, signed some insurance waivers, listened to another safety briefing, and then they were ready to go. Sal went and got their life vests and paddles and brought them back. Abby put on her vest and was surprised it fit perfectly, she also noticed that her paddle was a bit shorter than Ken's. She wondered why, but didn't say anything, she was going to save her questions for their guide. Before they headed down to the water, the guy who had picked them up from the airport asked to take their picture, "It comes with the package," he said.

Abby and Ken looked at each other, "Why not?" they replied. The guy pulled out one of those new Polaroid cameras, and took two pictures, one of the three of them, and one with just Abby and Ken. After the photos developed and were admired, Ken put them in his backpack.

When they finally got to the water, Abby saw what looked like a very small raft, maybe eleven feet in length.

Sal pointed to it and said, "That's our raft. She's a beauty, eh?"

"It looks kinda small to me," Abby replied.

"No, no, it's the perfect size for the three of us," Sal said in an excited voice.

Abby looked at Ken in surprise, he just shrugged his shoulders.

"The three of us? What about the guide?" asked Abby.

"You're looking at him," Sal answered with a big smile as he pulled the raft into the water.

"You've gotta be kidding!"

"Nope. Done it a million times," said Sal.

"Seriously, Ken?" Abby exclaimed.

"If he says he can do it, then I trust he can do it," Ken calmly replied.

"Seriously? I don't know, I'm an adventure girl, but what about safety first?"

Ken, knowing Abby was hesitant to set out with Sal as their guide, had an idea. "Okay, Abby, tell you what, pull out that rafting brochure and let's see what Sal knows. If he doesn't know the right answers word for word, we will get a proper guide from the rafting company."

"Okay, fine," she said.

"What say you, Sal?" Ken asked.

"Fine by me," said Sal, "Fire away."

Abby pulled the brochure out of her bag and started reading. "Okay, what is an eddy?"

Sal recited, "A spot in the river where the current goes against the river's normal flow, causing a slow down or even a stoppage. In fact, the first one we come to on this part of the river is in about an hour. It's a good place for us to stop for lunch."

Sal looked up at Abby with a smile. "How'd I do, Boss Lady?"

She jumped to the next definition, and the next and he answered each one correctly. Finally, she said, "Okay, okay, it seems like you know what you're doing, I'm in. Let's get this show on the road." She looked at Ken, he grinned, and off they went.

One of the questions Abby asked was about whitewater classifications. Sal told her that the Yellowstone River was usually around a Class

III, very adventurous, lots of rapids but overall, relatively safe for their skill level. He said Class IV and V were for very experienced rafters and Class VI rapids were a death trap, no one rafted at that level.

He was right about the Yellowstone River. Ten minutes into their trip, water was splashing from all sides, the raft rising and falling as it moved steadily with the strong flow of the river. Abby and Ken were holding their own, paddling as directed by Sal, who was barking instructions from the back of the raft. They were getting the full experience of a Class III ride. After an hour of almost constant maneuvering, including taking on a few rock gardens, Abby and Ken were in their glory, taking in all the river could give them. Abby's arms were starting to get a bit tired from the exertion it took to keep the raft on track. She had not realized how much work it would be, but she also had not realized how much fun it would be.

"When is lunch?" she yelled out to Sal.

"In a coupla minutes the eddy will be on the left, next to a small beachy area. We paddle over there and should be able to slow down enough to eat," Sal replied.

"I thought we would be stopped," Abby answered.

"I stopped there a few times, but I think the river is too high right now to stop safely. Either way we'll be able to put down our paddles and eat."

After a few minutes Sal barked out, "Hey, the eddy is coming up on the left get ready for lunch." As the raft started to slow down, Sal paddled them over into the slow-moving water of the eddy. They were on the left side of the river where it widened out, the extra room was what created the eddy that allowed them to take a break. In the middle of the river, the current was moving as swiftly as ever.

Ken and Abby secured their paddles under the thwarts and stretched their arms out, grinning at each other. Ken was reaching for the cooler when he heard a strange sound. It took him a split-second to realize it was a bullet, just as he heard Sal yell out, "What the fuck?"

Ken watched hopelessly as Sal fell backwards out of the raft and into the swirling water. Just like that his body disappeared into the river. Ken and Abby looked at the river anxiously, expecting him to pop up at any moment. They were in the calm area of the river, but no sign of him.

136

After a beat or two, Ken realized there might be more bullets coming. They were being attacked, but by who and why? He was proven right within seconds as he felt a bullet hit his body. His body jerked as he grabbed Abby, trying to cover and protect her with his body.

"Holy shit, those are bullets!" Abby yelled.

"I know. Get down, we're under attack!"

Ken's body jerked as another bullet hit him.

"Oh my God, are you hit?" Abby yelled.

"I'm fine. We have to get off the raft!" Ken shouted as he pulled her over the gunwale, away from where the shots were coming from and into the river. He felt a third bullet hit him in the leg as he was falling. He knew the only way to protect her was in the water. The shooter would have a very difficult time hitting them in the water. When they surfaced, they were both holding on to the raft and using it as a shield.

"What the hell, why is someone shooting at us?" Abby asked.

"I have no idea, Abby. We have to try and get downstream," replied Ken.

"What about Sal?"

"We can't help him right now. We need to get out of range of the shooter and get somewhere safe. NOW!"

They both heard a loud pop, and then another one. Bullets were hitting the raft.

"Quick," yelled Ken over the sound of the rushing water, "Help me push the raft into the current so we can move faster. The raft is only gonna be cover for another minute or two."

At first Ken wasn't sure that Abby fully understood the grave situation they were in, but as they started pushing the raft, he could see and feel her intensity to get to safety. If they were smart, they might have a chance. They both kicked hard in the water and slowly the raft started moving into the current and picking up speed. In just a couple of minutes, the raft was almost fully deflated and was taking on water.

"Take off your life jacket," Ken told Abby.

"No way, are you crazy?"

"No, I'm not crazy. It's bright yellow and will make an easy target."

"Shit, that makes sense."

"You can swim, right?"

"Yeah, I'm a good swimmer."

"Good, now take off your life jacket."

They both unbuckled their life jackets and let the current take them down the river. Almost immediately, they heard more shots being fired.

Abby looked at Ken, "You were so right."

Ken pulled Abby's face close to his and said, "Go under water, stay under as long as you can and swim as fast as you can. I'll be right behind you."

"I love you," said Abby, she kissed him quickly, let go of the raft and disappeared beneath the water.

Ken guessed the sniper's hide site was on one of the rock outcrops on the far side of the river. If they could get a couple hundred yards down the river, a clean shot would be much more difficult. Ken went under, swimming after Abby.

Underwater, Abby's mind was racing with random thoughts. *What the hell just happened? Was Sal dead? Who would want to kill them?* Almost twenty years on the force had put her in tight situations, but none like this. It took her a few moments to truly understand the danger they were in, but now she was in full survival mode. She swam as hard as she could, as long as she could, but she had to come up for air, her lungs were bursting. As far as the shooter knew, she could be anywhere in the river. If she was quick, it would be tough for him to get a lock on her. At least that's what she hoped. She said a little prayer, quickly surfaced, took a deep breath and went back under the water. *So far so good*, she thought. She couldn't see well under water, but it was easy to follow the current and the further away she got the safer she felt. *Just keep swimming, just keep swimming*, she repeated the mantra over and over in her head. Unknown detritus moved with her through the water and often bumped into her as she made her way down the river, going as quickly as she could. She surfaced for air several more times, but only when she absolutely had to.

Abby continued to move with the current until she encountered a rock pile, where she decided to try and get her bearings and look for Ken. The rock pile would give her something to hang onto and provide some cover. She broke the surface of the water and quickly scanned the immediate area. She did not see Ken and was not familiar enough with the river to know how far she had travelled. She decided to stand up to get a better look and to try and spot Ken. As she stood, her right foot slipped.

Ken was behind Abby, swimming with the current and looking for her underwater, but no luck so far. He too surfaced for air at the last possible moment, conscious that the shooter could get lucky, and hit him again. His old Army survival training had kicked in and he was able to keep himself calm as he swam through the water. He wondered where Sal was, and if he was okay. But mostly his mind was occupied with Abby, *Where was she? How was she?*

Abby's foot got stuck in a crevice between the rocks when she slipped. "Shit!" she said to herself. She vaguely remembered something in the safety briefing about keeping your feet up so this exact thing would not happen. Her head was now barely above water and as the current pushed her down the river, her body went under, it was a struggle to get her head back above water and get a breath. She tried to pull her foot free to no avail. She reached down under the water to try and move the rocks, but the current was too strong for her to get any leverage. Abby was starting to panic. She would get a breath with her head above water, then the current would push her under again, and she would have to swim in place to get her head above water and be able to take another breath. She had taken several breaths this way when all of a sudden something really big slammed into her and sent her under again.

Ken was still looking for Abby when he crashed into an object in the middle of the river. He grabbed on to the object and realized it was a body. He held on tightly and surfaced to take a breath. He went under to see who it was and as he saw Abby's face in terror, his heart started pounding in his chest. They were close enough that it was easy to see through the river water, so Abby pointed down at her foot and then started swimming to move her body up to take another breath. Ken had to fight against the current to stay with Abby. He couldn't hold on to her without keeping her under. He dove down to try and free Abby's foot, he tugged at the rocks, but they did not move. He grabbed her leg and tried to pull it free, tried to pry her foot out of her shoe. Nothing worked! He went up and grabbed another breath, on the way back down he scanned the river and saw a tree branch a few feet away, pinned between some rocks. He thought he could use it for leverage, but it could be water-logged and rotten from sitting in the river, he knew he had to try. Ken grabbed the branch and could feel rough bark; he took that as a good sign the branch wasn't rotten. Fighting against the current, he stuck the branch under the smallest boulder in the rock pile around Abby's feet. Running out of breath, he put his foot against another rock and pushed on the branch as hard as he could.

CHAPTER 30

After meeting Abby and Ken at the Chamber dinner and reflecting on the sense of danger he was feeling, Crajack knew he had to take them out. He decided that the rafting trip would be the perfect opportunity. Being a leader in the community, he was involved in many different organizations to help those in trouble, especially teenagers. To this end, he had been on many rafting trips with the local youth groups and was very familiar with the Yellowstone River, especially the part they were rafting today. Hitting moving targets, even for someone of his skill level, was never a guarantee. He decided that taking them out at the first eddy was the best option, it would be simple and quick.

He parked his SUV about a quarter mile from the shoreline point where he would set up to make the hit. Hidden among the rocks in that area, he estimated he would be about three hundred yards away from the raft when it would slow down in the first eddy, and if he got really lucky, the raft would come to a complete stop. First, he would take out the guide, then Ken, and then Abby, that would be the order, and he felt they would be relatively easy shots for him. Finally, he would sink the raft, hoping that it would be awhile before any bodies would be found. As he observed them coming down the river, Crajack saw that Ken's driver Sal, was acting as the raft guide. He had no problem killing an innocent guide, but this was even better, if all three of them were taken out, the only one who might report them missing was Dom, and Crajack knew that was something he wouldn't have to worry about for long.

Crajack lined up his target and fired the first round, it appeared that he hit Sal squarely in the left shoulder area, because he immediately fell into the river. He lined up Ken in his sights and fired, a smile crossing his face as he saw Ken's body jerk from the impact of the bullet. He got him! Ken managed to remain in the boat and was reaching for Abby, so

Crajack fired another bullet at him, and again saw him reel from the impact. He now turned his sights on Abby, lined up the shot and fired, Ken and Abby both fell overboard, but Crajack could not tell if the shot had found its intended target. *Dammit*, he thought. He fired a couple of shots into the raft so they could not use it as cover. He took out his high-power binoculars and for the next five minutes scanned the entire area around the raft and several hundred feet both up and down the river. He saw nothing. No bodies. He scanned the shoreline on both sides of the river and saw nothing. He knew he had hit Sal and Ken squarely, and felt he probably got Abby too. He felt confident about the kills, knowing if the bullets didn't finish them off, the river would take care of them. Of course, it would be better to see the actual bodies, but under these conditions, it just wasn't feasible. He started walking back to his SUV, already looking forward to his next victim later tonight.

CHAPTER 31

Abby knew her situation was critical. She could tell Ken was trying to move the rocks she was caught in, but the swiftly moving current was just making it too difficult. He came up for a breath and quickly went down again, not saying anything to her, not even looking at her. She could see him struggling under the water when all of a sudden, he lunged and threw his body into hers. The rock gave way! Her foot was free and they both started moving down the river again. Ken grabbed her arm and pulled her in the direction of the shore, they both started swimming at an angle towards the shore, using the current the best they could. After a few minutes, Abby could feel the current slowing down and she could sense the water was shallow.

Ken knew they needed to get to land and find some cover to fully escape the range of the sniper. As soon as the water allowed them to get up, Ken yelled to Abby, "Run to the shrubs along the edge and get behind them. Don't look back."

Abby sprinted out of the water and did as she was told, throwing herself behind a large, heavily branched shrub.

Ken stood up in the water and turned around, inviting another shot if they were still in the sniper's range. He wanted to know for sure if the danger point was passed. If the sniper could still see them, he would have taken the shot, but there was nothing. Ken figured the shooter was in the act of disappearing, probably confident he had killed all three. As far as the sniper knew, two individuals were hit. Sal and Ken for sure: that was visually apparent. The bullet aimed at Abby was on the mark, but they had been falling out of the boat and Ken had tried to block them, the sniper could not have confirmed a visual hit on Abby. The sniper probably thought that even if the bullets didn't hit Abby, she would have been swallowed up by the river and the rapids. That's what Ken would have thought if he put himself in the shooter's mind set. In the middle of a river with a rapidly moving current, most individuals would have panicked and drowned.

As Ken got to Abby behind the shrubs, he quickly grabbed her and looking her over asked, "Oh my god, are you okay? Are you hit? Are you bleeding?"

"No, no, I'm good. Nothing hit me. What about you? I saw your body jerk. You were hit. Let me check it out." Abby was pulling at his shirt trying to find where he had been shot.

"No, I'm fine, nothing happened, I'm not bleeding," he replied as he pulled her hands away from him.

"I saw it!" she yelled at him, "You probably don't even feel it yet. It's shock."

Ken held her hands, "Abby, look at me."

Abby stopped and looked at him.

"I'm fine. Nothing happened to me, okay?" Ken said calmly.

"Really?"

"Really."

"Oh, thank god!" Abby exclaimed as she grabbed him and held him tightly. After a moment she asked, "What the hell just happened? Did someone really just try to kill us?"

"Afraid so," Ken replied.

"That's crazy. What about Sal? Did you see any sign of him?" she asked.

"No, nothing." Ken responded. "But I have a feeling he's okay."

"A *feeling*? What does that mean?"

"Just that Sal can probably take care of himself. He has a certain … adaptability."

"God, I hope so," she responded.

Ken pulled off his backpack, reached inside and pulled out a water-proof bag. He unrolled it, pulled out his cell phone and a Smith and Wesson .45 and handed her the gun.

"Shoot anything that moves."

Abby was surprised at the appearance of the gun, did he expect something like this to happen? If so, why not tell her? Or was it his MO to always carry a gun? She wondered what else he had in the backpack. Was he the most prepared boy scout ever or what? She looked up from the gun and was about to say something when she saw Ken on the phone.

Ken had walked a few steps away, but she could hear him clearly. He was on the phone with their helicopter pilot, Joshua. The conversation was quick and precise. Ken was asking him to come pick them up where they were on the river. Understandably, Joshua was reluctant at first. She heard Ken say, "Ten thousand dollars," and within a minute he hung up the phone and turned to Abby.

"Joshua is gonna be here to pick us up in about fifteen minutes, I sent him our location."

"Are you paying him ten thousand dollars to do it?" Abby asked.

"Yes."

"That's crazy!"

"It's the quickest way out of here, and we need to vacate the area ASAP, who knows if the shooter is still in the area." Ken continued, "Let's move over to the trees by the clearing over there. That's the closest place for him to land and we'll be able to get to the chopper quickly."

Abby said nothing, just followed Ken and hunched down beside him when they got to the trees.

Ken said, "We'll get a room in town and stay there until we figure out what to do next."

"No, I want to go back to Billings."

"We can't."

"Why not?"

"Because the shooter probably thinks we're dead, so let's oblige him and not show up back in Billings until we have a plan."

"Okay, but we have to alert the police and the swift water rescue so they can start looking for Sal."

"No, we can't do that. No one can know we're alive. That's why I'm paying Joshua, not just for the ride, but for his silence as well."

Abby thought about it for a minute and figured it made as much sense as anything else did right now. Abby said, "Okay, we stay here, and we don't tell anyone. For now."

"Thank you." Ken responded.

"You're welcome. Now can you please tell me why you have a gun, why you aren't hurt, and why you seem so calm?"

Ken sighed and said, "Please, Abby, not now. I promise you I will tell you everything you want to know when we are settled in the hotel.

We need to figure out what is going on and come up with a plan. We have no idea what we are up against and we have to be very careful. Let's just focus on getting to the hotel quickly and quietly."

Abby begrudgingly agreed.

Just a few hours after the attempt on their lives, they were in a private suite, out of their wet clothes and into dry robes and slippers from the hotel, and the room service cart they ordered had just arrived. It was the first moment they felt like they could relax after their crazy river trip and being shot at. Looking at them, you could almost imagine they were on a romantic weekend getaway, but they weren't. Ken knew they had a lot to deal with and quickly, including finding out what happened to Sal. First though, he knew he had to respond to the numerous questions that Abby was going to ask, and he knew he would be telling her everything, all the secrets from his past, everything that he had never shared before.

CHAPTER 32

"Okay," Abby said, "I have some questions."

"Ask away," he quickly replied, he knew the questions would be coming.

"How is it you're not dead or at least bleeding? I saw you jerk back when the bullets hit you, you weren't wearing a vest ... so what the hell?" She continued rapid fire with more questions.

"Are you a robot, an advanced AI or something?"

"Or maybe you're an alien from another planet?"

"Do you have blood in you, or is it some alien green muck?"

"Do you even bleed?"

Ken held up his hands in a slowdown gesture, smiled and said, "Whoa, that's a lot of questions and you're not giving me a chance to answer."

"Okay, now's your chance. Give me some answers."

"You should probably get comfortable, maybe even get a drink or two, this is going to take some time."

"It's that bad that I'll need a few drinks? Jesus."

Abby got up and went to the room service cart. She grabbed a glass, a few ice cubes, and the bottle of scotch they had ordered with the food. She fixed a few pillows on one end of the couch, sat down, poured the scotch into her glass and looked at Ken on the other end of the couch. "Okay, I think I'm ready, so fire away. Oh, one last thing, can I interrupt if the story gets too crazy?"

"Yes, of course," he said, "One thing though, you better still love me when I finish telling you my story, agreed?"

"I guess you do remember me saying that."

"Yes, and I love you too. So, do we have an agreement?"

"For now, yes," she smiled and continued, "But I will let you know how my love holds up once I hear the story. I can be fickle."

"Okay," Ken took a deep breath, "Where should I begin? Let me start with answering your immediate questions. First, I'm not an alien from another planet."

"Well, that's a relief," Abby responded and sipped her drink.

"I do have blood in me, but I don't bleed. Bullets don't affect me like they would normal people. Actually, most things don't affect me like they do normal people."

This time Abby gulped a good portion of her drink.

"To go a step further, to my knowledge, I can't be killed by any typical means: guns, knives, disease, accident, whatever."

"What are you saying? That you're immortal?" She took another swallow of her drink and then poured more into the glass.

"No, not immortal, more like impenetrable. Does that make sense? I don't think I'm immortal, I've seen my body change over time, age a little bit, so I'm sure there is an end point in sight. I'm just not sure when that end point will come."

"I'm sorry, Ken, but that doesn't make the least bit of sense. It sounds like science fiction. How did this happen? When did this happen?"

Ken got up, walked over to her, gave her a soft kiss on the lips, helped prop up the pillows behind her and said, "Get comfortable. What I'm about to tell you is right out of a Twilight Zone episode and then some."

"I never did like that show, and so far, your story sounds impossible. But, you're not dead, you're not even bleeding, when you should be. Where are the clothes you took off?"

"Why?"

"Because I want to see them, that's why!" Abby demanded.

Ken went to get the clothes, he handed them to Abby. They were still damp. Abby found the shirt, held it close and inspected it. She found what she was looking for and put her finger through a hole one of the bullets had left. She said, "Open your robe please."

"Seriously? I'm trying—"

"Ken, if you want me to believe you, I need to see real, solid evidence."

He opened the robe so she could see his chest. She got up, placed the shirt against his skin, with her finger still in the bullet hole. She pulled the shirt away and kept her finger where it was, there was a faint bruising on his skin spreading out several inches from where the bullet had hit, but the bruise looked like it was weeks old, not hours.

"Is this where you got shot today?" she asked solemnly.

"Yes."

"And this is all that's left? This faded bruise?"

"Yes."

"The little you've told me already seems crazy and impossible, yet here I am with my finger literally on the evidence—bullet hole in shirt, but no bullet hole in body. It makes no sense," she shook her head in disbelief, "maybe it will when you fill in the blanks."

"Okay let me start, I'm not really Ken Stone, my real name is Keith Strickland. I was a Lieutenant Colonel in the Army during WWII. I was the Army's top covert operator used mainly for high-profile, black ops, I was good at it, really good at it, just as I am now. I had an experience close to the end of the war, that should've left me dead, but instead it changed my body, strengthened everything about it. I have physically aged a few years since then, I've noticed a few more grey hairs, literally though, just a few and some faint new lines around my face. They told me that for every ten years that pass, I age about a year."

Ken looked up at Abby, and couldn't read the expression on her face. She motioned for him to continue, but she didn't say a word.

"My last Army mission was six days before the Normandy invasion. I was already on the plane before I got to read the orders. I was to take out a German spy whose outpost was in the Andes mountains in Peru, of all places. I thought that was odd myself, but orders were orders, and they had to be carried out. Another thing I found out on the plane was that I was likely on a suicide mission, I had no help to extract myself, and I would have to hike out of the mountains on my own. Even Houdini would've had a tough time getting out. I knew the war was just about over, even if the invasion had problems, Germany was beaten, it was just a matter of time and bodies. My guess is, knowing victory was close, the Army brass wanted me removed. I knew too much and might become an embarrassment for them after the war.

"The mission failed before I even got on the ground when my plane crashed into a mountain short of the designated drop point. The young Captain flying the plane made a simple error that caused the crash. I can still recall the haunted look on his face when he realized what he did. When I finally came to after the crash, I had no idea where I was. My body was in agonizing pain and I could tell by looking at my wounds that I was close to death. And yes, I did bleed then, the blood was flowing because my stomach had been ripped open, my legs were clearly broken and I could barely move because of the pain. Strangely enough I wasn't scared, at least not of dying. Instead I was angry. I was angry at the Army for sending me on this suicide mission, I was angry at myself for the kind of life I had led the last ten years before the crash, but most of all, I was angry at God. Angry at Him for all the despair, misery and anguish he put in my life. I was yelling out at God with what energy I had, I was yelling what I would tell him if he dared to show his face. The yelling exhausted me and I passed out. When I came to again, imagine my surprise when I look up and see God finally showing himself to me. After a few seconds, as my mind cleared, I realized it wasn't God. It was a man, and there were others behind him. He bent down, said some things I didn't understand and started to rub something into my belly wound. All of a sudden, the pain intensified. It was excruciating. I screamed in agony and then passed out again, I didn't regain consciousness for more than a week."

Ken looked at Abby and said, "I think you should freshen your drink and get ready; the tale takes off from here."

Abby couldn't imagine where the story would go from here; it was already unbelievable. She poured herself some more scotch and leaned back to hear the rest of what Ken had to say.

CHAPTER 33

Ken continued … "When I finally came to, I was barely conscious. I remember slowly opening my eyes, trying to focus on something I recognized. Random thoughts flashed through my mind—the crash, my past in the army, my family."

Abby's eyes went wide at the mention of his family. Ken saw her reaction and said, "I was married before, back in the '30s. It was a long time ago. I promise I will tell you about that but let me finish this story first."

Abby, with a strained look on her face, just nodded and said, "Okay."

Ken continued, "I was in and out of consciousness for the next few days. I remember being fed, and having my bandages changed. I remember being grateful I was alive, even if I didn't understand why. On the mountain, I was certain my injuries were fatal, and when I came around from time to time, I could feel my body aching, hurting, from head to toe it seemed. There were two caretakers who tended to me, I remember feeling very safe with them, even though I still had no idea where I was, or who they were. Finally, I was able to stay awake for more than just a few moments. To my surprise, my caretakers spoke English, so communication was not a problem. Over a couple of days, they filled me in on my injuries, where I was, who they were, pretty much everything. I found it very hard to believe most of what they told me, but I was still so weak, I couldn't argue with them.

"They told me I had some very serious injuries, which of course I knew, and that it would take some time before I would be completely healed. I keyed in on the word completely, I hadn't thought that would be possible when I was laying on the side of the mountain. It was another two weeks before I could actually get up out of bed, and even then, it was just to sit in a chair by the window. I could feel the healing process taking place. It was like a buzz going through my body, like nothing I'd experienced before. Healing that should have taken many, many months, was happening much quicker. I didn't know why at the time, and I didn't care, I was getting better. It seemed like a miracle, and yes, it was one I was happy to accept.

"Every day, I'd get out of bed, walk a few steps around the hut, and then sit down in the chair. I would try to add a few more steps each day. My caretakers and I talked about anything and everything. In the beginning, I asked a lot of questions about where I was and who they were. I learned I was in the Andes mountains, in a village called Viracocha, and that my hosts were Incas, a people I thought were extinct. The only time they did not fully answer my questions was when I asked them how they were still in existence, and when I asked them how they had healed me. I was told all would be explained when the time was right. I accepted that because I really didn't have any choice.

"After about a month or so, I was strong enough to walk out of the hut and sit on a bench to enjoy the warmth of the sun. Although I was still weak, the healing process continued to be rapid and I was able to walk just a bit further every day. My muscles had atrophied some because of lack of use, but each day I felt my body was rebuilding its strength. As I took my small walks, I began to notice more and more of my surroundings. We were in a valley, with very tall mountains around us, there was a lot of vegetation, many different colors in the plants and food. I remember the food being quite good, lots of potatoes, more varieties than I knew existed, and prepared in so many different ways. I haven't had food like that since I was there.

"Within the village, there were many single-story huts, some larger two-story huts, and even larger buildings which were used for community gatherings. All of the buildings were set up along a remarkable road system, one that would work in any major city in the US. Everything seemed very organized. The weather was great, daytime temperature in the seventies, cool at night, almost always a gentle breeze. Later the weather would turn into winter, but even then, it was pretty mild. The valley seemed to be almost a magical place, where everything seemed to be the best of the best.

"I would say close to three months had passed when I finally started feeling like my old self. My muscles were getting stronger, I no longer had any soreness, tenderness or pain; all of my wounds had healed. The only noticeable remnant of my injuries is the scar you've seen that runs across my stomach. Now that my body was healed, my mind started to really wonder about what had happened. How had I been healed? How did the Incas still exist? How did they know how to speak English? What was my future? What about the war? Did the invasion happen? How did it turn out? Lots and lots of questions. I began to really pester my care-takers with all these questions. Their only response, and it was consistent from both of them, was that a tribe elder was the only one who could answer these questions and one would be visiting me soon. I really had no choice but to be patient, I was in the middle of nowhere and totally dependent on these people for my survival. Even now when I was fully healed, I wouldn't have any idea where to go if I wanted to leave. So, I was patient and I waited."

CHAPTER 34

"True to their word, an Inca elder came to see me within the week, his name was Hualpa. When I met him, I had an immediate affinity for him, like I knew him really well and we had been friends for a long time. We grew quite close during my time there. He came to see me every day for a week, we would talk for an hour or two as he answered all the questions I posed. Occasionally he would ask me questions, and I would answer them the best that I could. When he started to answer my questions, he wanted to start from the beginning regarding the history of his people, so I just listened. The story he told me is really just unbelievable, but I saw the truth for myself."

Ken looked at Abby to gauge what she was feeling. She met his eyes and said sarcastically, "Really, *now* it gets unbelievable?"

Ken sighed, "Abby—"

Abby interrupted, and said, "Please just go ahead and finish the whole story. Then we can talk about it."

"The city was founded by the ancient elder Melka, back in the 1500s, in fact Hualpa was Melka's grandson. It was a refuge from the Spaniards who were systematically destroying their civilization. Once the city was populated, they sealed themselves off from the outside world. The people lived in harmony, free from the oppression of the Spaniards. He told me I was the first visitor to ever breach or enter their city. Hualpa explained some of the ways of the people in Viracocha, how they lived simply and the rules they lived by. After a couple of days of talking about the past and how this village alone had survived, he finally started talking about what I really wanted to know—how was it possible that I was alive?

"Hualpa said that after some years being isolated in Viracocha, some of the elders had discovered a powerful force for healing. They had shared that force with me and that's how I recovered. Healing was one thing I thought, but death had literally been knocking on my door, and it was wide open. He said the herbs and tincture I was given on the mountainside were a highly concentrated form of the healing components. They could not bring someone back from the dead, but they could bring someone back from the brink of death. In the absence of any evidence other than my recovery, I believed him. Before he left that day, he also told me the combination had some other side effects, the body became incredibly strong, resistant to injury and disease, and also, it significantly slowed the process of aging. He said he was over four hundred years old, but looked around seventy to me. He left after that revelation, saying we would discuss it more tomorrow. He wanted to give me time to think about it. I heard what he said, but I didn't believe him, even with my miraculous healing, my mind would not, could not, fathom immortality, or near immortality as it turned out. Later, I would learn he was telling the truth and the evidence I saw with my own eyes finally convinced me to believe it.

"The next day Hualpa explained more about the healing medicine and the side effects. The original elders had found that when the water and a certain indigenous herb, known only in Viracocha, were consumed together, they had multiple effects on the body. The first thing they had noticed was the absence of sickness and injuries in one specific area of Viracocha. After some investigation, they found a special plant that only grew in one spot in the valley. The people in this area used the plants and vegetation around them for cooking and remedies. The elders assumed, correctly, that this special plant had something to do with the good fortune of health in this area. They started doing research and created a combination of herbs, including the special plant and gave it to certain families throughout all of Viracocha. Over a brief period of time, these families showed the same resilience to illness and injury the first group had shown.

"In the beginning, they didn't know all of the side effects, but over time they would learn. Hualpa continued with his story, and told me that one day, a young boy had a terrible fall from high in a tree to the rocky ground. The elders heard about the accident and brought the healing compound to the boy. He was unconscious when they arrived, with several broken bones, a huge gash on his head and a large, dark purple bruise blooming in his abdomen. It did not look good. They rubbed the herbs into the wounds and poured the tincture down his throat, but didn't know what would happen so they just hoped for the best. The boy was out for several days, but when he came to, his injuries seemed much less severe than originally thought. Within a few weeks he was getting out of bed and walking a few steps, and within a couple of months, he made a complete recovery. The elders thought the herbs might have been helpful but were not completely sure.

"One of them would visit the boy every few weeks to check on his progress, make observations and to try and figure out if the herbs had been a factor or not. A little over a year had passed and they began to notice that the boy had not seemed to age much over that time. Did the injuries affect his growth? Did the herbs affect his growth? They tried to figure out what was going on. They spent time with the families who lived near the special plant, and also with the families they had shared the herbs with. Trying to be objective, they agreed that these people also seemed like they weren't aging. They compared brothers to brothers and sisters to sisters, moms and daughters, but it's hard to see someone age because it happens so slowly. Only time would tell. The elders had not shared their theory with anyone, but two years after the accident, the boy still hadn't seemed to age, so they went to the Council and told them of their theory and concerns, and also, their plan.

"The elders wanted to move all of the people out of the area where the special plant grew and make it a sacred place. One reason was to preserve the plant, another was to make sure they understood what the plant did before more people were affected. The Council agreed to the plan after hearing their stories and seeing the evidence they presented. Over time, they found out that the herb did a lot of things. It significantly slowed down the aging process, it also increased the body's skin density a thousand-fold which prevented scratches and injuries from punctures. The healing properties worked at incredible speeds, speeds not even seen in today's medical world. Finally, they found that certain senses were enhanced in some people, not everyone had this effect, and for some it was hearing, others sight, but for many it was something the Incas call Suka, the ability to sense the true nature of a person. They didn't know how it worked, but just accepted it as a gift from their gods.

"The aging process was the one effect the Council wanted to control. Over time, they were able to calculate how the aging process worked—for every ten calendar years that passed, a person would age one physical year. The young boy who had fallen and been treated, did not reach puberty for thirty years after his treatment, the transition was very difficult for him. His friends and family grew up around him, and he still looked like a young boy and was treated like a young boy. In Viracocha, you were given the choice to accept the gift around the age of thirty-five or let life's normal process continue. The elder explained that some citizens thought the gift was also a curse: living a very long time had its downside."

"So exactly how old are you?" Abby asked.

"I am 108 years old," he replied solemnly.

"Wow, 108 years old," she echoed with a whisper. As incredulous as it sounded, she was believing him. "Please, continue."

"I still wasn't convinced of all he told me, and at the time I couldn't see any downside to living a very long life, if what he said turned out to be true. I learned later there was a price to pay for being nearly immortal. I asked Hualpa if the process could be reversed; could someone decide they didn't want to live forever? The answer he gave was puzzling, Hualpa replied, 'Yes and no. But I will explain all of that another time.' More secrets and more patience.

"Over the next three months I became an adopted citizen of Viracocha and was introduced to their farming enterprise and I became a farmer. I didn't mind. It was simple, but fulfilling work and it kept me busy. I had my own hut at this point, some friends, and my routine was the same every day. Up early, work a long day, a good meal at night and early to bed. Hualpa and I would see each other every few days, and he would continue to tell me more about the history of the Incas and of Viracocha. We grew very close.

"As I said, I didn't really believe what I'd been told, but as time passed, I began to notice a few things. For one, the work in the fields was very strenuous, but I didn't tire much and when I did, I recovered very quickly. My body felt stronger than any time I could remember. One of the strangest things I noticed was I was always working with my hands, but I didn't get any scratches or cuts that would be normal from farming the land, I should have, but I didn't. I decided to prove to myself one way or the other what seemed to be happening so one day I forced the issue. I tried cutting myself with a sharp knife, pushing it into my skin as hard as I could. I couldn't penetrate the skin. Nothing happened except a slight skin indentation and bruise which was gone the next day. That kind of freaked me out, so I left it alone for a little while. Then, while working to clear one of the fields, I dropped a huge rock on my foot. It should've been crushed, but I felt very little pain. When I looked at my foot, it seemed fine. I could move my toes, it was a little sore and a little bruised, but the bruise was gone the next morning. After that, I started to believe more of what I had been told.

"Hualpa and I talked quite a bit about the Council, I hadn't met them yet, they were mostly sequestered away from the villagers, with a few representatives like Hualpa to carry out communications and plans. He said the Council was considering me for a great honor, offering me the knowledge of healing they had learned. I said I already knew about the secret herb, but he responded by saying, 'We have learned more than that.' That was all he would say on the matter, despite the number of questions I asked him.

"Occasionally, I would get a terrible, uncomfortable feeling, like nothing I had ever felt before. I wasn't sure if it was a lingering effect from my injuries, or my healing or what, but it seemed to happen about the same time each day. As time passed, the feeling seemed to grow, and I was more able to identify it: a feeling of pure evil, a dark presence, this, I would come to learn, was what the Incas called Suka. When I had this feeling, I noticed some of the others around me seemed anxious too, we were all more on edge than normal. It almost felt like we were sharing feelings, but I know that doesn't make any sense. Also, no one ever talked about it, like it was a silent understanding among us to not acknowledge the evil presence. One day I realized I didn't sense the evil presence, and I didn't sense it the next day either. There one day and gone the next. I was fine with that and I hoped to never feel it again. Hualpa came to me a couple of days after the evil presence disappeared. I will never forget what he said, 'You are being summoned by the Council, they have a solemn request to ask of you.' Naturally, I had no idea what was going on, but it was apparent something awful had happened. I was led by Hualpa to the Council, where they shared the story with me."

CHAPTER 35

"Are you okay?" Ken asked Abby.

"Am I okay? You're telling me a story that is literally unbelievable, yet I've seen physical evidence that lends your story credibility. If your story is true, you're turning my world upside-down. Think about how that would make you feel. Am I okay? What do you think?"

"I understand your skepticism, I felt the same way when I first learned all of this. I will do everything in my power to show you the truth of it, I promise. I don't want to you lose you, Abby, and I don't want to keep anything from you ever again. I love you."

Abby just looked at Ken, closed her eyes and sighed deeply. When she opened her eyes a few moments later, he continued with the story.

"The Council told me that about two months ago, another outsider had found their way into Viracocha. Apparently, he had knowledge, or at least suspicions, of their possible existence. Imagine, two strangers in the span of a few months, when there had been centuries with no infiltration. Erik, that was the name he gave, had used an old entrance the Incas thought was blocked off, but over time the entrance had become accessible again. He was extremely sick and weak, I think he was probably dying of cancer. The Incas did what is their way; they gave him the same herbs and tincture they gave me and within weeks he was healing quickly. His body getting stronger every day, and if any of his senses were affected, as sometimes happened, he would have begun to feel that side effect. As he regained his health, the Incas came to sense and understand Erik's true nature: pure evil, diabolical evil, in every imaginable way. They missed this initially as his cancer was preventing them from being able to sense his true character. I then realized that the evil feelings I'd been sensing must've come from Erik, that I had been feeling his Suka.

160

"I was summoned because Erik had fled Viracocha, killing one of his caretakers in the process. Nothing like this had ever happened before and the Incas were not prepared to deal with this situation. Knowing my background in the Army, they thought I might be able to help them. I would have to agree to two conditions, no more no less. The first was to forgo the planned training and teachings about their healing knowledge. To me that was easy, I felt I'd been there long enough and was ready to get back to the world I knew. I wasn't interested in becoming a healer, but looking back now, that was probably a mistake. The second condition was much more interesting. The Inca Council offered me a special amulet. It was beautiful, pure gold with bright diamonds and other stones embedded in the design. It was actually two pieces, when you pulled off the bottom of the amulet, and then pressed the large stone in the middle, out came two unique metallic prongs, razor sharp and coated with a substance the Council told me would reverse the effects of the special herb. The prongs could pierce the increased density of the skin and allow the reversing agent to enter the blood stream, making the body vulnerable as it once was. They asked me to use it at my discretion on 'The Other' if I ever encountered him in the world outside of Viracocha. When Erik had fled and disgraced himself in their eyes, they would no longer honor him by using his name, from that point forward he was always referred to as, The Other. The interesting part was that they did not make it an order or a necessity for me to kill him, it would be my call. The Incas did not believe in the old proverb an eye for an eye, but they did believe in justice. I agreed to their conditions because I wanted out, and they were giving it to me without too much fanfare.

"I was preparing to leave when Hualpa came to visit me. He asked if I remembered the conversation about giving up the gifts of the herb. I said I did. Hualpa smiled and said, you realize the amulet is your answer, your way out if you choose it. It took me a minute to see what he was getting at. If a long life wasn't for me, I could use the amulet on myself to reverse the effects of the herb. I asked what would happen if I did that. He answered, you will be vulnerable to illness and injury, like you never had taken the herb, your body will age quickly and dramatically, to reflect your true age, and it will break down accordingly.

"Leaving Viracocha was a strange process. I was given a drug which rendered me unconscious, and when I awoke, I found myself in a hotel room in Lima, the capital of Peru. I was dressed in the clothes of the day and had a suitcase filled with more clothes, a huge cache of brilliant diamonds, some local currency and the few personal effects that had survived the crash. I felt great and couldn't wait to get back to the States. However, I quickly realized my situation would require some serious explaining if I went back to my old life. And if I really did not age normally—the jury was still out on that in my mind—how would I explain that? My elation at being out of Viracocha soon wore off as I pondered my uncertain future. I decided to attack this problem as I would any mission, come up with a game plan, look at every possible situation, and identify the strategies I'd need to mitigate the many risks. I spent the next four days walking, thinking, planning and re-planning my strategies. The next thing I did was catch up on current events, a lot had happened in the world while I was in Viracocha. When I had my plan together, I got a plane back to the States and began my new life. I had to adapt my lifestyle and strategies over time, but time is a luxury I have in abundance. The rest is a pretty boring history of my life, not worth going into. Fast forward some seventy plus years, and here we are."

"Wow, what a story," said Abby.

"I also have to tell you, I came here to Billings to settle some things, and then I was going to use the amulet on myself."

"What?!" cried Abby.

"Yes. A long life can be a curse, and it was for me, especially when you have no one to share it with. I was done. I didn't want to live anymore. I really had no reason to. And then I met you on the plane, and since that moment my plans have gone to hell and I've had more of a life in these past few days then in the past seventy years." Ken went over and sat next to Abby, took her hand, which she allowed, and gently kissed it.

"Wow," she said again, clearly dazed by this latest admission. "Is that all of it?" she asked in a calm low tone, almost a whisper.

"No, there is more, and it has to do with The Other."

"The Other?" Abby asked, "What about him?"

"Aren't you wondering who the hell tried to kill us just a few hours ago?"

"Honestly, Ken, I mean, Keith, I'm just trying to keep my mind from exploding with everything you've just told me. Now that you mention it though, I do wonder who the hell it was, and why they tried."

"How strange to hear you say Keith. No one has called me that in decades. Could we stick with Ken?"

"Sure, Ken it'll be, but right now I think that's the least of our worries."

Ken paused for a moment and then said seriously, "I'm pretty sure The Other is the one who tried to kill us."

Abby laughed sarcastically, "Okay, The Other has come from the past to hunt you down, right? I was with you, and believing most of your story, but now it's just too much. Come on, Ken, how do you expect me to believe all of this? You know everything you're saying sounds crazy. Even with the proof from your shirt and your injuries, it's a very tall tale to expect someone to believe."

"I understand what you're saying, Abby, but please believe me. I'm telling you nothing but the truth. I know how it sounds, but you're in danger and you need to take that threat seriously. Do you remember what I told you about Suka and about Erik?"

"Yes."

"Well, like I said, I'd hoped to never feel that evil presence in my life again, but I did, and it was just a couple of days ago."

"What?" she exclaimed, "When, how, who?"

"The night of the Chamber dinner, it was the same Suka I felt all those years ago, I'm certain of it. And I'm also certain he's the one who shot at us on the river, perhaps he also has the gift of Suka, or some other gift. He had to know somehow, I could be a threat to him. I don't know exactly who it is, but we can easily narrow it down."

"Narrow it down? There were a hundred people at the dinner, it will take days to narrow it down."

"Yes, there were lots of people there, but I didn't feel anything until the last three members of our table joined us, when the three of them arrived together, that was when I sensed the Suka, and I was honestly so startled by it, I didn't even think to try and figure out who it was."

"Well," Abby said impatiently, "Who were they?"

"Mayor Stockwell, Reverend Lephit and Chief Wagner."

Abby thought for a moment before she said anything. "That night at the dinner I would have found it hard to believe any of them could be full of evil, but after talking with my dad, and meeting with the Chief, I don't know. The Chief's name keeps coming up related to my dad's investigation, and he would have the skill set to shoot at us on the river. I just hate to think of any law enforcement officer on the dark side, it totally disgusts me."

They sat quietly for a few minutes, Abby still trying to digest everything she had heard.

Ken finally asked, "What's the decision of the jury?"

"The jury believes you, as much as they can," she said. "You can't be killed, you don't age, and you can sense other people's nature. That about sums it up, don't ya think?"

"Well, I do age, but very slowly."

"So, what would you say is your physical age? Because you look pretty good for a 108-year-old!"

"I would say my physical age is about forty-three."

"Okay." Abby paused here for a moment, "There is something else I need to know."

"Shoot," said Ken.

"What have you been doing for the past seventy years? I need to know that there are no more secrets between us."

"I have done many, many different things, and many I'm not proud of. Are you sure you want to know?"

Abby nodded solemnly.

Ken looked at Abby, took a deep breath and then turned his head away as he started this part of the story. "I think what I've done in the last three years or so is the most relevant, so let me start there. I know this is something I should have told you already, but I couldn't find the right time or place. I hope you can see that. The Ken Stone you know is not an art dealer, he is a man who has taken up his own crusade to rid the world of its scum and evil and the past few years, I have been working in the New York area."

Abby did not like where this was going, she was getting a knot in her stomach and a chill ran up her spine.

"I've removed some of the worst criminals around, drug kingpins, murderers, human traffickers, and just a few days ago, I took out Victor Panzetti and his crew." At this point, he turned back to Abby and looked into her eyes.

Immediately when Ken said Panzetti, Abby put it together, her entire body tensed and the knot in her stomach became a knife ripping her guts out. She jumped up from the couch and yelled at Ken, "You're the vigilante I've been chasing? Are you fucking kidding me?!" She started pacing around the room, Ken could tell she was extremely agitated. He hadn't seen her like this in the few days they had spent together.

"Abby, please …"

"Abby please? You don't get to say that to me. You don't get to talk to me. Just shut up!" she screamed at him, getting even more worked up. She turned away and Ken could hear her muttering under her breath, "Christ no, no, no. This cannot be happening." After pacing the room a few more times, she stopped in her tracks and said calmly and directly to Ken, "Answer me. Are you the vigilante I have been chasing in New York?"

"Yes, I am," Ken said solemnly.

"Oh my god, this is ridiculous, and ironic—I fell in love with the murderer I've been chasing for the past three years. I can't do this. I gotta get out of here." She went over to her wet clothes to get dressed.

Ken got up and followed her.

Abby yelled, "Stop, don't come near me." She took a few steps away from him. "I've gotta get out of here. I can't be with you, not now, not ever!"

Ken realized that there was no calming her down, when she learned he was the vigilante, it pushed her over the edge. He was worried for her safety and her life, so he took a more practical and honest approach.

"Abby, you can't leave," Ken said. "Your life is in danger. Don't you remember what we just went through?"

"Yes, I very well remember being shot at in the middle of the river. Right now, I would prefer that to staying here with you!" Some rational part of her realized he was right about the danger, but regardless, she still needed to be alone.

"Okay, okay, I'll leave. You don't have to move. You stay here. It'll be safer for you. Please try and stay calm," Ken said.

"Calm? You're lucky you can't be killed. I would've pumped six bullets into you by now." She realized her statement was absurd as she had no gun at her disposal. But she wanted to make sure he got the point. He did.

Ken knew his admission of being the vigilante was the catalyst that caused her to explode. No words would make any difference now. He gathered up his clothes and his backpack and at the door he turned around, "Abby, I am truly sorry."

"Stop!" she interrupted. "Don't say another word, and don't speak to me ever again."

Ken slowly turned around and walked out of the room, and out of her life.

When the door closed, Abby fell down into the closest chair, put her hands over her face and sobbed. Her Prince Charming turned out to be Charles Manson. What a goddamn disaster. She was glad he was gone; she would never be able to see his face again without being consumed by anger. As she cried, she hated that part of her was missing him already.

CHAPTER 36

Crajack was back at his retreat just a few hours after he saw his victims fall into the river. He had plenty of time before his next appointment, so he took a few moments to relax. He liked this trait in himself, always allowing extra time as a precaution, giving himself the opportunity to adjust and react to the unexpected and still stay on track. In this case, it wasn't critical, but he would take a small nap to clear his mind and remove any possible fatigue, which was the most common enemy he faced. From experience, he knew he couldn't be killed, so he didn't have the normal fears for those in his line of work. He laid down and thought about his plans for this evening.

Donna Stapleton was getting everything ready for tonight. A friend was coming over for dinner, and Donna wanted to make sure the evening was enjoyable and memorable for both of them. She had been doing a lot of research for Dominic regarding his theory about the numerous deaths, and the topic and potential suspect had been causing her a great deal of stress. She was hoping tonight she would be able to forget all about it, at least for a little while. Donna had never been married, and frankly, she liked it that way. She'd had a few relationships in her life, but really enjoyed being alone. Her solitary nature probably contributed a great deal to her career choice in Library Science. She went out regularly with a few men in town, but she wouldn't call them dates, because she really had no romantic interest in them. She expected tonight's dinner would be the same comfortable evening of talk and laughter, but she did have a very special surprise in store for her guest.

Dominic had been working most of the day, reviewing all the information he'd gathered regarding his current investigation. He had papers spread all over the kitchen table and had been getting more and more frustrated that he hadn't been able to find solid proof, right now it was all circumstantial. He looked up at the kitchen clock and realized it was getting late. It was time to go to the office and set up everything for tomorrow's paper, an early edition mostly covering the Chamber dinner. It would take him a few hours to get everything done, so he would stop on the way and pick up a good old-fashioned fried chicken dinner and a couple of cold ones. He liked working in the evenings when the place was quiet. Tomorrow he would revisit his files and continue to probe into the suspicious deaths, as well as the thin investigation file he had put together on the murder of Rabbi Kuperman, he was certain the evidence he needed was in front of him, he just needed to make the connection. And he was looking forward to another discussion with Abigail to see if she had come up with any new thoughts or ideas on the subject, especially because they'd hit a roadblock with Chief Wagner.

CHAPTER 37

It was exactly seven o'clock when Donna's door chimes rang. She briskly walked to the front door to welcome her guest.

"Right on time as always," Donna said, "Please come in and make yourself at home."

"Thank you, Donna. It's always a pleasure to see you. Thank you for inviting me to dinner," Crajack said as he crossed the threshold and leaned over to give Donna a kiss on the cheek.

"Come into the kitchen with me, I'll check on dinner and then we can sit on the deck and enjoy a glass of wine."

Crajack smiled as he followed Donna into the kitchen. "I brought a nice white wine. I hope you like it."

"Sounds delightful."

A few moments later, they were sitting on Donna's deck, enjoying the summer evening.

"The food smells delicious, Donna. If I may ask, what are we having for dinner?"

"We're having one of your favorite dishes, lamb chops. I did some homework and checked around to find out what you like," she said as she smiled radiantly.

Crajack thought, *Too much homework, you stupid fool!*

"I've been looking forward to this evening. It was long overdue," Donna said.

"So have I," he said as the rush of adrenaline started.

It was almost two hours later when they finally finished the last course, a wonderful dessert of homemade strawberry short cake and vanilla ice cream.

"Donna, that was the most delicious meal I've eaten in a long time. You went way too far just for me."

"Nonsense, it's the least I could do for a good friend like you. It's just a small token in return for the friendship and kindness you have shown me over the years." Donna had drank a little more wine than she was used to. She was a bit tipsy, but not fully drunk. She still had her wits about her and a full understanding of the situation, a good meal with a nice man, hopefully one she could please before he left. The surprise had been on her mind for quite a while; she was sure he would be pleased and gracious, so she decided now was the time to get bold.

"You know what? Let's forget about cleaning up right now. Do you mind if I go into the bedroom and change into something more relaxing? Then we can continue the evening if it's okay with you. I have a very special surprise for you."

Crajack was taken aback. Was she suggesting what he thought she was suggesting? He never would have thought Donna would make a first move. He decided to play his part and see how far she took it, just to amuse himself. He was *certain* how the evening would end, she just thought she knew how it would end.

"Donna, please, that's not necessary."

"Nonsense. I've been planning this for a long time."

"You have?" Crajack said surprised.

"Yes, I have. I hope you know how much I value our friendship. I thought this would be a good way to show you that."

"Really?" he asked.

"Yes, really," she replied.

"Okay then, if you are insistent. Go ahead while I finish my wine."

Donna smiled broadly and said, "Be back in just a few minutes," as she walked into the bedroom.

Not many things surprised him, but this one had. He never envisioned Donna pointing the evening in this direction. He went into the foyer and picked up his black bag lying by the umbrella stand. He had discreetly put it there when he entered the house. Donna's eyes had been riveted on him and the bottle of wine, so the act was unnoticed by her. He put his hand under the false bottom of the bag and pulled out a Colt .45 with a silencer attached. He put the gun behind his back tucked into his pants, completely out of sight from anyone looking straight on. He took another sip of wine, thinking he wanted to take care of Donna quickly. It was Dominic he wanted to suffer, not her, she was more of an innocent bystander. And even though she had shown some signs of being naughty this evening, she was still one of those good people that he really despised. But now Crajack was feeling a bit horny. Maybe he should give her what she wanted first, a good fuck, and then kill her. He looked at his watch. There would be enough time.

"Would you mind getting me a glass of wine and then come in here and make yourself comfortable?" Her voice was so alive, so wanting. He was leaning towards accepting her sexual gifts.

"I'll be right in, Donna." He poured some wine into her glass and carried it into her bedroom. The lights were low. He couldn't see well enough to tell what she was now wearing.

"Surprise!" Donna said as the room lights came on. She was standing in the middle of her bedroom, still dressed in the same clothes, holding a painting that appeared to be a portrait of him.

"This is for you! I've been working on it over the last six months. It's my first portrait. All of my previous work has been confined to flowers and fruits. What do you think? A good resemblance?" Donna stood there, holding the painting and smiling so proudly.

Crajack stared speechless, gawking at the amateurish portrait, a horrible attempt to capture him. It looked like a paint by numbers hack job. Jesus, how could he have read her signals so badly? She was an overabundance of good. Seriously? A painting? Rage started to build within him. He was pissed off at himself for being surprised.

Donna, still grinning from ear to ear said, "I bet you never had anyone paint your portrait before."

He started to laugh, pleasantly at first. The laugh turned into a snicker and then became menacing.

Donna didn't know what to make of it; he was not acting like himself. As she looked into his eyes, she saw what seemed like hatred and a cold chill went up her spine. She was confused and scared. Did she offend him? Was the painting that bad?

"Are you okay, you seem—"

"Shut up!" he screamed at her. Crajack was no longer able to keep up the charade of his cover persona; his rage was growing by the moment. Focusing on the real task at hand, he reached behind his back and calmly pulled the gun out.

"What are you …," she whimpered when she saw the gun, and then a look of understanding overtook her face and she could not finish her sentence. She stood up tall and straight, knowing what was coming. "He was right," she said quietly.

"Yes, Dominic was right, my dear, and now you will pay for meddling in my affairs." He felt the rush of adrenaline as he took aim at the center of her head. Donna was frightened and trying hard not to show it. They were staring each other in the eye when Crajack fired the gun at her head. She fell back, dropped the painting and stared blankly up. Death was instant.

Crajack walked over to where she had fallen, staring cruelly at her body for a moment. Then, without another thought to his victim, he began the process of eliminating any traces of him ever having been there. For most killers, this is where the mistakes are made, but not for him. He had planned exactly how the evening would go, and even with the surprise innuendo, that turned out to be a stupid painting, his plan was solid. Ten minutes later, any and all traces of Crajack were nonexistent. The house was clean, so on to his next victim he went, smiling and humming along to the music in his car. As he drove away, he had only one lingering thought, *Really? A fucking portrait?*

CHAPTER 38

Dominic had spent the evening knee deep in getting the early edition out for the next morning. The office was empty as he liked it. Unless there was an emergency or a breaking story, the paper usually closed down around 8:00 PM. Dominic was just about finished with his last task, updating the society page related to the Chamber dinner. He looked up at the grand old clock that had been in the office for over fifty years. It read 11:00 PM. *Jesus, where did the time go?* His mind started to wander to his investigation of the deaths and also to the murder of Rabbi Kuperman. He was certain the killer would strike again and wondered if he was working on a time table.

Dominic saw the lights of the car as it pulled up in front of the paper. The lights went out, and he heard the car door open and close. He wondered who the hell could be coming here at this time of night. He doubted it was anyone from the paper, they would have called first, to make sure he was still there, but maybe someone saw the lights on. Dominic went to the front door, opened it up and greeted his guest, "Well, this is a surprise, what brings you here so late at night?"

Crajack smiled and said, "Hello, Dominic. I figured you might be working late, getting the paper ready for tomorrow. Do you mind if I stop in for a while? I've got a few things I'd like to talk about, sooner rather than later if possible."

"No problem. Don't mind at all. I was just about done. C'mon in. There might even be some coffee left. You want a cup?" Dominic was curious about the late-night visit and wanted to know the purpose.

Crajack quickly canvassed the office to ensure Dominic was alone, and how best to set up the crime scene to deflect suspicion from himself. He was feeling the rush again. He'd already taken out four people today, and soon he would add Dominic to that number. Not a bad day for a world-class hit man.

"Don't mind if I do, Dominic, especially if it's strong."

"Oh, it's strong all right, probably put hairs on your chest. It's been sittin' for a while now." Dominic walked back to the coffee area as Crajack followed. He poured two cups of coffee and asked as he turned around, "How do you take your—", what he saw stopped him mid-sentence.

Crajack was standing in the center of the room pointing a gun with a silencer right at Dominic's heart. Dominic was not one to panic or fold under pressure, and he wasn't about to now, not yet anyway, so he tried to play it cool and calm.

"What's with the gun?" he asked.

"I think you know why I have the gun, at least you and Miss Head Librarian were working on figuring it out, right?"

Dominic's brain was starting to put everything together and his face fell with the simultaneous realization that his theory was right: there was a killer in Billings, and that the killer knew Donna had been helping him in the investigation, she was going to suffer the same fate as he if she hadn't already. In an effort to give himself some time to think his way out of the situation, Dominic put a puzzled look on his face and asked, "Figure what out? I have no idea what the hell you're talking about. Now put that damn gun away."

"Stop the bullshit, Dominic, I wrote the book on how to lie, so don't insult me by lying to my face now."

Fear really started to creep into Dominic's head as Crajack's voice and demeanor changed in an instant. He knew he was in trouble, very serious trouble. His only hope was to stall him and maybe someone would come by the paper, but at this time of night, that wasn't very likely. Fear or no fear, Dominic wasn't the kind of man who would back down, so he did what he was trained to do, he started asking questions.

"How long have you been crafting this public persona, throwing every suspicion away from you?" asked Dominic.

"A very long time."

"Who are you, or maybe I should ask who were you before this incarnation?" Dominic asked.

"My dear Dominic, if I told you who I really was, you'd have a heart attack or stroke and I don't want that. Let's just say I'm from the past."

"Are you the one who killed the Rabbi?"

"I guess it doesn't hurt at this point to tell you the truth. Yes, I killed Rabbi Kuperman, the worthless Jew!"

"Jew? The ones I'm investigating are all Jewish. Why are you only killing Jewish people? It doesn't make any sense."

"It doesn't make sense? It makes perfect sense to me! Too bad for you though. If only you had a little more time in your investigation, you might have found a few other suspicious deaths here in Billings."

"I thought there must be others that I hadn't found yet," Dom said thoughtfully. "Who else have you killed?"

"I'm not giving you a play by play summary, suffice it to say that I've had the great pleasure of eliminating other undesirables like the Rabbi."

"So Jews are undesirables? What does that even mean?"

"Think about it a second, Dom."

They stared at each other across the barrel of the gun. Finally, Dominic said, "I don't understand. Can you explain it to me?"

"Dominic, Dominic, you're the big-time editor, you should be able to figure that out. Let me give you a hint. It's an old feud, a passion I have from a previous life. I hate the motherfuckers, and the hatred runs deep in me."

Dominic didn't understand the explanation, *A previous life?* But he did understand the current situation and he knew he was probably not going to make it out of this alive. Was there some way for him to leave a clue? His mind focused on how to leave some sign for his daughter, something only she would understand, he knew he couldn't trust the police in this instance. Dom kept thinking, *Keep him talkin' and don't panic, because it won't help.*

Dominic said, "There are plenty of people that I hate, but I don't go around killing them."

Crajack wasn't interested in hearing Dominic giving him a lecture about who he should kill and why. "Well, let's just agree that we're different people, Dominic. And I really am glad to finally tell you the truth. I have hated you since our first meeting. That, plus the fact that you came way too close to blowing my cover, along with the meddling library fool, is cause for me not only to kill you, but to keep you in agony right down to your last breath."

Dominic was grasping at straws to keep this maniac talking, "So what are you, a White Supremist, or a Skinhead or Nazi or something?"

Crajack took a step towards Dominic as he said, "A Nazi? Yeah, you could say I'm a Nazi. That fits pretty well."

Dominic tried to take a step back, but bumped into a desk. Still trying to stall, he makes a reasonable leap and asks, "Probably goes back a long way doesn't it? World War II? Your father? Your kind of hatred runs deep, something you grew up with." Dominic thought, *This psycho is probably the son of a Nazi trying to carry out his father's legacy.*

"I'll tell you, Dominic, you might actually have been able to figure it all out. Lucky for me, you don't have any more time. I'm on a tight schedule here, and as much as I want you to die in agony, I need to be going, I've been here long enough."

"So, you're just gonna shoot me right here, right now?"

"Yeah, that's my plan. Just think of the headline—Newspaper Editor Killed in Office Putting Out His Last Edition. Oh, but who will write the story if you're not here?"

"You won't get away with this."

"Sure I will. I already have, dozens and dozens of times."

"Not this time. My daughter will figure it out, she's a—"

"She's dead, Dominic," Crajack cut in. "I took care of her and her boyfriend earlier today. It has been a pretty good day for me if I do say so myself."

"No way. I don't believe it!" Dominic shouted, "A pissant like you could never outsmart my daughter."

"Hate to tell you but they never even saw it coming. And I've had enough with the talking." Crajack took three quick steps and slammed the gun into the side of Dominic's head, he dropped unconscious onto the desk and then his body slid to the floor. Crajack put two bullets into Dominic's chest. He looked at Dominic for a moment, not liking his last words, like it was a prophecy. He thought, *Damn, I should have made sure to see the bodies!*

CHAPTER 39

On the third ring Ken was awake enough to pick his phone up from the nightstand. He was hoping it was Abby, that she had calmed down and wanted to talk to him. He was still reeling from the argument they had and the fact that she had thrown him out. He couldn't leave her, knowing she was in danger, so he'd gotten a room on the same floor as hers to be close by, just in case. The screen showed it was 6:15 AM, and the caller was unknown, he declined the call. Five seconds later the phone rang again. Someone obviously had his private number. This time he answered the call but didn't say a word; he just listened, he could hear breathing, but the person on the other side of the call said nothing. Someone would have to give in.

Ken finally lost his patience and barked, "Who the hell is this?"

"Boss, it's me."

"Sal, you son of a bitch," Ken said, relief in his voice. "I knew you were alive. Thank god. How did you manage to get away?"

"It's a long story, Boss, but I'm okay. How's you and the Boss Lady?"

"We're fine, Sal, thanks. Where are you right now?" Ken didn't want to discuss what had happened between Abby and him. No need for Sal to know, not just yet.

"Before I get into my location, Boss, I got some really bad news."

The news he gave Ken was a game changer; it was as bad as it could get. He would have to get Abby to talk to him, at least to tell her the news. The attack on the rafting trip had not been a fluke, and their lives were in serious peril until they eliminated the threat. But first, they would have to figure out for sure which one it was: the Chief, the Reverend, or the Mayor. Whether she liked it or not, he wasn't going to leave Abby's side until the threat was over. At that point, if she still wanted nothing to do with him, so be it. He got dressed and went to knock on Abby's door.

His knock brought no response, so despite the early hour, he knocked much harder and longer, still no answer. He still had his room key, it was in his pocket when he left the room to Abby last night. He didn't want to use it and violate Abby's privacy, but he had no choice, so he slid the card in the slot. The knocking had roused Abby from her sleep, but not from the bed. She saw him as he stepped through the door into the room.

Instantly on high alert she yelled, "What the hell are you doing here?"

"Abby, please, just give me a minute. I have something very important to tell you."

"I don't want to hear ANYTHING you have to say," she said as she gave him a death stare, "Now get out!" She got out of bed and headed towards him and the door to ensure he left immediately.

"Abby, please, I got a call from Sal."

The surprise of hearing that Sal was alive, stopped her for a moment. "Sal's alive?" she said hopefully.

"Yes." Ken responded. "He's okay and back in Billings. He gave me some information you need to know."

"Knowing that Sal is alive is great news, but I absolutely don't want to hear another word of what *you* have to say." She finished walking to the door, opened it and indicated that Ken should leave.

He had not wanted to be so blunt, but he clearly didn't have a choice, "Abby, it's about your dad."

Abby's face went pale and Ken could see her entire demeanor change, he glimpsed what she must have looked like as a little girl. She just stared at him, not able to say anything, thinking the worst. Ken gently took her hand, closed the door and led her to sit down on the couch.

"Abby, I'm so sorry. Your father has been shot."

"Is he dead?" she asked softly.

"No, he's at the hospital. The early cleaning crew found him at the paper a little while ago. He was shot twice in the chest and is in surgery right now. Abby, he's in critical condition. It doesn't look good. I'm so sorry."

Abby stood up and said, "I have to get to the hospital. I have to see him."

Ken held Abby's arm and said, "Abby, it's not safe for us out there, remember? Someone tried to kill us yesterday and then tried to kill your dad. If we rush right over to the hospital, we might be running right into a trap."

"I DON'T CARE!" Abby screamed at him as she forcefully pulled her arm away. She started to sob. Ken reached for her to pull her into his arms, but she resisted, pounding her fists into his chest, over and over again. Ken held on to her as she pounded away.

Abby's crying lasted only a few minutes. Ken had maneuvered her back onto the couch and was holding her. She took a deep breath and sat up, pulling away from his arms. The look on her face was different. The anger that had been directed at him was no longer there. She looked Ken in the eyes and said, "I have to go to the hospital to see my father."

"I know you do, and you will as soon as we can. We just need to spend a few minutes coming up with a plan to keep everyone safe, agreed?"

"Yeah, okay."

"Abby, I need you to know that I'm not going to leave your side until this business is over. After that, if you want me gone, I'm gone. I want to keep you safe whether you're with me or not."

Abby looked at him for a long time and finally said, "Tragedy certainly has a way of changing things, doesn't it?"

"What do you mean?"

"Last night I couldn't bear the thought of you. Today … I don't see how I can get through any of this without you."

Ken raised his eyebrows in surprise and looked into her eyes hopefully.

Abby continued, "I don't think I really know how I feel right now, and maybe when this is all over, I won't want to see you ever again. But right now, I need you, and *goddammit,* some part of me still loves you."

CHAPTER 40

Sal had arranged an SUV for Ken and Abby and it was waiting for them when they got downstairs. They had agreed a helicopter might bring unwanted attention and they needed to stay under the radar, their adversary thought they were dead, and it was best to keep it that way. It would take a couple of hours to drive back to Billings, but they felt it was the safest way. Shortly into the drive, as the sun was rising higher in the sky behind them, Abby filled Ken in on the investigation her father had been doing on the suspicious deaths and how he believed the Chief was the primary suspect.

"He really thinks Chief Wagner is a killer?" Ken asked.

"Yes, he does. After my visit with the Chief, I wasn't convinced. I told my dad I would think on it. But it seems very coincidental that after my visit with the Chief, we get shot at, *and* my father gets shot!"

"I think at this point we have to assume the Chief is a killer and that he is The Other from Viracocha. He shot at us and he shot your father. He thinks we're dead, so we have an advantage. First thing we need to do when we get to Billings is to surprise him and confront him. I'll call Sal and ask him to find out where he is." Ken went to make the call but was interrupted by Abby.

"No!" Abby yelled, "I have to see my father. I have to see him before we do anything else. Who knows how much time he has left?"

"Abby," Ken said calmly, "I know you want to see your father, but it's not a good idea. It's not smart. It puts us out in the open again. I need to protect you, and it will be much easier to do that if we keep the element of surprise on our side."

"I don't care if it's not a good idea. I have to see him, Ken."

Ken glanced at her and saw the look on her face. There would be no persuading Abby to do anything other than go immediately to see her father. "Okay, we'll go see your dad. I have an idea. Let me call Sal so he can help us out."

"Thank you," Abby said sincerely. She was holding out hope that her father would be okay and that he would wake up and be able to confirm exactly who had shot him, although Abby was pretty sure she already knew who it was.

Abby stared out the window, her head was absolutely spinning with everything that had happened in the past twenty-four hours. First, they were almost killed on the rafting trip, then Ken's unbelievable story about the Incas and what he was, the fight they had—although she realized the fight was one-sided—the awful news about her father being critically wounded and then finally her somewhat forced reconciliation with Ken. It all sounded like it came out of a mystery novel or something. She laughed when she realized it was enough material to keep a shrink busy for years. Then she thought about her sister, Gina.

"I have to call my sister," she said quietly.

"I didn't know you had a sister," Ken responded.

"Gina. She and my dad haven't spoken in years. She got into some bad stuff when my mom died; that's what caused the rift. She has totally straightened her life out and she's been a doctor in Minneapolis for almost a decade, but Dad is stubborn and still doesn't want to have anything to do with her. It was the same for me, but I reached out to her several years ago and we talk and text now. But I haven't seen her in person in a very long time. We kept saying we needed to get together. We just never made it happen, and now there's no choice." *If only Dad and Gina had had a chance to reconcile*, thought Abby.

"When you talk to her make sure you tell her not to talk to anyone. We still need to keep a low profile. Also, make sure we know what her travel arrangements are. I'll have Sal pick her up."

"Okay, will do," she replied with a strained smile as she dialed the phone.

The phone call with her sister went easier than she expected. Gina handled the news better than Abby would have guessed, maybe because she had so little time to react. After a few minutes of sisterly discussion, Abby asked Gina to take the earliest flight she could get into Billings. Abby also told her to be prepared to stay in Billings for a while, that there was a lot going on. Abby could tell Gina was a bit confused about the need for all the instructions, but to Gina's credit she went along with it. Abby wondered how much more Gina would need to know. This wasn't her fight, and she didn't want to put Gina in harm's way. Whatever questions she had, and she probably had a lot, would wait until they met face to face.

CHAPTER 41

As she ended the phone call, Gina Steel took a deep breath, that was a lot to digest in a ten-minute phone call. She hadn't spoken to Abby in a couple of months, and she's been estranged from her father for a very long time. With one phone call, that was all about to change. She agreed to everything Abby had asked her without a second thought. It was pure instinct. Her sister who she loved, now and always, needed her, and her dad was in intensive care, possibly dying. She had to be there for them. The past was the past and it was today that mattered, this was a motto that had guided her for many years. She was constantly reminding herself: you can't undo yesterday, but you can improve for tomorrow.

She went online and quickly booked a flight to Billings. Then she had two things to take care of. First, to let her practice know she would be away for a few days, maybe longer. Fortunately, she had a backup for just this type of emergency, a doctor friend who she fully trusted to take care of her patients. Second, what to pack and for how long? She hurriedly threw some things into a suitcase, enough for a week or so. If she needed more, she would get it.

A few hours later, she was boarding her flight. Once the plane had leveled off, she had her first sip of club soda. Iced tea was her drink of choice since she was a recovering alcoholic, but it wasn't an option on the plane. The woman next to her had headphones on and appeared to be deep into an audiobook. That was fine with Gina; she wasn't into small talk. She settled into her seat and thoughts of her dad brought back a lot of memories for reflection. She flashed back to her first stint at college.

Up to that point, life had been normal without any serious ups or downs. She had a great relationship with her younger sister Abby, even though they were polar-opposites. Abby was always more outgoing and really loved life in the city. Gina was more of an introvert and was uncomfortable at large social gatherings. Abby had her share of boy-friends and was into sports, while Gina spent most of her time cracking the books and hanging out in the library. Regardless, they got along well, sincerely loved each other, and made compromises when they had to in order to avoid typical sibling conflicts. That all changed when her mother was murdered.

Abby had her issues with it, but Gina spiraled completely out of control. Within a few weeks she had dropped out of school and was getting more and more into drugs and alcohol. A lot of the details were faded, but one thing was sure: she had hit rock bottom and the road back was not easy. The first day of her new life was the day she stood up in her first AA meeting and said, "Hi my name is Gina and I'm an alcoholic." That was the day after she and her dad spoke for the last time. She didn't know it at the time of course, but that had been a very difficult conversation and it was what finally prompted her to seek help. She got clean, went back to college, got accepted to Johns Hopkins medical school, and graduated with honors. She had fought her way back to a good life, vowing never to succumb to her demons again. She opened her own practice where her primary mission was simply to help sick kids. It had taken awhile to build her practice, but now it was thriving.

A few years after her practice started, she felt she was ready to try dating again. She found out that what attracted her to someone was their inner self. She liked people that were loving, compassionate, understanding and willing to compromise in order to sustain a friendship and then a relationship. The gender didn't really matter. She had two serious and lasting relationships. The first one was with a minor league ball player, who she met at the gym. He was a great guy and she enjoyed being with him very much. After a few years, neither of them seemed to be ready for a deeper commitment, so the relationship ended, but very amicably. Her second serious relationship was with a fellow physician, a woman named Amanda, who she met at a medical conference in Miami. The love was real, but as sometimes happens, life got in the way. In this case, it was their devotion to their professions. They were each so committed to their medical practices, they found they had little time for a real relationship to flourish. They agreed to remain friends, but they ended the relationship. Gina realized that in terms of today's labels for people's sexual preferences, she was the classic bisexual. It was the person, not the gender, that mattered to her. Her train of thought was broken by the plane's captain as he announced that they were starting on their approach into Billings.

Gina checked her seatbelt and then her mind went back to the phone call from Abby. It was strange and maybe even a little mysterious. Her dad's condition was straightforward, but he'd been shot. How did that happen? And why had Abby asked her not to tell anyone where she was going or why? It was curious to say the least. And Abby wasn't picking her up. She told Gina someone named Sal would be getting her. When Gina asked what he looked like, Abby had just said, "You'll know him when you see him, don't worry about it." She felt like this trip had more in store than what was on the surface, so she told herself to be prepared for anything. As the plane touched down, she wondered what this guy Sal was like.

CHAPTER 42

Ken had asked Sal to figure out a way that could get into the hospital and into Dominic's room without being seen. He wanted to keep the element of surprise on his side, and he was convinced it would be safer for everyone if The Other still thought they were dead. Their adversary was formidable, but so was Ken, and with the Amulet, he had yet another advantage. As they pulled up to the back entrance of the hospital, Sal was waiting for them in his car. They were in a remote area with little traffic, so they pulled up right next to him and they all got out.

"Sal, I'm so glad you're okay!" Abby said giving him a big hug.

"Thanks, Boss Lady. It takes a lot more than a coupla bullets to get rid of me. Glad you guys are okay too, and I'm real sorry 'bout your dad."

Ken and Sal shook hands and gave each other the typical one-armed bro hug. "You look good Boss."

"You too, Sal, you too," Ken responded. "As usual, thanks for setting this up for us."

"No problem, Boss. It was easy."

"Seems like almost anything is easy for you, Sal. Not sure how you do it."

"I know a few guys who help me out once in a while. No biggie."

"We have a lot of things to talk about when we're done here."

"I figured, Boss."

"Listen, we need you to go to the airport a little bit later and pick up Abby's sister. Her name is Gina. I'll text you her flight info. She'll be here early afternoon. When you pick her up, bring her back here. I'm sure she'll want to see her dad, okay?"

"You got it, Boss."

"Ken," Abby said impatiently, she needed to get inside and see her dad.

"Okay, right, we're going now. One thing first," Ken said. "No matter what happens in there, we need to keep a calm and cool head, okay?"

"What are you talking about?" Abby asked.

"Your dad is a victim of a crime. the chief may be there now, or walk in at any moment. If that happens, just keep cool, we don't want to tip him off that we suspect him of anything."

"Suspect him of what?" Sal asked confused.

Ken glanced at Abby who nodded, so Ken continued, "Okay, I'll tell you, but we don't have time for any questions, okay?"

"Sure, Boss."

"We have reason to believe the chief is the one who tried to kill us on the river," said Ken.

"What? You gotta be kidding me!"

Ken gave him a look.

"Okay, Boss, no questions." Sal handed them a bag that contained hospital scrubs, doctor jackets and ID's, one set each for Ken and Abby. Through one of his connections, Sal had gotten the latest update on Dominic. "Your dad's outta surgery and is in intensive care, top floor of the hospital," he said. "One other thing I gotta tell ya."

Abby's face went pale, thinking it had to do with her father. "What?" she asked.

"Donna Stapleton was also killed last night."

"What?! Oh my god, she was working with my father on his investigation, how did the chief know that?" She looked fiercely at Sal and then Ken and said, "We seriously need to take this asshole down."

"We will, Abby. I promise," Ken said reassuringly.

They changed in the SUV and walked into the hospital like they belonged there.

Dressed as doctors, Ken and Abby entered the ICU. They could see a Billings police officer standing guard at Dominic's room. Sal had advised them the officer was there to make sure no unauthorized visitors entered his room: Chief Wagner's orders. The officer gave Ken and Abby a quick look, but their fake IDs and hospital attire were good enough for him, so he let them in without a word.

As they entered the room, they saw a nurse attending to Dominic. He had numerous tubes and monitoring equipment attached to his body and was on a ventilator as well. Abby started to cry as she realized he wasn't breathing on his own. She immediately went over to his bed and held his hand.

Abby said to the nurse, "I'm his daughter, Abby. Can you tell me what his prognosis is?"

The nurse's face softened when Abby revealed she was family, she responded, "I'll get the doctor for you. She'll be able to answer all of your questions."

"Please, just tell me what you know," Abby pleaded.

"I'm sorry. I'm not supposed to," the nurse responded.

"Please, can you just tell us the basics? How did surgery go?" Ken asked in a bold matter of fact tone.

A little surprised by Ken's tone, the nurse responded automatically, "Surgery went as well as could be expected, but there is a lot of damage and he lost a lot of blood. The next twenty-four hours are crucial."

"Can he hear us?" Abby asked.

"Maybe. It's always good to talk to them," the nurse answered. "Unfortunately, he hasn't moved or made any sounds since he's been here."

Abby leaned over and lowered her head to Dominic's ear. "Dad, it's me, Abby," she said in a low whisper.

Dominic didn't move, no change in his facial expression either, but Abby was certain she felt his hand squeeze hers.

"He knows I'm here," she said.

Just then one of the monitors attached to Dominic started to beep. Abby looked up at the nurse in fear.

"It's okay. It's normal for the monitors to beep if he shows any type of reaction. It's a good thing." She smiled reassuringly at Abby and then left the room.

Abby leaned over Dominic again and whispered, "I love you, Dad." Again, she felt him squeeze her hand. She had tears welling up in her eyes as she sat down in a chair next to the bed and continued to hold her father's hand. Every so often she would glance up at the monitors that were tracking Dominic's vitals, but nothing changed. Ken just let Abby be with her dad, and for the next twenty minutes, the only noises in the room were from the machines. He occupied his time thinking of different scenarios they could use to confront the chief. Then they heard a discussion taking place outside the door to the room. Ken looked at

T
HE CURIST

Abby, who returned his gaze. They were on high alert, not knowing who was about to come in the room.

Finally, a light knock on the door, and Reverend Harold Lephit walked into the room. The reverend quickly looked from Abby to Ken, and Ken saw a look of surprise pass over his face. *Perhaps he wasn't expecting anyone in the room,* thought Ken. And then the full force of the evil Suka hit him and Ken had to use all of his willpower to keep from showing any reaction. *Oh my god, we had it all wrong,* Ken thought. *The reverend is The Other, not the chief!*

Crajack, in his reverend persona, was shocked to see Ken and Abby alive. How did they survive? He knew he hit Ken at least three times with the sniper rifle. The prickly sensation was back and spreading throughout his body. *Keep calm,* he told himself, *They have no idea who I am.*

With great restraint, both adversaries kept their feelings hidden. Abby had no clue what was going on with either of them internally. Ken realized he needed Abby to act normally towards the reverend, so he would have to lie about the Suka. The reverend calmly shook Ken's hand and turned to go to Abby. As he did so, Abby glanced over to Ken and he gave a subtle shake of his head to indicate no Suka as she expected. Ken also realized that The Other must have thought he killed both of them, so finding out they were alive had to be a shock, but he didn't show any emotion. *This guy is cunning,* he thought, *I have to stay alert and patient.*

Crajack walked over to Abby and said, "I'm so sorry, Abby. I can't believe anyone would want to do this to Dominic. It's shocking and tragic."

"Thank you, Reverend. Thank you for coming to see him."

"Of course, my dear," Crajack replied. He then walked over to the other side of Dominic's bed, gave him a blessing, and proceeded to recite a small prayer. *Must keep up the façade,* Crajack thought to himself.

"Tell me, Abby, what have the doctors told you?" Crajack asked.

"It's not good," she replied. "They said the next twenty-four hours are critical. Unfortunately, he's closer to death than recovery, barring a miracle …"

"Well, I never rule out miracles, my dear, not in my business. I've seen some amazing things in my life." Abby didn't know it, but Crajack was actually referring to his transformation with the help of the Incas, his sarcasm made him chuckle internally. "So, don't give up hope," he said, continuing his charade.

Crajack was glad to hear that Dominic's demise was almost certain. He wasn't ready to defend himself in case Dominic could somehow convey who had shot him. A few minutes later, he was politely excusing himself, telling Abby not to hesitate to ask for any assistance. And of course, he promised to pray for Dominic's recovery.

As Crajack was walking out, Ken asked him in a low whisper if he could talk to him outside about possible arrangements in case Dominic didn't make it. Ken made sure that Abby didn't hear him. She was focused on whispering in Dominic's ear hoping for some response.

"I'll be back in a few minutes, Abby. I'm gonna walk the reverend to his car."

Abby turned to him and gave a nod of acceptance.

Ken felt he had to confront The Other now, on neutral ground. He wanted to gauge his adversary, now that he knew for certain who it was. He was also desperate to secure Abby's safety. Could he make a deal with The Other?

Crajack was a little surprised at Ken's request but had no reason not to go along with it. He wanted to hear what Ken had to say. He felt there was something special about Ken, but he didn't know what it was. Then it hit him, was Ken like him? Did he have the magic of the Incas? *What a twist that would be*, he thought, slightly amused at the notion.

CHAPTER 43

Ken and Crajack got in the elevator. No words were exchanged on the ride down to the lobby. As they walked off the elevator, Ken finally spoke, "Why don't we go to the quiet room on this floor, see if we can have the room to ourselves."

"I'd rather not," Crajack replied. "How about we talk in my car. It's right outside the main door. I parked in the clergy spot."

"Sure, that's fine," Ken replied. As soon as they were both settled in the front seat of Crajack's car. Ken went on the offensive; he didn't want to mess around with this guy.

"That was some performance you gave to Abby up there in the hospital room. You didn't miss a beat with your reverend act. Maybe even worthy of an academy award. Especially since you thought you killed us on the river."

Ken's statement surprised Crajack. If Ken had figured that out, he was not a typical adversary. He wondered again if Ken had the Inca magic. He decided to play it straight with Ken, "Yes, I must admit it was a pretty good performance. I've had a lot of practice, but thanks for the compliment. And you're right, I thought you were dead. One out of three, good in baseball but not in my line of work."

"Sorry, Reverend, but you are actually zero for three. Sal is alive and well."

"Really? Kevlar, I presume?" said Crajack.

"Bingo."

"Well, that explains why Sal is alive, but why are you still alive? You weren't wearing Kevlar, were you? I counted at least three hits."

"Bingo again on both counts." Ken responded. "Let's just say that this isn't the first time our paths have crossed."

Crajack studied Ken's face as he thought about what Ken just said. He wondered, *Could it really be?* Then with blinding speed, Crajack whipped out a small pistol with a silencer and fired three shots point blank into Ken's chest. Nothing happened, no blood, no scream.

"So, you are like me with the gift of the Incas," he said in a matter of fact tone.

"I am nothing like you," Ken said harshly through gritted teeth.

"I guess that explains how Dominic's daughter survived. You took the hits. Well done," Crajack said sarcastically. "I guess next time I'll have to make sure to see the bodies. At least the bodies of your lackeys, not sure what I'm going to be able to do about you though. You're obviously the soldier I heard about during my time with the Incas. It's a shame we never got a chance to meet. Maybe we could have formed a partnership."

"That would never have happened," Ken quickly replied.

"Maybe, maybe not. I'm sure you've done your share of killing over the years, so really, we aren't that different from one another. You may have different reasons to kill, but you're a killer just the same."

Ken said nothing. He wanted the conversation to be one-sided for a while, let the Reverend get more comfortable and maybe over-confident as well.

"Now me, I kill for money, plain and simple. And I'm very, very good at it. My clients would give me excellent references, but that doesn't really happen in my line of work, if you know what I mean. If we're being totally honest, I kill a little for fun too." This last statement put a wicked grin on Crajack's face.

"Listen, Reverend—"

"Stop it, no more reverend from you. Call me Crajack."

"Crajack?" Ken asked a little confused.

"Yeah, Crajack."

"Okay, whatever. Listen, Crajack, I want some assurances from you."

"Assurances? What kind of assurances?"

"I want your word that you won't make any more attempts on Abby and Sal's lives ever again."

"And why would I make a promise like that?" Crajack asked.

"Because I have something that you could use, something from the Incas, something that you never received." Ken wanted to stir his curiosity.

"Bullshit," Crajack responded. "I have all I need—money, power, health and immortality."

"Not quite," responded Ken, "Slow aging, yes, but not immortality. Now, I *do* have immortality. I stayed in Viracocha to receive that final gift, you didn't. You made an early exit. Your mistake unfortunately, but that can be fixed." Ken paused for a moment, "I'm sure you know it's inevitable that Father Time will still get you. You basically are living a slow death, no matter how you slice it."

Crajack never looked at his aging process in that way. To him, it was a gift and his adversary was twisting it into a nightmare. *Very cunning*, he thought.

"You say you're immortal. How do I know you aren't lying?"

"You don't."

The honest response tweaked Crajack's interest. He had wondered many times if there was more to gain if he'd stayed with the Incas. "So, how can this mistake be fixed?"

"No more info until I have your word."

"You ask a lot. I can somewhat understand your feelings for the girl, but why Sal?"

"He's very resourceful, believe me, and he has grown on me, become a good friend, something you wouldn't understand."

"Yeah, well, sorry to say I don't believe anything you've told me."

"Why would I lie?" Ken asked. "I have nothing to gain and you have nothing to lose."

"Look, I'm sure you have the same, shall we say, abilities, as I have. I should have known from the dinner. I felt something wasn't right that night. You probably did as well."

"I did."

"So where do we go from here?" Crajack asked. "You want to kill me, but you can't, I want to kill you, but I can't. But I can kill Sal, Abby and Dominic, they're loose ends. I can't have them out there knowing about me and you realize that. So, I think you made up a desperate story to try and convince me to spare them, and it's just not gonna happen."

Ken stared at Crajack for a moment with a look of pure disgust on his face. "Then I guess we're finished here."

"Okay then, good talk," Crajack said with a sardonic smile on his face.

Ken got out of the car, slammed the door and walked back into the hospital, wondering if the Amulet would really do what the Incas said it would do. Abby's life depended on it, Sal's too!

As Crajack drove away from the hospital, he was thinking about Ken and his story. First, it was crazy that they crossed paths, two men with the magic of the Incas, in Billings of all places. Second, the idea of true immortality was very appealing; he just didn't believe that Ken had it in his power to give him immortality. And finally, Crajack wasn't about to make a deal to spare any lives, he knew he had to take out Sal and Abby, and Dominic if he managed to pull through. He wasn't sure what he was going to do about Ken though, he had to think on that a bit. For now, he was keeping all of his options open.

CHAPTER 44

Sal got to the passenger pick-up area a few minutes before Gina's plane arrived at the gate. It took some doing and more money than he thought it should, but he finally got the house plans for the reverend's mountain retreat that Ken had asked him to acquire. In his rush to complete that task, he forgot the sign he'd made which read *Gina Steel*. Now he'd have to try and figure out which one she was.

The Billings Airport was small. Sal waited between the terminal and baggage claim, hoping to be able to identify her. A stream of people began to flow out of the terminal's secure area. No one looked happy, flying was such a bitch these days. He figured it must have been a shit flight. After ten minutes, the flow of people slowed down, and he had not been able to identify her. He wondered if she was even on the flight. Maybe he missed her? He would give it a couple more minutes and then head over to baggage claim and look for her there.

He was scanning the people standing around him one last time, when the terminal door opened and *she* walked out. Sal was stunned as he stared at the woman who had just emerged. She was a looker! He hadn't known what to expect, but this was certainly not it. Abby was a looker too, but even plainly dressed in jeans, a man's button-down shirt and her brown hair up in a ponytail, Gina was more beautiful than her sister. She was a little taller than Abby, and her statuesque face looked like it came out of a magazine after being air-brushed to perfection, but this was no air-brush job, it was the real goods. Her body had curves that would shame the letter 'S'. Sal wasn't the only guy gawking at her. She was turning the heads of most of the limo drivers, all of them praying she was their ride.

Sal came out of his trance just in time to save Gina from the wolves. He, the least likely looking person to be her chauffeur, walked over to her, did a little bow and said, "Sal Chieffo, at your service, Ms. Steel. I'm here to get you to your dad on the double."

She looked at him and smiled, somewhat surprised and somewhat curious. She wasn't sure what she had been expecting, but it wasn't Sal with a heavy New York accent. Despite being dressed in a sport coat, over a Wonder Woman t-shirt, wearing baggy jeans with his hair a mess, he exuded a warm sincerity. He instantly made her feel safe and at ease. "Hello Sal," she reached out her hand, "Please call me Gina. It's a pleasure to meet you."

He took her hand and they shook, lingering for a moment. Sal's face had a glazed look on it, like a puppy dog in love.

Gina put her arm through Sal's and said, "Let's get my luggage. It's not much. One suitcase and a carry-on that I didn't feel like carrying."

Sal led her to baggage claim, her bags were circling on the belt just as they arrived. Ten minutes later they were in the car, bags stowed and halfway to the hospital to see Dominic. The conversation during the ride was limited, but not forced, as they got to know each other a little bit.

"Do you know my dad?" she asked.

"Yeah, we're friends. I drive him around some. He's a great guy. I'm really sorry 'bout what happened."

"Thank you, Sal. That's very kind of you. Do you know my sister from New York?"

"New York? Nah, met her here in Billings a few days ago."

"Really? I got the impression you were old friends."

"Nope, just a few days, but they been really long days."

"Oh," was all she said. *Long days?* Gina wondered what that meant but did not pursue it. Figures Abby would find a guy like Sal, a New Yorker, here in Billings.

As they drove, Gina gazed at the snowcapped mountains in the distance, with the backdrop of the deep blue Montana sky. The sun was starting to think about its descent, the light in the east changing ever so slightly, some scattered clouds floated in the sky, a very peaceful scene. *No wonder Dad retired here. It's beautiful. God, I hope he's going to be okay!* She really hated the fact that she had not reconciled with her dad. Maybe she should have pushed harder to reconnect with him. Having Abby back in her life was a wonderful gift, even if they didn't really see each other much. *He just has to pull through so we can fix our relationship. I don't want it to end like this for him or for me.*

CHAPTER 45

When Ken returned from the parking lot, he found Abby in the same position as when he left. He decided that telling Abby about the reverend could wait. For now, dealing with Dominic on his apparent death bed was enough for her to handle. Another few hours wouldn't make any difference, and surprisingly, she didn't ask him about it. They sat in a peaceful silence for a while. Every now and then a nurse or orderly would come in to the room to perform a task, but mostly it was just them, being there for each other and for Dominic.

The next time the door opened, it wasn't another hospital employee, Sal and Gina walked in to the room. Abby looked up, saw her sister standing there and immediately got up to embrace her. They held each other for a few moments, not saying anything. Tears were welling up in both their eyes.

Gina pulled away first and said, "Oh my god, Abby, it's so good to see you. It's been way too long." And then she pulled her into another hug.

"Gina, I'm so sorry you had to come here like this. Dad hasn't come out of his coma yet. They don't know if he ever will," Abby told her through her tears.

"Hey now, he's gonna be fine. That's what we all have to believe, okay?"

After being apart for so many years, Abby loved having the feeling of her older sister taking care of her. She had not realized how much she missed her. Once the flow of tears subsided, Abby introduced Gina to Ken. They embraced each other with a strong hug, Ken holding on until Gina let go.

"I am truly sorry about your dad," Ken said softly.

"Thank you," she replied. "Listen, I'm gonna see if I can talk to the doctor."

"Check with the charge nurse. Tell her you're a doctor too!" said Abby.

"I will if I think it'll help. I'll be right back."

Ten minutes later, Gina walked in with Dominic's doctor. Introductions were made all around.

Gina started by saying, "Dr. Green has given me a full update on everything they have done and are doing for Dad. He's in very good hands." Gina could see the relief on Abby's face.

Dr. Green then said, "Dr. Steel and I have agreed that Dominic needs his rest. That means I'm going to restrict visitors to one at a time and only for a few minutes each hour."

"What?" Abby exclaimed. "He needs his family around for support. He needs us."

Gina went over to Abby, gently took her hand and said, "Abby, I know it's hard to think of leaving him right now, but that really is what's best for him. You look like you could use a rest. Why don't you go home, shower, eat, take a nap? Whatever you need. I will stay here with him."

Again, her older sister was looking out for her. Abby took a breath and realized she was exhausted. The last two days were beyond anything she had ever been through. She looked at Ken, who nodded in agreement. The pause allowed the thoughts of the past two days to come rushing back. She realized she was lucky to not have seen the chief yet, and they had to come up with a plan, quickly, so they could take him out with the Amulet. She finally gave in and said to Gina, "Okay. On one condition—you come back to the house with me. I think I'm gonna need you more than Dad does right now."

Gina hesitated, "Are you sure?"

"Yes, I'm sure." Abby turned to Dr. Green, "Okay, we'll let him rest, but you have to promise to call if anything changes good or bad."

"Of course," said Dr. Green, and then she left the room so they could say their goodbyes to Dominic.

Abby turned to Sal, "Sal?"

"Yeah, Boss Lady?"

"Can you get someone to come and stay with my dad? Visit him whenever they allow. I'd feel much more comfortable with that arrangement, than with trusting them to call us if anything changes."

"Sure, no problem, I got the perfect guy," responded Sal as he pulled out his phone to make the call.

CHAPTER 46

When they left the hospital, Ken suggested they all ride together in Sal's car, and everyone agreed. What he didn't tell them was he thought they would be safer together as a group. He didn't know what Crajack would try, or when, but he assumed Crajack wouldn't be backing down. Sal got behind the wheel, Gina to his right and Ken and Abby climbed into the back. As it turned out, the drive was the perfect opportunity to start bringing Gina up to speed on all the events of the past week, Abby felt very strongly that Gina deserved to know the truth, all of it, even the unbelievable stuff about Ken. Sal would learn a few things too.

"Oh, Abby, I can't believe it's been so long. It is so good to see you even under these terrible circumstances." Gina continued, "I'm so glad Ken was here for you so you weren't alone. Did you two come out here for a vacation to see Dad? I'm sure this isn't what you expected!"

"Not exactly, Sis. I only met Ken five days ago, Sal too," Abby said.

"What? You just met each other? You act like you've known each other forever."

"Well, now is as good a time as any to get you caught up on everything. Sal knows most of it, but he's gonna learn a few things too."

Sal looked at her through the rearview mirror with raised eyebrows.

Abby said, "Yes, Sal, there are some things we've learned that you're not up to speed on yet. Okay, some of this might sound crazy, so please just hear me out, okay?

"Okay," Gina replied.

Abby started with her Dad's phone call to her in New York and recapped what had happened in the past few days, leaving out the stuff about Ken. No one interrupted as she spoke. Abby couldn't read the expression on Gina's face when she finished. After a moment or two Gina said, "You were shot at?"

"Yes, we were. Luckily, none of us were hurt. I wish I could say the same for Dad." Abby started to cry. Ken put his arm around her and held her for a few minutes.

"You can't blame yourself, Abby. You didn't do this." Gina told her, then asked, "I can't imagine what the last twenty-four hours have been like for you. I'm so sorry. I'm afraid to ask if that's the whole story."

"It's not. Someone who was helping Dad research his story, Donna Stapleton, was also shot last night and was killed. We got the news about Dad early this morning. That's when I called you and then we headed back as quickly as possible. And here we are now."

"Do you have any idea who is doing this?" Gina asked.

"Actually, we do have a suspect."

Sal raised his eyebrows in surprise as he looked back to Abby again. This was news to him.

"Police Chief Wagner is our suspect," Abby said with venom in her voice.

Ken realized he still hadn't told Abby that the reverend was not only their suspect, but had confessed to shooting Dominic and Donna. He cleared his throat and said, "Abby, it's not the chief."

Abby turned to look at him like he was crazy, "What are you talking about?"

Sal pulled in to Dominic's driveway right as Abby asked her question. No one made a move to get out of the car. They were all waiting to hear what Ken had to say.

"I was going to tell you, but it didn't feel right to do it at the hospital."

"Tell me what?" Abby asked, a little angry.

Ken continued, "Do you remember when Reverend Lephit visited today?"

"Yes."

"The second he walked in the room, I felt the Suka. I instantly knew it was him. I just held it in, because I didn't want to tip him off."

"What? Are you sure? He was barely on our radar."

"Yes, I'm absolutely sure."

"You let me talk to that monster? You let him comfort me! How could you do that? You know all I want to do is kill whoever is responsible for hurting my father. How could you do that to me, Ken?" Abby turned to the window as tears started rolling down her face.

"Abby? Abby. Please look at me," Ken said as he gently took her hand. "You are vulnerable to him. I couldn't take a chance he would hurt you right in front of me. I had to play it cool. You understand that, don't you? We need to take him out, but we need a plan first. We can't go after him half-cocked."

Abby finally looked over at Ken, saw the sincerity and love in his eyes and let out a big sigh. "I understand what you're saying, but I really wish you had told me."

"I'm sorry." Ken said.

"Uh, Boss," Sal interrupted, "What the hell is a sooker?"

"It's called Suka, spelled S-U-K-A," replied Ken.

"Okay, Suka, whatever, what the hell is it?"

"So, there is a little more of the story to tell. Mainly, how I know who the killer is and why he's so dangerous to all of us. Why don't we all go inside, rather than stay out here in the car all day, and I'll tell you the rest, all of it, okay?"

They all agreed and got out of the car. Gina took Abby's arm and held it as they walked to the front door.

The four of them were seated comfortably in Dominic's living room with stiff drinks in their hands, except for Gina who just had iced tea. Gina had chosen to sit down next to Sal on the sofa. It was her first move to let Sal know that she liked him. Abby caught on, Sal didn't, and Ken was only focused on the story he was about to tell.

Ken looked at Abby and she started, "Please listen to Ken carefully. He's about to tell you a very strange story, but I promise everything he says is true, and I believe every word of it."

"I think we're already in the middle of a very strange story. Not sure how it could get stranger," Gina said in a matter of fact tone.

Sal stared at Abby and then Ken, he was quiet but had an expectant look on his face.

Ken began the story of Viracocha, Suka and The Other, and did not stop for the next thirty minutes. When he was done, Sal shook his head in disbelief, Gina just stared into space contemplating all that she just heard.

Sal said, "Boss, Boss Lady, I love ya both, but this is one crazy story. Immortality? The Incas? Reverend Lephit is a killer for hire? What the hell? What kinda play are you going for?"

"No play, Sal. I know it's hard to believe, but it's the truth. Well, I'm not truly immortal, I do age, just very, very slowly and my body is very resistant to injury. Sal, how do you think we got away from him at the river? I'm not sure why you were wearing Kevlar—apparently there is a lot I don't know about you—but I wasn't wearing it. He hit me with a few shots on the river, but I was able to protect Abby and get us off the boat because the bullets had no lasting effect on me."

"I just don't know, Boss. And what was that crap about Rev. Lephit killing people for money? That's just crazy. I mean I'm no church guy, but I met him a few times. No way he's a killer."

Ken decided that he had to show Sal something that would convince him of the story. "Sal, can you please give your Glock to Abby?"

Abby looked surprisingly at Ken. He just nodded. This was the quickest way to make them believe the story.

"Uh, okay, Boss," Sal hesitated for just a second and then gave Abby the weapon, making sure the safety was on.

"It's loaded, right, Sal?" Ken asked.

"Wouldn't be much good if it wasn't, Boss."

Gina was now intently focused on what was going on in the room. Abby had stood up and was holding the gun pointed directly at Ken, who had also stood up.

"Abby, what're you doing?" Gina shouted in alarm.

Ken nodded again and Abby fired two shots point blank into the middle of Ken's chest, the force of the bullets could be seen in the reaction of his body.

Sal recoiled and yelled, "Boss Man, NO!"

No one moved or said anything for a beat or two. Finally, Ken turned towards the sofa and pulled up the shirt he was wearing, and as bright as could be, there were two large crimson bruises starting to form, but no blood and no holes!

Sal and Gina stared at the bruises, then at each other, and back at the bruises again.

"Holy hell," Sal whispered to himself as he made the sign of the cross.

Ken then stretched out his shirt to show them the holes the bullets had made in it. Gina got off the sofa and went to examine Ken's shirt and the bruises.

"I don't believe it," she said. "Or rather, I don't believe this is happening, but I guess I *DO* believe your story now." She went back to the sofa and sat down.

Sal said, "I believe you too, Boss. I can't really argue with a demonstration like that." He then turned to Abby and said, "You sure can pick 'em, Boss Lady."

The joke gave them all a much-needed moment of levity as Abby quipped back, "You got that right. I was hoping for a nice quiet insurance salesman."

Ken brought their attention back as he said, "Now, we need to come up with a plan to kill our very formidable adversary."

"Well, we ain't gonna do it with bullets, not if he's like you," Sal wisecracked.

"Actually, that's exactly how we're going to do it," replied Ken.

CHAPTER 47

With all eyes on him, Ken pulled the Amulet out of his pocket and held it out for them to see. It was suspended from a beautiful gold chain, Ken grasped the bottom of the Amulet and pulled it off. Then, he very carefully pressed the stone to show them the razor-sharp prongs that came out. Gina gasped in surprise. She wasn't expecting deadly sharp points to come out of such a beautiful piece.

"This is what we're going to use on Crajack," said Ken.

"Who the hell is Crajack?" Abby asked confused.

"Rev. Lephit is Crajack. He bragged to me about being a highly paid hit man, and told me to call him Crajack. Remember how I talked about The Other in Viracocha? The Other is Crajack, one and the same."

"That sounds better to me than callin' him Reverend," quipped Sal. "But, Boss, hows that little thing gonna help us?"

Ken explained to them the final secret he had from the Incas, the power of the Amulet to reverse the immortal-like effects in Crajack. Gina quickly realized that it would have the same effect on him were it to pierce his skin and asked, "Ken, could you please put that away now that we've all seen it?"

"Of course," he said as he put the Amulet back together and put it in his pocket.

"Okay, Boss, that little thing is gonna help us, but how we gonna get close enough to use it?" asked Sal. "And are you sure that it will work, it's been a while, maybe it's got one of those shelf life things I find on most of the food I eat."

"Look, everything the Incas told me has been true so far, I have to believe this Amulet is the real thing." Even though he sounded confident, the same thought had occurred to him several times. *Did the Amulet really have the capability to do what the Incas said it would do?* Everything depended on that one point being true. If it wasn't, Sal and Abby wouldn't make it out of this alive!

"I tried to convince Crajack that I had something he didn't, true immortality, but he didn't buy it. He is over-confident and doesn't think he can be killed. We are gonna use those weaknesses to our advantage. Tomorrow, we show up at his place and just knock on the door. I think showing him the Amulet will convince him to let us in, he's gonna want to take a look at it since he's never seen it before. Once we're inside, I'll keep him talking. I need the two of you," indicating Abby and Sal, "to keep quiet, no matter what he says. Can you do that?"

"Sure, Boss."

"Yes," replied Abby.

"What about me?" Gina asked.

"Gina, we're going to need you to be our medical team in case things go south. Abby and Sal are, of course, vulnerable to bullets, so we need to be prepared in case they need medical attention. Are you up for that?"

"Absolutely," Gina responded confidently.

"Okay, I'm gonna have to get close enough to him to pierce his skin, so there's probably going to be a fight. I need the two of you with me so you can shoot him once he has been stuck with the Amulet. I'm gonna have to keep him from trying to take you guys out, so I'll have my hands full."

"I want to put the bullet in him that finishes him," Abby said fiercely.

"I'm with you on that one, Boss Lady."

"Okay then," said Ken. "We're all in agreement that we take the offensive, we walk right up to the house and invite ourselves in for the final confrontation."

Everyone nodded their heads in agreement.

Never one to let life and death get in the way of a meal, Sal piped up, "Anyone else hungry?"

"I'm starving, now that you mention it," Gina replied.

"I have no idea what's in the kitchen," Abby said.

"No problema. We'll order something, whatcha want?" asked Sal.

"Sal, no one delivers out here."

"Don't worry 'bout it, Boss Lady. I'll get one of my guys to bring it to us. Chinese?"

They all agreed on Chinese, gave Sal their orders, and he went to make the call. Ken walked over to the front window and peered out intently. Abby went over to him and put her arms around him, and they just stood there for a few minutes, enjoying the feeling of each other.

Ken finally spoke, "Life is weird. I was sent to kill the German spy Erik Wendt seventy-five years ago, and it looks like I'm finally going to get the chance to complete that mission." He pulled a very old picture out of his wallet and showed it to Abby. "See that guy?" Ken asked, pointing to Wendt.

"Yes," replied Abby.

"That's Erik. This picture was given to me with my mission orders, not sure how, but it survived the crash and I've carried it with me every day since then."

"Ken," Abby said anxiously, "is the other guy in the picture who I think it is?"

Ken looked down at the picture and then at Abby, "Yes, the other man in the photo is Adolph Hitler."

"Holy shit," said Abby in awe of the connection.

The food arrived and they devoured it like they hadn't eaten in days. Despite the fact that Dominic was still in critical condition and that they were about to face a potentially lethal mission tomorrow, the mood was light and enjoyable. Afterwards, they broke up into two camps, Ken and Sal stayed in the dining room to review the house plans they had gotten on Crajack's mountain place, and Abby and Gina, feeling a bit nostalgic, went back into the living room and began delving into old photo albums, laughing, crying a bit and recalling mostly happy memories.

"Is this everything you got, Sal?"

"Yeah, Boss, that's it."

"How accurate do you think these plans are?"

"I dunno. He's pretty far out there, so he coulda had stuff done that he never registered or got permits for. The footprint of the house has gotta be the same, but who knows what he done inside."

"Agreed," Ken said. "It seems pretty straightforward, but we have to be prepared for anything. I'm sure he has security measures that aren't in these plans, but it doesn't look like he's tried to build a fortress. Again, he's arrogant and thinks he can't be killed. That, and the Amulet, are the only things in our favor."

As Abby and Gina started looking through the last photo album, Ken decided to take a break and joined them on the sofa to look at the photos. The album was very old. All of the pictures were in black and white and seemed to be from the time before Dominic was even born. Abby remembered looking through this album once with her mom, but that was many years ago and she only remembered bits and pieces. Half-way through the album, she came across some photos of men dressed in military attire.

"Gina, look, I think this is our grandpa with some of the men in his unit. He served in WWII. I remember Dad always talking about him."

Ken leaned in closer to study the photo.

"The stories about my Gramps are legendary in my family. His unit was involved in the Normandy invasion and most of the men in his unit died that day."

"As many great patriots did," Ken said solemnly.

"Yes, too many men. But the strange thing is, for some reason he wasn't with his unit for the invasion and never told anyone why. He just said he was on a different mission, one he couldn't talk about. It was all very strange, and he took his secret to his grave. Dad always felt that he carried the burden of not being with his men when they met their fate on the beaches of Normandy. Dad said that Gramps hoped his mission had been worth it. Again, we never found out. I guess I should be thankful. Him living is why I'm here now."

Ken looked intently at the man Abby pointed out, he was a corporal standing with some other men in front of a car. The photo is faded, and grainy, but Ken has a flash of recognition and says, "Oh my god, it's him!"

"Him who?" Abby asks.

Ken took the album and held the photo closer to his eyes to make sure, "Yes, that's him. No doubt about it!" he said excitedly.

"You knew him?" Abby asks in awe.

"Remember I told you about my last mission, the plane crash, the Incas. I didn't tell you about the driver who took me to the plane. It didn't seem important, but now, the driver was a corporal who was taken away from his unit to get me to that plane. A corporal who could drive like the wind from his racing experience before he enlisted. It was your grandfather!"

"Are you sure?" Abby exclaimed.

"Yes, I'm sure," Ken said looking her directly in the eye. "A hundred percent sure."

"That means Gramps is responsible for both of us being here. Crazy."

"Christ," Ken said. *Was this divine intervention, or a coincidence, or a little of both?*

"You can't make stuff like this up," Gina said.

"Can't make what up?" asked Sal as he joined them.

Gina explained the connection between the photo, her grandfather, and Ken.

Sal looked at Ken and shook his head, "Like Alice said Boss, your story gets curiouser and curiouser. Anything else you gotta tell us?"

"After this last discovery, I honestly have no idea," Ken said.

CHAPTER 48

The next morning everyone was up early, and together they prepared and consumed a full breakfast—eggs, potatoes, bacon, sausage and lots of coffee. Abby called the hospital to check on Dominic and was told there was no change in his condition, his vitals remained stable. After breakfast they went to work on their assigned tasks. Abby and Ken cleaned and loaded the weapons, as well as prepared extra clips of ammunition for each gun. Gina detailed to Sal what medication and equipment she would need if someone did get shot or otherwise injured when they went to see Crajack. Sal of course, had a guy who could get him what he needed in just a few hours. Sal also had the responsibility of taking care of Crajack's mountain retreat after they killed him. The plan was to demolish the house, make it look like a gas leak caused an explosion and killed Rev. Lephit, just another tragic accident.

Later that morning, they gathered in the living room to go over the plan one more time. Again, Gina positioned herself next to Sal. This time he noticed and the smile on his face told it all. Abby smiled also, but Ken was still oblivious to the bond growing between Sal and Gina, a bond that was growing very quickly. It was just around 11:00 AM when they got a call from the hospital. Gina took the call in the other room and returned after a few minutes.

"That was the doctor."

"What did she say?" asked Abby.

"She just did rounds and said Dad was waking up a bit. They took him off the ventilator and he's breathing on his own. All of that is great news, but he's not completely out of the woods yet. I just want you all to be aware of that. And we can visit him if we want."

"Oh my God," Abby exclaimed. "That's awesome news!"

"Great news. Why don't we head out and visit him before we head to Crajack's?" Ken replied.

"Sounds good to me. Let's go." Gina said.

Ten minutes later they were in the car headed to the hospital. Ken was in the back seat going over the approach in his head. He knew initial dialogue would be key. He needed to keep Crajack focused on just him, so Sal and Abby needed to keep quiet. Cross conversation between the four of them would only cause confusion and would play into their adversary's hand. Ken hoped the Amulet would be enough to tweak Crajack's interest and distract him, at least long enough for Ken to make his move. He knew Abby and Sal would do their part when the time came, of that he had no doubt. *Would the Amulet do what they needed?*

The stop at the hospital was quick but positive. Dominic looked so much better simply because most of the machines he'd been hooked up to had been removed, Abby held one hand and Gina the other. He opened his eyes a few times and squeezed their hands, a tear fell from his eye as he was looking at Gina. He wasn't strong enough to speak, and his throat was irritated from the ventilator, but the expression on his face was all they needed to know how he felt. They left him with words of love and encouragement and promised to visit later. They didn't share a word of their plan for fear of causing him a setback in his recovery.

In the parking lot downstairs, the four of them split up, Gina went to the van that one of Sal's guys had delivered. It had been transformed from a basic cargo van to a makeshift ambulance and had everything Gina had asked for. Ken, Abby, and Sal climbed into the SUV they had left at the hospital last night. They didn't want to take Sal's car. The two vehicles pulled onto the road and headed towards the mountains, the van following the SUV. A little under an hour later, the SUV pulled off the road and on to the driveway that led to Crajack's sanctuary. Gina and the medical van were safe a few miles down the road, out of harm's way.

Crajack was working in his study when the perimeter alarm went off, letting him know someone was headed to the house. He looked at the video cameras and smiled to see Ken, Abby and Sal on their way to him. *How foolish. He has made it too easy for me to take out his lackeys. He has brought them directly to me!*

Sal stopped the SUV twenty yards from the house. There was nothing ominous about the house. It appeared to be just a mountain retreat, one of hundreds you would find in the mountains around here. "Doesn't look like much to me, Boss."

"Looks can be deceiving, Sal," Ken replied.

Ken walked up to the front door and rang the doorbell, which was equipped with a camera and microphone. Ken knew that Crajack could see and hear them.

A few moments passed before Crajack answered, "Well, well, I see our conversation yesterday didn't scare you away."

"Not in the least. I told you I need to secure the safety of my team and I'm here to do just that."

"And I told you that you have nothing that interests me. I have everything I need."

Ken then pulled out the Amulet and dangled it in front of the camera so Crajack could see it in full detail.

"I know you didn't believe me about the extra gift I have, so I thought I would show you. They say seeing is believing, right?"

Crajack was stunned to see the Amulet, he knew immediately it was a true Inca artifact. The gold, jewels and detailed design could be nothing else. He had looked and looked, but had never come across anything as beautiful as the things he had seen in Viracocha, until now. His interest was tweaked, but he still didn't believe the immortality story.

Ken paused for about thirty seconds to give Crajack time to examine the Amulet. "So, what do you say? Let me in and hear my proposition. You have nothing to lose." Ken wondered if he would bite.

There were another few moments of silence and then Crajack said, "Okay. I'll come and let you in."

"No tricks," Ken said.

"No tricks," Crajack responded. "I won't need any, I assure you."

A minute later Crajack, dressed in all black, opened the door and escorted them down the hallway into the kitchen. He went around the center island to the refrigerator, pulled out a bottle of wine and asked, "Would anyone care for a glass of Riesling?"

Ken stood at the island directly across from Crajack, Sal was a few steps back to his right, and Abby a few steps back to his left. "No, we're fine," he responded.

"Suit yourself," Crajack said as he shrugged. "It's very good." He poured a glass and took a sip, savoring the wine before swallowing.

Ken wasn't sure what to make of his adversary's laid back and casual manner, he reminded himself to stay open to all possibilities and then said, "Enough of the social pleasantries. Let's get down to business."

"I told you yesterday, no deal." Crajack continued, "Nothing has changed in the last twenty-four hours to make me change my mind."

"I showed you the Amulet. It can grant you full immortality."

"Yeah, you showed me the Amulet. It's an Inca artifact, I can see that, but I have no reason to believe it does what you say it will. Convince me."

"Convince you?" Ken asked doubtfully.

"Yes, convince me."

"And when I do, you'll guarantee my friends' safety?"

"Maybe."

Ken took a deep breath. He had to continue with the story, keep Crajack focused on him, so he decided to try and surprise him by using his real name. He pulled out the Amulet and said, "Okay, Erik, let me explain how this works."

Crajack had a weird look on his face as he said, "Before you start the show, my friend, I'm curious as to why you're calling me Erik?"

"First, I am not your friend," Ken said between gritted teeth, "And second, I'm calling you Erik because that's your name. I know all about you, Erik Wendt. Didn't you ever wonder why there was a WWII American soldier in Viracocha? I was on a top-secret mission to take you out in Peru. I had all the intel on you I needed, the secret bunker in the Andes, your life as a professor, how you were hand-picked by the Nazis to search for Viracocha."

Crajack was staring at him, looking a bit confused.

"I even have a picture of you. It came with the mission orders." Ken threw the picture down on the counter in front of Crajack.

Crajack picked up the picture, looked at it for a moment and then started to laugh. A full-throated, body laugh which almost had him doubled over.

Ken quickly glanced at Abby who shrugged. He then asked, "What's funny?"

"This," he said, indicating the picture, "This is funny." He continued to laugh.

"Why is it funny?" Ken asked, annoyed.

"Oh, you fool. You have a picture of me alright, but Erik? Erik, or should I say his remains, if there are any, are lying deep in the mountains of the Andes."

Ken was now the confused one, but he had to keep his mind focused. And then, the reality of the situation and what Crajack said clicked in his brain and everything suddenly made perfect sense to him. "No, it can't be."

"Yes, it is so. To save you asking a lot of questions, I'll give you the short version. Almost everything recorded in history about my death is false. It was all a ruse. I was dying of cancer and had a doppelgänger put in my place, no one knew about this. Erik's early work and theories interested me, even more so once I knew I was sick. So, I gambled that it might be true and with nothing to lose, I got on a plane to Peru. As soon as we entered Viracocha, I disposed of Erik, poor lad. He wanted so badly to see if his theories were correct. The rest I think you kind of know. My only regret was the outcome of the war. I have to say the Allies really did kick our ass."

"Ken," interrupted Abby, "Could it be true?"

Crajack looked right at Abby and said, "Yes, my dear, it is absolutely true. I am Adolph Hitler!"

"What kind of bullshit is that?" asked Sal who had never seen the old photo.

"He can speak!" Crajack says to Sal. "Yes, it's true. Here, take a look for yourself," he said while handing the picture out for Sal. Sal didn't move from where he was, so Ken took the picture and gave it to Sal, who examined it closely. "Come on now. It's not like I didn't give anyone a clue," Hitler continued.

"What are you talking about?" asked Abby.

"Come on now, my dear. You're a detective, right? Are you good at puzzles, anagrams specifically?"

Ken was completely shocked at the revelation. *Could it really be Hitler?* he thought to himself. The two men in the picture, Erik Wendt and Adolph Hitler were roughly the same height and build, and without the ridiculous moustache, most people wouldn't be able to pick Hitler out of a three-person lineup. It would explain the intensity of the evil Suka he felt when he was around this guy. He had killed millions and had been given the power to carry on for decades, how could the Incas have done this? They had to know what kind of a man he was. Ken suddenly decided it didn't matter; they were going to take him out whoever he was. Things had gotten out of control, and he had to rein everything back in and now.

"Holy shit," Abby exclaimed after working it out in her head. "Harold Lephit, it's an anagram for Adolph Hitler!"

"Excellent work my dear," Hitler exclaimed. "You win the prize!"

"Fuck you," responded Abby.

"Such harsh language from a lady. The world sure ain't what it used to be, is it?" Hitler said, taking another sip of his wine.

"Okay, okay," Ken said, "Everyone settle down, we still have some business to do here and I would like to get it finished once and for all, no matter who you are."

Over his shoulder Ken asked, "You good, Abby?"

"Yeah, I'm good."

"Alright then," Ken said.

"So now there is the question of the magical Amulet, right? How are you going to prove to me that it works as you say it does?" Hitler asked Ken. "And what about everything I have done? Can you assure me no one is going to seek revenge, not for Donna or Dominic? How is the old chap by the way? Shame it didn't turn out as I planned."

Abby couldn't hold it together any longer, she pulled her gun out, pointed it at Hitler, and took a few steps forward.

Hitler laughed, "I'm sure you know that gun will not harm me."

"We could always test that theory if you like," Abby responded, her face filled with hatred.

Without taking his eyes off Hitler, Ken backed up a few steps, put his hand on top of Abby's outstretched arms and tried to guide her to lower the gun. He whispered something to her that no one else could hear and she finally complied, lowering the gun to her side.

"No revenge. What's past is past," Ken said. "It can't be changed. It's the future I care about now. She can't do you any harm, neither can Sal, so why are they any concern of yours?"

"They are loose ends. And loose ends can sometimes bite you in the ass. Dominic and Donna were loose ends. That's why they had to go."

"And Rabbi Kuperman, was he a loose end?"

"No, he was a continuation of the final solution!" Hitler screamed in exultation. "I hate him and his kind. You should've been there to see the look on his face when he realized I was going to kill him. I think the modern term for it is *priceless*."

"You're right about one thing," Hitler continued, his face and voice suddenly changing to one of menace, "We do need to come to an understanding. I'm glad we finally met, but I'm going to be leaving Billings, and I never want to see you again. I don't care what you do, just stay out of my way. I may not be able to kill you, but there are things I can do to make your life, literally, a living hell. But these two lackeys you brought with you, I see no value in keeping them around. They need to be dispensed with immediately."

"You still haven't heard my offer. My companions stay with me, and again, I want your assurance that nothing happens to them, at least not at your hand or by your doing."

"Okay, you made your point. Let me hear this wonderful offer of yours. What does that pretty medallion thing do?" Hitler had always wondered if he left something, on the table, so to speak, by leaving Viracocha the way he did. He couldn't think what it could be, he had near immortality, no sickness and had amassed great wealth. He thought he had it all.

"It's not a medallion. It's an amulet."

"Whatever," Hitler interrupted.

Ken continued, "The Amulet gives you permanent immortality. Right now, you're aging, only about a year for every ten calendar years, but still aging. With the power of this Amulet, you will never age a day beyond today," which was basically the truth Ken thought. "I have not aged one day since 1946, the year I received this final Inca gift."

"So, for the lives of your two lackeys, you're willing to share this with me?"

"Not share, trade. I will give you the Amulet if you promise to spare their lives. You will then be as me, completely immortal and able to live forever."

"How do I know you aren't lying?"

"What reason would I have to lie?" Ken asked. "If I'm lying, they're dead. We both know I can try and stop you, but one way or another you would eventually get to them."

Hitler considered what Ken said and agreed there would be no reason for him to lie. Ken stared at Hitler, Hitler stared right back. Two professional killers not flinching or showing any emotion. Who would give in first? It seemed like an eternity, but was only a few moments before, finally, the silence was broken.

"Okay, so what's the secret of the Amulet?" Hitler asked.

Ken was pleasantly surprised, what he had predicted was exactly what was happening, Hitler was over-confident and arrogant, and that would give him the chance he needed to make his move. *Gotcha*, thought Ken. "It's all here on the symbols. See for yourself," said Ken as he held up the Amulet.

"Hand it to me and I'll take a look," said Hitler.

"Sorry, but the Amulet doesn't leave my possession until we have a deal," as Ken pulled the Amulet back.

Hitler paused for a second, something didn't feel right to him, that prickly sensation of his was going at full force, and he decided to completely trust it.

"Sorry, no deal. I'm tired of this game," said Hitler as he pulled out his Glock and shot Abby!

CHAPTER 49

Abby screamed in pain as the bullet tore through her right shoulder. Ken was totally caught by surprise at the shot but recovered quickly and went on the attack. He pulled the Amulet apart and pressed the stone to extend the prongs as he leapt across the counter at Hitler, trying to stick him in the arm. Hitler moved much faster than he expected, and Ken missed with the Amulet, but was able to knock the gun out of his hand. Both men were now on the same side of the countertop, facing each other. Ken again thrust the Amulet, but Hitler side stepped the attack and landed a firm blow to Ken's torso, but it had little effect. This time, Ken decided to charge at him with the full force of his body, hoping that the Amulet would pierce some part of Hitler's body in the collision. He charged at Hitler like a linebacker going after a tackle and they both crashed down to the ground. Ken was trying to hold on while Hitler was trying to squirm out from underneath him. They were both on the floor, rolling over each other, wrestling more than exchanging blows. Ken expected the strength but was surprised with the quickness and agility of his opponent. This guy was his equal and he realized that trying to fight him and hold the Amulet in his hand was a serious handicap.

Hitler was finally able to squirm free and while still on the ground, he pulled a gun from an ankle holster and fired out three shots before Ken was on top of him again. Two of the bullets found a mark, Abby was hit again, this time in the leg, and the last bullet whizzed by Sal's right ear, taking some of his earlobe with it. Ken was able to knock the second gun away, but it didn't go far.

"You, stupid fool. You've just signed the death warrant of your friends!" Hitler screamed.

Ken was desperately maneuvering his body, trying to get in a position where he could thrust the Amulet's pointed prongs into Hitler's flesh. Hitler tried to reach the gun on the floor, causing Ken to extend his arm to knock it away, but the move was a decoy! As Ken reached out to knock the gun away, Hitler changed direction and pulled a Glock from a second ankle holster.

Ken was in a bad position to try and knock the gun away, so he shouted, "Sal, Abby, he has another gun!"

Sal quickly flipped over a nearby table as cover and pulled Abby over so they could both huddle behind it, hoping the table's thickness would protect them. Hitler got off a few more shots, two of them hitting the table, before Ken tackled him to the ground again. They were like two robots fighting, equal in strength and stamina, exchanging blows that had no effect on the other.

"Ken," Abby yelled, "Get this guy. We're both hit."

Abby couldn't tell how serious Sal's injury was, but she could see he was bleeding profusely from the right side of his head. Hitler looked up hopefully to see how much damage he'd caused, and it gave Ken just the opening he needed. Using every ounce of strength he could muster, he used one of his special forces moves and succeeded in flipping Hitler over and getting him into a headlock. Hitler knew a few moves of his own and used a scissor move to put extreme pressure on Ken's headlock but couldn't break it. With all the focus he could muster, Ken kept the hold on Hitler, positioned the Amulet in his hand just so, and then simultaneously released the hold and stabbed the Amulet into Hitler's exposed neck.

"I got him!" Ken yelled. That was the signal for Sal and Abby to empty everything they had into Hitler.

Hitler froze where he was, stunned that the Amulet had penetrated his skin. He could not understand how it happened. He pulled it out of his neck and threw it down. Sal and Abby pulled out the weapons they were carrying and started firing. Abby, on one knee, hurting and bleeding, let loose a complete clip, fifteen shots in all.

Nothing happened to Hitler.

This time Hitler lunged at Ken, he was furious, and they again start exchanging blows. Ken's mind was racing as he was fighting. He watched as the bullets had no effect on Hitler, and his heart sank—he had no way to protect Abby and Sal now. *The goddamn Incas*, he thought, *the Amulet was our only hope.*

Hitler spied one of the guns lying on the floor and went after it. Ken knew he had to keep Hitler away from the gun so he couldn't shoot Abby or Sal again, so he raced Hitler to the gun, and his hand got there first. But Hitler kicked the gun out of his reach and then kicked Ken in the face and raced after the gun again. Ken scrambled on all fours to the gun but did not get there in time. Hitler was now holding the gun and it was aimed at Abby. Ken was afraid to rush him again for fear of him firing. The room was completely silent, except for their heavy breathing, as everyone tried to understand the new dynamics of the situation, now that Hitler had the gun back.

The silence was broken when Hitler starts to laugh. "Wow, that was the most fun I've had in years, watching you guys think you can take me out."

He walked slowly over to Abby, grabbed her by the hair. "Say goodbye to your bitch," he said to Ken as he aimed the gun at her head.

Ken watched in horror. He saw the tortured look on Abby's face, the tears in her eyes. She stared straight at him and he stared right back. They had this final moment with each other.

Gunshots rang out and Ken closed his eyes in despair.

Suddenly Hitler let out a low growl of pain, bending over slightly.

Ken opened his eyes and saw that Abby was fine, he then saw Sal, and realized Sal fired again at Hitler, and this time, it had an impact.

"What's happening?" Hitler groaned. He put his hand on his stomach, feeling something warm and sticky and pulled his hand away. To his astonishment, he saw blood on his hand, not much, but blood nonetheless. It was a sight he hadn't seen in over seventy years. At the same time, he suddenly felt a strange sensation flowing through his body, eventually he recognized the feeling as pain. Then his legs started weakening. The gun felt like it weighed a hundred pounds as he dropped it to the floor.

"Sal, empty everything into him. The Amulet is finally working," Ken ordered.

Hitler paid no attention to Ken's words; his mind was clouding up as the pain and weakness accelerated. *What's happening? This can't be the end*, he thought.

Sal emptied his clip into various parts of Hitler's body. Blood was pouring out of him like it was going through a sieve. Hitler fell to both knees, hunched over, head down. "All this for a broad," he mumbled.

Abby loaded another clip into her gun, stood up weakly and went over to Hitler, still on his knees in a puddle of his own blood.

"I owe you," she screamed. "For Donna," as she fired a shot into his chest. "For my Dad," firing another shot between his eyes. "And one last one for everyone else you killed, you fucker."

With each shot his body shook.

When she fired the last bullet, he finally fell over. Dead.

Ken walked over to her, held her tight. "It's over," he said. "The Incas came through."

"Wasn't so sure there for a while, Boss," answered Sal.

"We need to call Gina and get you medical attention," Ken said looking at Abby and Sal. "You're both bleeding."

"It's just an ear nick, Boss. No big deal. Boss Lady needs more fixing than me."

"You sure you're good to go?" asked Ken.

"No problem," Sal responded.

"Okay, then start the wheels rolling like we discussed."

"On it."

Ken turned slowly to survey the scene and Hitler's body when Abby screamed, "Oh my god, NO!"

"What?" Ken asked alarmed.

"The Amulet, *it pierced your body!*"

CHAPTER 50

Ken carefully turned his head until he could see the Amulet sticking out of his shoulder. "Damn, it must have happened when we were fighting."

"Let me pull it out," Abby said reaching out her hand.

"No, don't touch it," he quickly replied. She stopped in her tracks. "Let me do it."

He slowly moved his hand to the Amulet, grasped it gently and pulled it out. There was no doubt it had pierced his skin. He took a deep breath, put the Amulet back together and placed it back around his neck.

"Do you feel anything?" Abby asked.

"No, nothing yet … look, we can't worry about me now. Whatever is gonna happen is gonna happen. It can't be changed, and we still have a lot to do."

Sal was just hanging up the phone.

Ken asked, "How long?"

"Five minutes Boss."

"Okay, let's leave this horror show."

"What about the body?" Abby asked.

"Leave it. It's all being taken care of, right, Sal?"

"Right, Boss."

They went out the front door together, and in a few minutes, Gina showed up with the medical van. Right behind her was another large black van with three of Sal's associates in it.

Gina got out of the van and ran over to Abby, "Oh my god, get in the van. What happened?"

"We got him, Sis, but we didn't get away clean," Abby said as they walked to the van.

"I can see that. Just two bullet wounds then?"

"Yeah for me. Sal's hit too though."

Gina froze for a moment and turned to look at Sal. He smiled at her, "I'm fine, just a flesh wound, promise."

"Okay then," Gina replied to Sal. She helped Abby get into the van, "Let's get you fixed up, Sis."

Abby looked around the van in amazement, "Where the hell did you get this hospital on wheels?" Abby asked since she had not been involved in any of the discussions about it.

"Where do you think?" Gina said as she pointed at Sal. "It's all his doing."

"I should have guessed," Abby quipped.

Over the next few hours, Sal's men did what Ken had asked for. They disposed of Hitler's body and wired the mountain retreat with C-4 for decimation. There would be little to no trace of the body or the explosives or anything for that matter. It would be blamed on a bogus gas leak. The explosion happened later that night, well after they had all left the property.

The story that came out in the local paper about the explosion summed up everything nicely. Reverend Harold Lephit was missing, and it was assumed he was killed in the explosion, although significant remains could not be found. Chief Wagner signed off on the investigation, putting any wild rumors to bed. The murders of the Rabbi, Donna, and the attempted murder of Dominic were never solved.

That night, after another visit to the hospital, they all settled back at the house. Dominic's condition was continuing to improve, so they didn't feel the need to spend the night with him. At first there was relative silence as they sat in the family room, trying to take in all that had happened.

Finally, Gina broke the silence and asked, "So, what the hell happened in there? Obviously, everything did not go as planned."

"That is the understatement of the century," Abby replied as she pointed at her bandages.

"As missions go, it was pretty much as we scripted. I just underestimated the skills of our adversary," Ken replied.

Abby rolled her eyes and looked at Ken, "Really? Just as we scripted?"

"Yes, exactly as we scripted. I look at it like this: our mission was accomplished and we all came out alive. What more can you ask for?"

"I would like to script nobody gets any bullet holes in their body, what about that?" Abby asked.

Ken chuckled and said, "Okay, next mission, I promise we'll write the script to ensure no one gets any bullet holes."

"No more missions!" Abby and Gina exclaimed together, and they all had a good laugh. It helped to relieve their tension and from that point on, the words started to flow.

"Gina, there's a little more to the story of what happened in the house," Abby said as she looked at Ken.

Ken replied, "We have to tell her everything, including what happened to me."

"Wait, what happened to you? You came out of there without a scratch," Gina asked Ken.

"Not quite," Ken responded. He took a second to assess, but he still had no feeling that anything within him was changing … or did he? "We used the Amulet successfully, but during the fight, I somehow managed to get the Amulet stuck in my shoulder."

"Oh my God, are you okay? What's gonna happen to you now?" Gina asks.

"I'm okay right now. Haven't noticed any changes. What's gonna happen? I really have no idea. We know the Amulet works, otherwise we'd never have been able to kill Hitler. All I remember is that the Incas told me the Amulet piercing the skin would cause the body to age rapidly until it reached its natural age, but I don't really know exactly what that means."

Gina stared at Ken with a confused look on her face, "Kill Hitler? What are you talking about?"

Ken, Abby and Sal all exchanged glances, they still couldn't believe it themselves that Rev. Lephit was actually Adolph Hitler, or at least he claimed to be. Abby said to Gina, "Yes, it's true. I know it sounds crazy.

Let me tell you what happened." She proceeded to tell Gina all that they had learned from the reverend.

When Abby was finished, Gina said, "That's unbelievable. Literally, who would believe that story?"

"No one," Ken chimed in. "That's why we all have to agree to never tell anyone about it. As far as the world is concerned, it was Rev. Harold Lephit who died in that house. No one ever needs to know that Hitler lived for decades after the war. Are we all agreed?" he asked as he looked around the room and everyone nodded their assent.

Gina took a deep breath and said, "Okay, the reverend was really Adolph Hitler, and Ken was stuck with the Amulet and is no longer immortal. Is there anything else you need to tell me about what happened? Big or small?"

"No, sis, that's all," Abby replied with a hint of a smile touching her face.

"Then let's get back to the Amulet." She turned to Ken, "You honestly have no idea what will happen?"

Ken shook his head and said, "No idea. I don't feel any different right now. I'll let you know if I do. I'll let you all know. Until then, I guess we have to just wait and see."

Tears started down Abby's face, not a lot, but they were noticeable.

"Hey, hey, no crying," Ken said as he took Abby's hand. "We don't know what's going to happen. It could be days or years. It took a few minutes for the Amulet to do its work on Hitler, so maybe it will be a slow process. Until we know anything, let's just try and relax, get some rest and take care of each other and Dominic."

"Okay, my love," Abby replied and then kissed him.

CHAPTER 51

As Ken laid in bed that night, waiting to fall asleep, he thought about what the Incas had said regarding the Amulet: *You will begin to age rapidly.* But they never explained exactly what that meant. His belief was that his body and mind would rapidly change to catch up to his true age. *I guess we'll find out in the morning,* he thought.

When Ken woke up, he looked over to see that Abby was still asleep. He got up and went to the bathroom to do his morning business, a quick glance in the mirror told him all he needed to know, he looked like he'd aged ten years overnight! He sighed and said to himself, *Okay, now I know what we're dealing with.* He figured he had a week at most before his body would shut down from old age or disease. He made a quick decision on how he wanted to spend those days and then got on the phone to make arrangements. Once he was done with his calls, he went over to the bed and watched Abby sleeping for a few moments, then he sat down on the bed and gently woke her.

"Good morning, handsome," Abby said sleepily as she rolled over to face him.

"Good morning, love."

Rather than say anything, Abby just started to cry when she saw Ken. She noticed immediately the difference in his face, his eyes, his hair, and she was filled with despair.

Ken wiped a tear from her check and said gently, "I told you yesterday no crying, remember?"

"Oh, honey …"

"Abby, sweetheart, please don't cry. I'm pretty sure now that I only have a few days left, maybe a week, but we are going to make the most out of them, okay?"

"What are you talking about?"

"Come with me and let's wake Sal and Gina. I'll tell you all what I've arranged."

"Arranged? You already planned something? Did you know this was gonna happen like this? Why didn't you tell us last night?" Abby said, angry now, her emotions all over the place.

"No, I didn't know this would happen. I had an idea it might be like this but didn't want to scare you in case it turned out differently. And I just made the arrangements this morning."

Abby sat up and hugged him fiercely, "God, I love you!"

They stayed like that for a bit, and when they separated, Ken looked deep into Abby's eyes and said, "I love you too, so much."

After a few moments Ken asked, "Are you ready?"

Abby nodded, got out of bed and put on a robe, then they headed down the hall to Sal's room. They knocked, and then knocked again, but got no response. Then they heard Gina's door open behind them and, "Boss, what's up? It's too—" Sal stopped in mid-sentence when he saw Ken as he turned around. "Holy shit, Boss, you look old."

"Thanks, Sal. You look great too," Ken replied, smiling a bit at his joke.

"Boss, sorry, I didn't mean nothin'. Do you feel okay? Man, this is crazy."

Gina then popped her head out from behind Sal, took a good look at Ken and immediately went into doctor mode. She went back into her room, grabbed her bag and said to Ken, "Follow me."

All of them ended up following Gina into the kitchen. She directed Ken into a chair and immediately took all of his vitals, measured his reflexes and asked him a series of questions. "Other than the fact you look like you aged ten years overnight, everything looks good. This is because of the Amulet?" she asked.

"Yes," Ken replied.

Now that she was done being a physician, Gina sat down hard in one of the kitchen chairs and said the same thing Sal had, "This is crazy. Do you mind if I monitor you on a regular basis? I don't have to if you don't want me to."

"I want you to do it," Abby quickly said and looked at Ken.

"That's fine with me," Ken said as he looked around the table at the sad faces of Abby, Sal and Gina. He needed to lighten the mood, so he continued in an upbeat voice, "Pack your bags, folks. We're gonna spend the next week in style and relaxation."

They all stared at him and Abby said, "You want to go on vacation? Are you insane?"

"Yes to vacation and no to being insane. Look, I'm not gonna be around to collect any social security benefits, but we absolutely can make the best of the time I have left, okay?"

Sal was the first to speak, "Okay, Boss, whadya got in mind?"

"Well, I own a sixty-acre ranch in the Jackson Hole Valley—"

"You own what?" Abby asked incredulously.

Ken chuckled and said, "As I was saying, I own a ranch in Jackson Hole. The house has six bedrooms, all master suites, with gorgeous views of the mountains and the Snake River. I already called, so the property manager will have everything ready for us when we arrive. Food, drink, the whole works."

"Sounds wonderful, but are you sure that's what you want to do?" Gina asked.

"Yes. That's where I want to spend my last days with the people I love, and that's all of you. There will be a Gulfstream ready at 10:00 AM to fly us out there."

Abby asked, "What about my dad?"

Ken paused for a moment. He hadn't thought of Dominic. He turned to Gina and asked, "Do you think he could come with us in his condition?"

Gina considered his question for a moment. "If he's the same or better than yesterday, it could be possible to transport him without setting him back, but he would have to be flown with special equipment and a medical team. It would be cost prohibitive to do that."

"Money ain't a problem," Sal quipped, "Believe me."

"Sal's right. I don't care what the cost is. We just need to make arrangements for it. Sal, can you and your associates make it happen?"

"Sure, Boss, no problem."

Abby gave him a hug and a kiss and said, "Thank you." Gina did the same.

VINCENT CALFAPIETRA & JULIE DONOFRIO

"Okay, Sal, pick a couple of your guys who are most loyal."

"They're all loyal, Boss."

"Right. I assume they will be doing the flying?"

"Good assumption," Sal quickly replied.

"Well, they're welcome to stay at the house with us, or I can put them up wherever they like, just let me know."

"Will do, let me start making the calls."

"Okay then, let's move on this. I want to be on the jet as soon as possible."

Three hours later, Ken, Abby and Sal were in the air on the way to Jackson Hole airport. The flight time was just over an hour, so they would be at Ken's ranch by lunchtime. The jet with Dominic and Gina was leaving a few hours later but should arrive before nightfall. Gina had insisted on flying with her father, which made Abby feel much better about flying him out to be with them. Before they knew it, the three of them were walking through the large, heavy oak front doors of Ken's sprawling ranch house. The house was amazing. All the rooms were large and roomy but had a cozy feel. There was a game room as well as a small movie theater and everything was decorated with a beautiful western theme. The views were absolutely breathtaking with the mountains all around and the Snake River running through the backyard. Next to the river there was a large, partially-covered deck, outfitted with a small kitchen, fire pit, comfortable chairs and a fishing station. The Jackson Hole Valley was truly stunning; they couldn't have asked for anything more.

"This is absolutely gorgeous, Ken," Abby said.

"I know. I only wish I'd spent more time here."

"No!" said Abby, "I will have none of that, no wishing for things you didn't do or pining for the past. Let's just enjoy ourselves, keep everything positive, okay, love?"

Ken gave her a gentle kiss and said, "Okay, Boss Lady."

No one had yet mentioned that Sal was in Gina's room last night; they had enough on their minds. But now they needed to get settled and Ken had to make the room assignments, "Sal buddy, should I give you your own room, or …" Ken just left the assumption hanging in the air.

Sal's face turned bright red as he said, "Uh, I think one room for me and Gina would be okay, Boss."

Abby walked over to Sal, kissed him on the check and said, "I'm happy for you both."

The tension left Sal's face and he grinned. "Yeah, we sure are a mismatched couple, but they say opposites attract. It's a ying-yang thing or something like that."

With that said, they went to their rooms to get settled, agreeing to meet in thirty minutes for lunch on the back deck. Lunch was a beautiful buffet spread with a variety of dishes, something for everyone. They stuffed themselves like they hadn't eaten in a week. Afterwards, they stayed on the deck, admiring the view and enjoying some good wine. A couple of hours later, but much earlier than expected, Gina and Dominic arrived at the house. Hugs were exchanged all around and then Dominic got settled into his makeshift hospital room to rest. The travel had tired him out, but other than that, he was in good spirits and glad to be with them. Gina had told him part of the story during the trip, so when he saw Ken, he was shocked at his appearance, but not surprised.

The four of them settled on the back deck and Ken pulled out a piece of paper, which contained some notes he had jotted down on the plane. "My dear friends, I thought about what I want to do over the next few days, with you all of course, things I've always wanted to do, but somehow never managed to find the time or the opportunity. It might sound a little corny, but here goes: I want to enjoy the outdoors and your company, so I'd like to do some fishing, some boating, have a skeet shooting competition, BBQ outside, roast marshmallows, play some cards, maybe even throw in a game of Parcheesi or Yahtzee, simple stuff, but fun. Oh, and watch some movies. I love movies, but I never really watched a lot of them, so we'll all pick our favorites and watch them together. How does that sound?"

Abby smiled and said, "It sounds wonderful, darling."

"I'm in," said Gina.

"Me too, Boss," chimed Sal.

"Can I pick tonight's movie?" Abby asked excitedly.

"Sure, hon, what do you want to watch?"

"I want to watch *Wonder Woman*. I have heard a lot of good things about it and it got a ninety-three rating on Rotten Tomatoes."

"Then *Wonder Woman* it is. We'll watch after dinner."

They spent the rest of the afternoon talking, visiting Dominic and just enjoying the company and the scenery. Ken spent about an hour alone in his den, but other than that, he was with Abby every second. Sal and Gina didn't stray far from each other either. Dominic was doing well but was sleeping a lot. This was to be expected and would probably be the case for the next couple of weeks, but everyone could tell he was happy to be with them. No one talked about Ken's condition, they didn't need to. They could see the impact in his face. Later on, they gathered in the dining room for a scrumptious dinner and then retired to the movie theater to watch the evening's feature film, *Wonder Woman*.

As they got into bed that night, Ken said, "I didn't expect that movie to be so good, but it was."

"Totally agree," said Abby, "It was a fantastic movie!"

"This is the first time I have seen Gal Gadot, and she's beautiful. Her smile alone would be worth the price of admission, and I think she was perfectly cast as *Wonder Woman*."

"Beautiful? Really? Better looking than me?" Abby challenged.

Just as Ken was about to respond, Abby put her hand over his mouth and said, "No need to BS me, I'll admit she may be a teeny, tiny bit better looking, but she has the benefit of hair, makeup and wardrobe folks. How's a regular gal like me ever going to be able to compete with that?" Abby could barely get the last words out before she broke out laughing.

Ken laughed with her, "Thank you for not making me answer that question."

The next three days passed in much the same way. They would do a morning activity, enjoy a scrumptious lunch, take a nap, which Ken needed more as each day passed, and then they would play cards or games in the afternoon, followed by dinner on the deck and an evening movie. Sal and Ken caught an abundance of Cutthroat Trout and Smallmouth Bass, Gina won the Yahtzee tournament and, under protest, Abby was declared the winner of the skeet shooting competition. Sal turned out to be a ringer in Parcheesi and after three games no one would play with him anymore.

Everyone could see the changes in Ken, which were noticeable each morning. Ken's hair was the easiest change for the naked eye to see, but there were also new lines on his face, his gait had slowed, and he tired more quickly with each passing day. What was less obvious were the changes within Ken's body. His left knee had developed arthritis, so he

230

limped a little in the mornings. He was getting headaches, which had never bothered him before, and a few of his teeth started to come loose. He was feeling things he had not felt in seventy years, pain and discomfort. But he carried on like a trooper, and since Abby had told him when they arrived to keep it positive, he had not once complained. A few times when he and Abby were alone, he shared what he was feeling with her, what hurt, what was unexpected, but he told her these things as facts, not complaints.

It was the morning of the fifth day at the ranch, Abby and Ken were still in bed.

"How about we take it easy today?" Ken said, "Maybe just get comfortable on the back deck or by the river and watch nature do its thing? I'm feeling kind of lazy and old this morning," he chuckled.

"You're looking good to me, big guy," Abby said, forcing the words, "But sure, a day of doing nothing is fine by me."

"Thanks, hon," he replied.

Abby got out of bed and said, "I'm gonna hop in the shower."

"Can you do me a favor first, my love?"

"Sure, what can I do?"

"Ask Gina to come by. I have something I want to give her. It's important."

"Of course, I'll go get her and then leave you two alone while I take a nice long shower." Abby sensed that whatever Ken wanted with Gina, he would want to be alone with her.

Gina followed Abby into the room five minutes later. "Good morning," she said brightly.

"I'll be in the shower, you two," said Abby as she walked into the bathroom.

"Good morning, Gina. Thanks for coming," Ken said graciously.

"No problem. Are you feeling okay?" she asked.

"Yes, tired and achy, but feeling fine. That's not why I asked you here."

"Why did you ask me here?"

"I need you to do something for me." He pulled three envelopes out of the nightstand drawer and handed them to her. There was one addressed to each of them: Gina, Abby and Sal.

"What are these for?" she asked.

"I need you to give these to each of the recipients when the time is right, but you must open and read yours before you give any of them out, okay?"

"How will I know when the time is right?"

"You'll know. Trust me, you'll know," he said sadly. "Can you do that for me?"

"Of course," Gina said as she took the envelopes and her eyes welled up. She gave him a gentle kiss on the cheek and realized he was right, she would know when the time came, and she thought it would be soon.

That afternoon, having gone through several bottles of Riesling and almost a gallon of iced tea, Abby and Ken were sitting side by side on the deck, Sal and Gina were off to their left a bit also sitting side by side. The view was beautiful, the sun bright and a few white fluffy clouds crossed lazily in the deep blue sky as they sat and watched. Ken was thinking about his life, about the Incas, and about Abby. He thought she was holding up pretty well, and the last few days on the ranch meant more to him than he thought he had a right to ask for, the laughter, the fun, making love, even the simple act of watching movies and enjoying a glass of wine.

He was holding Abby's hand but his hand no longer had the steel grip of a few days ago. In fact, it hardly had any grip at all when he felt a sudden twinge ripple through his body.

"Abby, I love you," Ken softly whispered.

"I love you too, Ken, and I always will."

"I know," he struggled to say as his eyes closed and his head drooped to the side. He was gone.

CHAPTER 52

It was quite a few minutes before Abby let go of Ken's hand. She wasn't sure if it was real or imaginary, but she could feel the warmth leaving his body. Not a sound had been uttered, but Sal and Gina sensed a change and looked over at them. They saw the tears in Abby's eyes and realized that Ken had passed. Sal and Gina pulled their chairs over to Abby, not saying anything. Gina held Abby's other hand and Sal had his hand on Gina's leg for comfort and support.

Watching someone you love die is not easy. In Ken's case, it was with mixed blessings. They knew he was going to die. The surprise element and shock were missing, but the grief and finality were still there. The changes they saw in Ken's body were remarkable; he had aged so rapidly in just a few days. His hair was totally white, and his face was that of an old man, soft, wrinkly and somewhat drawn.

"He went quietly," Sal said, "No pain."

"No regrets," added Gina. "His way."

"I guess," Abby said, struggling to say anything through her tears.

After a little while, Sal said stoically, "I think I should start doing what the Boss Man asked me to do when he passed."

"I need a little more time," Abby said.

"No problem, Abby. Whenever you're ready," Sal replied.

Sal and Gina got up, kissed Abby on the head and went into the house to give Abby some time alone with Ken and her grief. When she finally came into the house, she nodded to Sal, indicating that he could do what needed to be done.

"Sis, will you come sit by the river with me?" Abby asked Gina.

"Of course."

Gina took Abby's hand and they walked down to the deck by the river. For the next couple of hours, they stayed by the river, not talking a whole lot, Abby occasionally sipping on a glass of wine. They just stared out at the beautiful, panoramic view of the mountains as the river ran past them.

When they had arrived at the ranch, Ken had confided in Sal what his wishes were after his death. He didn't think Abby would be up to the task, and he was right. Over the past few days, Sal had made the necessary arrangements. Ken's body was cremated that night, and the next day his ashes were returned to them at the ranch in a plain brown box. Ken wanted them to spread his ashes into the river behind his house, and that is exactly what the three of them did as the sun was setting behind the mountains. They all had tears in their eyes. There was no fanfare, no memorial service, no burial. A few moments later, Sal handed Abby a picture. It was the polaroid of her and Ken that had been taken the day of the rafting trip.

"Where did you get this?" she asked Sal.

"Boss Man had it in his pocket. I thought you would want it."

"Thank you, Sal. I think this is the only picture of him I have. Thank you."

Later that evening, Gina went to her room and pulled out the three envelopes Ken had given her. She thought now was the right time, so she opened her envelope, pulled out a sheet of paper and started to read.

> Dear Gina,
>
> If you are reading this, we both know what has happened. Let me start by saying it was a privilege to meet you. You are a first-class lady all the way. Why you and Abby hadn't seen each other for so long is not important now. What counts now is that you two are together, and I feel you will be for the rest of your lives. I see a beauty in you that's rare today. This beauty inside you is strong and compassionate, maybe even stronger than Abby's. You know about my gift called Suka. It's not always a strong sense or feeling I get, but in your case it is. You radiate a very powerful good, something I have only come across a few times. Your sister has it also, and in many ways, Sal does too.

The three of you make a hell of a team, and I need you to be the strong one to help Sal and Abby with the difficult and potentially dangerous tasks I'm asking of them. They will talk to you about it, and they will seek your counsel. Just give them the best guidance you can and all the support they need.

Finally, I have seen you and Sal grow very close in just a few days, similar to Abby and I. I'm so happy for both of you, especially for Sal. He needs someone like you in his life.

God bless and remember my spirit will always be with you.

Ken

Tears were streaming down Gina's face. So much said in just a few words. She picked up the remaining two envelopes, thinking about the phrase *difficult and potentially dangerous*. What did he mean by that? Many thoughts crossed her mind, but none that made any sense. *I'll find out soon enough*, she thought. She went out to the living room to give Sal and Abby their letters from Ken. Sal was on the phone when she walked in. She put up her hand to indicate he didn't have to hang up, but he did it anyway.

"Call ya back in a few," Sal said. "What's up, babe?" he asked Gina, using a new moniker and she liked it.

"Ken wrote you a letter before he died, and he asked me to give it to you."

"Holy crap! Boss Man talkin' to me from the great beyond."

"I got one also, and I've already read it. There is one for Abby too. Where is she?"

"She went to her room just a few minutes ago."

"Okay, I'll bring her letter to her, and I'll leave you alone to read yours."

"You don't have to, babe. I don't mind."

"I think it's best," Gina replied, "We can discuss them after we've all read them."

"Okay, babe," he replied. Sal opened his envelope, pulled out the paper and began to read.

Sal,

Hey man, you're reading this because I didn't make it. I think we both realized I bit the bullet when the Amulet pierced me during the fight with Hitler. That's what you get for being careless. I want to thank you for always being there for me, since the day we met at the airport. No matter what I needed or when, you were Johnny on the Spot.

We never talked about your background, and to be honest I didn't need to know. I have a pretty good feeling it was with some government agency with initials for a name. You truly are one of a kind. There aren't many people in the world with your skills, resources and contacts and I am forever grateful that you shared them with me. Now that I'm out of the picture, I'm asking you to provide Abby and Gina with the same support you did me. (And congrats on getting together with Gina. She's a keeper for sure!) This support may wind up being a full-time job, kind of like a permanent Guardian Angel. I have the feeling that's okay with you, and that it will be an ongoing adventure! And so you know, it gives me great peace of mind to know you will be looking out for both of them.

I've had a lot of time to accumulate wealth, and I've done well with my investments. All of these resources will be at the disposal of Abby, you and Gina. You won't have to worry about money ever again, just don't spend it all on those football wagers you sometimes make! I have listed the banks and account numbers below, as well as the passwords and codes you will need to be able to get to the money. There are also a few safety deposit boxes with some gold, diamonds and bearer bonds. I estimate the total value to be around two billion dollars, lots of compound interest, if you know what I mean.

Finally, here are the latitude and longitude coordinates you will need to help Abby complete the mission I have offered her. She may decide not to do it, and that's fine, but if she does, she can't do it without these coordinates. She will get together with you when she's ready to execute what I hope is the adventure of a

*lifetime. Both you and Gina will have to help her get through it.
Again, Abby will explain once she reads her letter.*

*That's it, my friend. Remember I'll be with you guys in spirit
now and forever. Be safe.*

Ken

Sal put down the letter. He was saddened by it, but at the same time
it gave him hope. He had seen death and been near it many times in his
life, only luck and good fortune had spared him from meeting the grim
reaper. The idea of being the guardian angel to both Abby and Gina
appealed to him. *Will do, Boss,* he thought to himself.

Gina went to Abby's room to give her the letter, but she was sleeping. She left the letter propped up on the nightstand where she would
easily see it. The next morning when Abby woke up and looked at the
clock, she couldn't believe it, 8:00 AM. She had slept for over twelve
hours. She rolled over and swung out of bed and immediately saw the
envelope. She hadn't seen a lot of it, but she recognized Ken's handwrit-
ing. Out of habit, she glanced around the room to see if anyone was
there, but of course it was empty and eerily quiet. She grabbed the envelope, propped a pillow behind her back and opened it.

Abby,

*I'm so sorry I'm not there for you any longer. We were both
blessed and cursed, but I would not have traded one second of my
time with you for anything in the world.*

Abby started to cry, and put the letter down for a minute, trying to
gather herself. She sat up a little taller, fluffed the pillow and picked up
Ken's letter again.

*Knowing the end is near, I have been looking back and feel
like I've lived four lives. The first was as a young army officer, a
good man, a family man, serving his country with honor, you
would have liked that guy. Unfortunately, he died the day his wife
and son were killed. The second life was short lived as Lt. Col.*

Keith Strickland, a vengeful Army assassin who used alcohol, drugs and women indiscriminately. His soul was lost and he died on the side of a mountain in the Andes.

The longest life I lived was as Ken Stone, a transformation created by the Incas. I was never really at peace during this life. I had times of contentment, but nothing to live for. That is kind of ironic considering the near immortality I had. I was a conflicted soul, some good, some bad. I could have used the Inca gift to do so much more, but I used it to feed my need for revenge. And I justified my killing by taking out the bad guys, but I really was not that different from Hitler, we were both killers, plain and simple. I lived on the dark side of life with an occasional peek into the light. That was not the intent of the Incas.

My best life started when I met you on the plane. It didn't last as long as I would have liked, but I have absolutely no regrets. I fell in love with you about ten seconds after we started talking. I saw and felt in you the goodness and compassion that I had forgotten existed. I saw a beautiful woman that I wanted to spend the rest of my life with and I did. You brought me back to life again, not the Incas. The days I spent with you were a better life by far than the seventy plus years the Incas gave me. I truly love you, never forget that.

"I won't," she mumbled to herself. "I love you too."

Life moves on, and you must move on with it.

A few more things, my love. I have asked Sal to look after you and Gina. I have asked Gina to look out for you and Sal. And of course, I'm asking you to look out for the both of them. I have given Sal information about my financial holdings, which are substantial. He will help get things transferred and setup however you desire. Lastly, Abby, I offer you the chance to do what I didn't do. There was one thing about the Amulet I never told you. It is basically a free pass back into Viracocha. Whoever brings the Amulet back to the hidden city will be fully accepted by the Incas. That person will be given all the gifts the Incas have to offer. I hope you will take my suggestion to go there, and I hope you will use the gift in a way that I didn't, that you will use the gift to help mankind.

So, my love, I leave you the Amulet. It's in the wall safe behind the large picture of the sunset in the dining room. You can be that person! Take up where I failed. I know it's a lot to ask after all you've been through. Please know that I am fine with whatever you decide to do. Take some time, refocus your life, talk to Gina and Sal. The three of you are a team now, and you can accomplish anything and everything you put your minds to.

Never change, Abby. You are perfect. Know these two things, I will always be with you, and you are the love of my life.

Love, Ken

Abby finally put the letter down as tears fell from her eyes. It took her awhile to let the impact of the letter sink in. She picked it back up and read it for a second time, paying more attention to Ken's mention of the Amulet and going back to Viracocha. Questions were flowing through her mind. She needed to get with Gina and Sal to see what their letters had said. Her future now appeared to be very different from anything that she had expected. *Thank god for Gina and Sal,* she thought.

CHAPTER 53

Six months later

It was early on a Sunday morning. The Gulfstream was cruising above the Andes mountains approaching the drop spot, the coordinates Ken had left. She had been training for this jump for the last few months and they had practiced it over a dozen times in a remote area of California. Sal was with her in the back of the plane, tracking their location, he would give her the signal when it was time to jump. In addition to the training and practice jumps, her jumpsuit was equipped with a state of the art, laser-guided GPS that had an accuracy within one meter. If the coordinates were right, she would be saying hello to the Incas very soon. This was the third day they had attempted the jump. The previous efforts had been aborted when they encountered poor weather conditions that would make the jump extremely dangerous. Today the weather was perfect.

She was scared shitless. *I can't believe I'm doing this*, she thought to herself. *You better be right, Ken!*

"Thirty seconds," Sal yelled. "Be safe. I'll see you on the flip side."

"Take care of my sister while I'm gone, okay?"

"You got it," Sal replied.

She blew him a kiss goodbye and focused her attention on the jump. She leaned out the open door and felt the air rushing by her at an incredible speed. "Jesus Christ," she mumbled, "What the hell was I thinking?" She stopped looking down and touched her jumpsuit where the Amulet was safely secured.

"Now!" Sal yelled.

She jumped and yelled out, "Here I come!" Her eyes wide open, she wanted to remember every moment of this jump, good or bad.

Her training had been intense, but the real thing was always different. Using the GPS on the way down was a little tricky, but she had been trained on what to do in almost every situation. She would be in communication with Sal from the plane but expected that link to fail during the last few thousand feet of her descent. They had tried to study this geographical area with the latest in satellite imagery and other cutting-edge technology, but they had never been able to get clear data and pictures. There was something about the terrain of this area and the atmospheric conditions that helped to keep Viracocha hidden from the outside world.

Finally, she landed. Within a few minutes, she was approached by a small party of people. She assumed they were Incas. At first, they seemed hesitant to approach her, but once she pulled out the Amulet and showed it to them, everything changed. She was immediately treated with something like reverence as they escorted her into their village. No words were exchanged, and she wondered if anyone spoke English. They had when Ken was here, but that was seventy plus years ago, a lot could have changed.

The greeting party brought her to the home of one of the elders, who to her amazement, started speaking English. He asked her how she came by the Amulet, and she explained how she had met Ken and everything that had happened in Billings. The Inca elder introduced himself as Hualpa, and said he had known Ken as Keith and in fact had been the one to give him the Amulet. She told him why she had come to the valley, what she wanted her mission to be and how she wanted to use the gifts they offered to make a difference in the world. From that point, until the day she left, she was treated as one of them.

CHAPTER 54

A few years later

Abby, Gina and Sal were gathered in the theater room at the Jackson Hole ranch, which had now become their permanent home base. They were getting ready to watch a special news story on the charitable foundation they had created together, and that they were all very proud of. The picture was on, but the volume had been muted so they could chat.

"Sal, you're recording this for us too, right?" asked Abby.

"Yep."

"Wasn't somebody supposed to bring popcorn?" asked Gina jokingly.

"Yeah, Sis, you were supposed to!" Abby said.

"I guess I walked into that one," Gina said smiling.

"Hey ladies, here we go," said Sal. He turned up the volume as the World News Exchange logo popped up on the screen indicating the program was starting.

> Hello, this is Alyson Leonard with WNX bringing you a special report on an organization that has the whole world buzzing, The Strickland Foundation for Health. In just a few years, under the guidance of the woman they call The Curist, this foundation has made incredible contributions to the medical field, some even say they have accomplished miracles. They have done it in an unusual way, using a process they call Collective Participation. The Foundation has brought together the best minds in pharmaceutical science to research and find cures for our most common deadly diseases. But they don't stop there, they freely and willingly share their data, research and findings with any person, company or university who

is interested. As a non-profit organization, the only thing they are interested in are results. This is a quantum change from how most for-profit, pharmaceutical companies work, where they keep their data and research under the tightest security available. Even before the foundation was started, public trust in pharmaceutical companies was at an all-time low, it seemed all Big Pharma was concerned with was profits. With their unique approach, this foundation has received an incredible amount of support both in the media and in the hearts and minds of the people.

Their process seems to be working as they have developed a vaccine for leukemia that has a ninety-eight percent efficacy and their Breast Cancer vaccine is in final trials and is showing almost a ninety-nine percent efficacy. The sharing of information seems to be the difference maker in their success. They share their data, and more and more researchers are using that data to make small advances, and in turn, they are sharing their findings with The Strickland Foundation. No idea, thought, or breakthrough is too unusual for them to investigate and the results are speaking for themselves. Not to mention that the vaccines they create are provided free to anyone who wants to get one. That's right, I said the vaccines are free! Now that you know the basics, let's go back to the beginning, when the foundation was started and introduce you to the people who are making it happen.

They watched for the next hour. When the show ended Sal turned off the screen.

"Well, I think it was a pretty fair story. Fairly accurate," Gina commented.

"Agreed," said Abby. "From experience we know we're never going to make everyone happy. We just do the best we can."

"Pretty good press," Sal chimed in.

Abby paused for a second, gathering her thoughts to ask a question she had thought of many times, but never voiced. "Sis, does it ever bother you that I couldn't do it? Go to Peru and visit Viracocha? That it was you instead of me?"

"Hell no," Gina responded. "After Ken died, the three of us discussed it and agreed you would go. We had a good plan in place. But when you found out you were pregnant? Forget it, there was no way you were going, and it didn't make sense to wait. It had to be me."

"I know you're right, Gina, but—"

"No buts, Abby!" Gina put her hand on Abby's and gave it a soft squeeze. "We both did the right thing. And now that I have the gift of the Incas, I'll be around a long time to make sure the foundation you created—"

"The foundation *we* created," Abby interrupted.

"Okay," said Gina, "I'll be able to make sure the foundation we created continues the amazing work."

"Ken was right when he said near immortality was a blessing and a curse."

"Yes, he was. But I have the Amulet for when I'm ready to call it quits." Gina said touching the Amulet around her neck.

Just then Ken Jr. ran into the room and jumped on his mom's lap. He was closely followed by Dominic who had been teaching him how to fish that afternoon.

"Hi, Mom."

Abby planted a big kiss on his cheek, "Hi to you, big guy. How was fishing?"

"Fish are stinky." Ken Jr. said, scrunching up his face to show how stinky.

All of the adults started laughing at his funny face. Despite everything they had been through in the past few years, life was good.

EPILOGUE

Riley Flood was just about finished loading the SUV with everything she would need for the day's events. It was her responsibility as the assistant manager of the twins' soccer team to make sure the soccer equipment, lawn chairs and cooler with drinks and snacks were available when needed. This was her Saturday ritual, a job she unfortunately inherited when her husband passed away four years ago. The twins, Mandy and Kelley, who were now twelve years old had gotten used to their dad being gone, at least outwardly. *That's the great thing about kids*, she thought, *they continue to move on, a lot better than she had.*

"Okay, girls, it's time to go," she yelled out to them from the car. The twins popped out of the garage followed closely by Vader, their five-year-old Yorkie. He was the star of the family, all eight pounds of him, and everyone knew it.

Once on the road, Kelley asked, "Mom, why are we leaving so early?"

"We have to make a stop at the pharmacy on the way, honey. Today is the day we're registered to get the leukemia vaccine being offered. Even with an appointment, I expect a long line, so I want us to get there early."

"Is this the new medicine that everyone's talking about, Mom?" asked Kelley.

"Yes, honey, and it will make sure almost nobody will get sick and die from leukemia ever again."

"Like Dad did?" she asked sadly.

"Yes, honey, like Dad."

It was a bold claim, but Riley believed it. She knew more now than she ever wanted to know about leukemia, but she'd read the articles, learned about the trials, and even though she didn't have a medical background, if the vaccine did half of what was claimed, it would be a tremendous improvement. With leukemia being the number one cancer in children, young families and their children would probably benefit the most. They would get to live regular lives, go on vacation, and just be kids, rather than live in a world of doctors, hospitals and treatments.

"Is this medicine from the lady they call The Cutest?" Kelley asked.

"She's called *The Curist!*" Mandy said, sounding a little annoyed.

"That's what I meant." Kelley retorted.

"Some people at school say she's an angel. Is she mom?" Kelley sure was full of questions today.

"I don't know, honey, but she cares about all the people in the world and has dedicated her life to helping people."

"Isn't that what angels do, Mom?" Kelley asked.

"I guess so, honey."

"So, she is an angel!" Kelley said triumphantly.

Riley did not reply. She just smiled at Kelley in the rear-view mirror.

Mandy, who had been quiet so far stated, "I'm gonna meet her one day. I wrote her a letter and told her that Daddy died of leukemia, and now because of her no more daddies will ever die like he did. I said I would like to meet her and thank her for what she's done. I found her address online."

"That's not where she really lives, sweetie. It's just a way to get mail to her."

"I know that, Mom! But still, she'll read my letter, I just know it."

"You know she's a very busy lady and she may not have the time to meet you. So, try not to be disappointed if it doesn't happen."

"No, Mom, she'll read it and come."

"I certainly hope so, sweetie. I'd love to meet her too," said Riley, giving her daughter hope she herself didn't believe.

Ten minutes later they arrived at the pharmacy, and there was a line waiting to get in, just as she expected.

Two days later the doorbell rang around 5:00 PM.

"I got it, Mom," Mandy yelled out.

Riley checked her watch and wondered who it could be, "Wait for me, Mandy. We'll both answer it."

When Mandy opened the door, her face lit up in amazement. She rushed out and gave the woman standing there a big hug.

"I told you, Mom. I told you she would come!"

The Curist held out her hand to Riley, "Hi, I'm Abby Steel."

Riley took her hand with a dazed look on her face. "Hi," was all she could get out.

The Curist looked down at Mandy, who had finally let go of her and said, "You must be Mandy."

"Yes, I am. And you are The Curist."

"Yes, but you can call me Abby," she said smiling. "May I come in?"

"Of course," Riley said. Abby walked in holding Mandy's hand as Riley closed the door.

"Mom, who is it?" asked Kelley who was walking towards them with her face focused on her phone.

"You must be Kelley," said Abby.

Kelley looked up and surprise lit up her face.

"See? I told you she would come," Mandy said again, as she led her new friend to the couch.

The four of them talked for an hour or so, friendly and funny and sometimes sad conversations. They showed Abby some photos of their father, and she was touched in a new way. She wished she had been able to help this family, but it wasn't meant to be.

Abby finally looked at her watch. "It's time for me to go. I have very much enjoyed meeting you ladies and talking. Thank you."

"Oh, can't you stay a little longer?" both twins asked in unison.

Laughing, Abby said, "I'm sorry, but I can't."

"She's a very busy lady, girls," Mom said. To Abby, "We really can't thank you enough for this visit. It means the world to Mandy and Kelley, and me."

"It meant a lot for me too," Abby replied, smiling with soft grace in her eyes.

"Can you sign our school yearbooks?" the girls asked.

"Girls," said Riley.

"No, it's okay, I would love to," replied Abby.

The girls ran into their room and grabbed the books, she signed them both, handed them back and then said her goodbyes. Her car was waiting at the curb, Sal was driving. The Curist turned around and waved one last time, Riley and the twins were huddled together on the front porch waving back at her.

Back in the kitchen, Mandy turned to her mom, "She really is beautiful, Mom, almost as pretty as you."

Riley blushed. "Yes, she is beautiful."

"She's taller than I thought," Kelley interjected.

"Yeah, I agree, and she's taller than she looks on TV," answered Riley.

Mandy opened her year book to see the inscription The Curist wrote, "Come look Mom, look at what she wrote!"

Mom went over and read the inscription, which was the same in both yearbooks.

To Mandy and Kelley,
Good luck to you and best wishes for a great life.
Love Abby "The Curist"

Made in United States
Orlando, FL
29 December 2023

41854934R00157